THE DARK HOUR

THE DARK HOUR

K.J. YOUNG

This is a work of fiction. Names, characters, organizations, places, events, and incidents are either products of the author's imagination or are used fictitiously.

Interior illustrations by Caitlin O'Dwyer

ISBN: 978-0-9864164-3-9

WALGRAVE'S
ASTOUNDING WONDERS

PERFORMING DAILY
AT THREE AND EIGHT

PREPARE TO BE AMAZED!
YOU WON'T BELIEVE YOUR EYES!

For those who sleep with a nightlight

CHAPTER ONE

We seek an enlargement of our being. We want to be more than ourselves.

—C. S. Lewis

His day starts with a job interview. If he gets the position, it will change his life.

When Mark Norman climbs onto the bus that July morning, he's greeted by the stench of body odor and wet hairspray. He scans the rows as he walks, hoping to avoid the most obvious offenders, and takes an empty seat in the back. The bus chugs along, passengers getting on and off, the heat of the day already ruining everyone's mood. Street noise and hot air pour in through half-open windows. When he's nearly to his destination, an oversize man with a crew cut and horn-rimmed glasses sinks down next to him. He holds up a newspaper and turns to Mark. "What do you think? Is Jimmy Carter going to get the nomination?"

This is just the type of bullshit small talk Mark tries to avoid. "Couldn't say." He looks out the window.

"Did you hear that Lindy Boggs is gonna be presiding over the Democratic National Convention next week? Lindy Boggs! Never thought I'd see a woman running things. What's this world coming to?"

"Don't know."

"Jimmy Carter." He points at the newspaper photo, a weekly bus pass clutched between his fingers. "A grown man going by the name Jimmy. What's that all about? I'll be damned if I want some peanut farmer running the country. The way he talks, too, like some mealymouthed hick. That might fly in other parts of the country, but no one's gonna buy it here in Wisconsin. The whole thing makes me sick."

Mark takes a piece of paper out of his back pocket and unfolds the crumpled page, keeping his gaze downward. He senses that the big man still has his eyes aimed his way.

The guy huffs in irritation. "Cat got your tongue?"

"Not really."

"If you don't want to talk, you shoulda just said so."

"Okay, then. I don't want to talk."

"Now that wasn't so hard, was it?" he says, giving Mark a smug look.

Asshole. Mark clenches his fists and takes a deep breath.

When the bus stops at Clarke Street, Mark stands and pushes his way out to the aisle. As he heads down the steps, the driver says, "Have a good day," in a not entirely convincing way. Behind him, the door of the bus hisses shut before it rumbles away. Mark opens his hand and smiles down at the bus pass he liberated from his annoying seatmate. *Score!* He tucks it into his back pocket for later use.

Looking up and down the street, he compares the printed address on the paper with the buildings in front of him. Taking it all in, he frowns. "No fucking way," he mutters. She sent him *here*? It has to be a mistake. He isn't familiar with all the neighborhoods in the city, but this one has to be the absolute worst. The storefront windows are covered with iron bars. The sidewalk ahead of him is a stretch of patched and crumbling concrete. Graffiti covers the glass panels of the telephone booth on the corner. It's eerily quiet, too, with little traffic going past.

This just feels wrong.

He is all wrong, with his navy dress pants, his tie pulled down a little so that he can leave the top button of his too-small dress shirt undone. Instinctively he knows that with his shiny shoes and neatly parted hair, he's conspicuously overdressed. Anyone can see he doesn't fit in.

It occurs to him that he could leave. Cross the street, wait for the next bus, and head home. His gut says this is the best plan of action. Too bad it isn't an option.

Mark turns the paper over. Looking at the directions scrawled on the back, he walks to the corner and turns onto the sidewalk running alongside Bartleby Street. Halfway down the block, he spots the place. When he's directly in front of it, he stops to look up, gaping.

The woman at the placement agency called it a grand old house, and the name—Alden Manor—confirms her description, but he didn't expect this. Before him stands a stately mansion, crowded on either side by what looks like warehouses. An old glamorous dame escorted by two nondescript brutes. The mansion is three stories of brown brick, with points reaching to the sky. Between each story, the brick façade is interrupted by a decorative band of stone detailed with angels and stars. Steps up to the entrance lead to a covered porch fronted by a row of three stone arches. Curved terra-cotta tiles top the roof. In another lifetime, this would have been a hell of a house, a place where the wealthy would gather to clink champagne glasses and discuss business deals, but now, positioned between two industrial buildings in the worst part of the city, it looks run-down and angry.

Still, at one time this place belonged to someone with serious money.

While he stands taking it all in, a man's voice yells out, "You don't wanna be going in there." Mark turns to see a lanky man with a gray-haired ponytail leaning against the neighboring building, one foot back against the brick. The man brings a cigarette to his lips; the tip glows red. He exhales and stares at Mark through a cloud of smoke.

"Oh yeah? Why's that?" Mark asks.

"People go in that house, they don't come out the same."

"Really."

"You don't believe me?" He throws back his head and laughs, a gold canine tooth glinting in the light. "I seen it with my own eyes. Bad things happen to folks who go in there."

Mark gives him the once-over. Tie-dyed tank top, hemp necklace, and jeans with patches on each knee. Birkenstock-clad feet. Nothing to recommend him. Mark doesn't take advice from aging hippies. "Thanks, but I'll take my chances."

The man shrugs. "Suit yourself. Don't say I didn't warn you. Name's Doug, by the way."

"Sorry, but I have to go. Got an appointment." Mark glances at his watch. *Right on time.* He heads up the steps. "Check you later."

"Of course you have an appointment," Doug says, his voice gleeful. "They all do. Every single one. You won't be in no hurry once you see what's waiting for you. They're gonna get you."

They're gonna get you. Words a child would use. Who would fall for that? *Stupid hippie.* Standing before the front door, Mark's glad to be out of the morning sun and in the shade of the porch, even if it has the atmosphere of a catacomb. *Now to do it and get through it.* Mark needs to be employed, and in this job market, there aren't many prospects. Overall, he has a good feeling.

Mark bangs the heavy iron door knocker against the strike plate three times. When the door abruptly opens, he's staring at a young woman about his age.

"Hello," he says, putting out his most winning smile. "I'm Mark Norman. I have an appointment."

"You're late, and they don't like it when you're late." She steps aside to let him come in. He notices then that she is petite, with dark-brown hair pulled back into a severe ponytail. Her pale face, absent of any makeup, highlights a scattering of freckles across her nose. She wears a white peasant top and red-checked flare-legged pants. Around her neck a gold cross hangs off a delicate gold chain. In a second he sizes her up: she's a real good-girl type. A paragon of virtue. Probably wanted to be a nun just like Sister Mary Agnes, her third-grade teacher at St. Joseph's Elementary School.

"I'm right on time." Mark glances at his wristwatch. Inside the house it is noticeably cooler than outside, but a little humid too, making it a cool dampness. He sizes up the space, taking note of a grand staircase leading up to the second floor.

"Just barely." She makes a face. "They like you to be early. They're interviewing several candidates, and they don't want any of them to overlap."

He was supposed to be early? Why didn't Beverly at the job placement agency inform him of this? She was so smooth, telling him he was a sure thing. "You're just what they requested," she said looking through the file. "Young, tall, strong, healthy." She held one hand to the side of her mouth as if confiding a secret. "Off the record, they also want a young man who is handsome, with no family ties. For round-the-clock availability, I would guess. They specifically said to send candidates no older than twenty-five." She nodded approvingly, as if he was clever to be on the short side of twenty-six. "As soon as I heard their requirements, I thought of you."

Mark was flattered that Beverly mentioned his good looks, but now, standing across from this young woman in the dimly lit entryway of Alden Manor, surrounded by walls of dark paneled wood, he wonders what he's gotten himself into.

The young woman beckons for him to follow her down a long hall. As they walk, she asks, "Have you ever done this kind of work before?"

"Not yet," Mark says.

She doesn't comment on his lack of experience, but begins to spit out instructions. "Don't talk too much. Wait for them to ask the questions and then answer directly."

"Okay."

"The last guy who came tried to impress them. That didn't go over well."

"Got it. Nothing impressive." He smirks. "I'll try to tone it down."

She stops, and he almost walks into her. "If you have an attitude, you won't get the job." Her tone is flat.

"Look," he says, annoyed at being chastised. "I'm not even sure I want the job."

"You want the job," she says with a sigh. She keeps walking, talking to him out of the side of her mouth. "It pays more than you'd get anywhere else. Plus, you owe your girlfriend your share of two months' rent, and she's getting impatient with you. I'm thinking this is your best bet."

"Hey!" Mark says, incensed. "How do you know that?" He thinks back to Beverly and her bullshit talk about confidentiality. She said that everything he told her was just between the two of them, even miming the locking of her lips and tossing away the key. He'd be within his rights to go over to the employment agency and give her a piece of his mind when he's done here. Not that he will, but the idea has appeal.

The young woman shrugs. "You won't have any secrets in this house." She approaches a set of double doors and ceremoniously opens them, leading the way in. "This is the blue room," she says. Inside, dark woodwork covers the lower half of the wall, while blue patterned wallpaper rises above it to the ceiling. The tall windows are curtained with a gauzy white fabric.

On the opposite end of the room, a fireplace with bookcases on either side takes up the entire wall. In front of the fireplace, a sofa faces two tall-backed chairs, all of them a tufted blue print. Nothing is stained or worn, and yet the room strikes him as being dated and dingy. The one thing of interest is a wheeled drink cart holding various bottles of liquor, as well as martini glasses and cocktail napkins. Based on the well-stocked drink cart, Mark thinks that maybe the owners of this house aren't stodgy after all.

"Wait here," she says, pointing to one of the chairs. "I'll go get them. They're eager to see you."

Mark sits down. He isn't sure what he was expecting today, but it wasn't this mansion with its oppressive dampness and dim hallways. Depressing as hell. *I'm not even sure I want this job.* He lets the thought roll around in his head. And then he thinks of her reply, that the pay is good and that he is two months late on the rent. Granted, it *would* be nice not to hear his girlfriend rag at him day after day. *Get a job. Get a job. Get a job.* Like it's so easy. Like he hasn't been pounding the pavement trying to do just that.

The problem isn't getting a job. It's getting the right job, one where he's not working among lowlifes supervised by idiot managers. Mark hasn't had the best luck with jobs, so he may as well wait and hear what they have to say.

CHAPTER TWO

When the young woman returns, she is accompanied by an elderly man and woman who shuffle in on either side of her. Their gait is unsteady, as if they're afraid of stepping on a slippery spot. Mark is familiar with all the euphemisms to describe old people—senior citizens, golden oldies, retirees—but these two are about twenty years beyond that. One foot in the grave, and the other one sliding toward the edge. The man is bald on top, with a friar's fringe of gray hair. He wears baggy, old-man dress pants and a long-sleeved white shirt with a striped tie. He walks haltingly with a cane and has a slim build and a long, deeply lined face. The young woman, who Mark realizes has never given him her name, towers over the old lady, who has liver-spotted hands and baby-fine white hair with an unnaturally wide part. The younger woman helps the old lady into the room, one arm looped around her waist.

"Here we are," the young woman says in a monotone voice. "This is Mark Norman." She situates the lady on the sofa, while the man settles next to her, propping his cane in between them.

"Excellent, Lisa." The man's voice is unexpectedly vibrant. "We'll take it from here."

"You sure?" Her forehead furrows. "I can bring you drinks. Iced tea? Lemonade?" She looks at Mark, but he doesn't respond. He's here to talk about a job, and then he is leaving. A beverage adds a complication he doesn't need.

The man leans forward and grasps his knees. "That won't be necessary." He waves a hand. "Off you go." She leaves, *reluctantly*, Mark thinks as she passes him. After she closes the doors behind her, the man says, "Lovely girl, that Lisa, but she fusses a bit much. I think she believes that her efforts are the sole thing keeping us alive." He chuckles. "As you might have guessed, I'm Roy Walgrave, and this is my sister, Alma."

"It's nice to meet you, Mr. Walgrave and Miss Walgrave. I'm Mark Norman." He gets up and shakes their hands. The old man's grip is surprisingly strong, although the feel of his fingers reminds Mark of chilled bones wrapped in crepe paper. He's never cared for old people, associating them with decaying bodies and failing faculties, but he tries to get past that now, making a point to meet their gaze. Both of them have dark eyes that stand out despite the slight distortion of the thick-lensed glasses they both wear. He sits back down. "I'm guessing you have some questions for me?"

"You would be right about that," Mr. Walgrave says. "Beverly from the agency seems to think you are just what we're looking for."

"I hope so, Mr. Walgrave."

"You can dispense with the formalities. Call me Roy, and call my sister Alma."

"All right then. Roy. I've never worked as a home health aide, but I learn quickly and promise you that I would do a good job." He feels the way their stares bore through him. It makes him so uncomfortable he almost wishes for that beverage after all. It would help to have something to do with his hands.

"I'm sure you'll be fine." Roy has a gruff, friendly voice. "I expect the job will probably be different from what you're imagining, but I think we're easy to work for, and I know it will be an excellent experience for you."

"Terrific. I'm always up for a challenge."

"And the pay will more than compensate you for some of the, shall we say, more *unsavory* duties?" He chuckles as if he's made a fine joke.

"I see." Mark tries not to think about the unsavory duties. The likelihood is that they involve bodily fluids or brushing the old guy's dentures. If any of these chores go beyond his tolerance level, he's fairly certain he can foist them off on Lisa. As much as women protest, he finds that if he makes a show of being incompetent, they revel in picking up the slack.

"We'd like to start with a few questions, if you don't mind, Mark."

"Sure thing. Fire away."

Roy leans forward, tenting his fingers. "Beverly says you're twenty-five-years old, and you live in an apartment on Alcott Avenue."

"That's correct."

"But you don't live alone?"

"No, I don't," Mark says. "I live with my girlfriend, Monica. She runs a catering company." Technically, Monica is a banquet waitress and bartender, but Mark prefers his version of the truth.

"Are you engaged?"

Mark shifts his feet, uncomfortable, half-annoyed. *Living in sin.* That's what this old guy is getting at. "No, we're not engaged."

Roy asks, "Do you have any tattoos?"

"Me? No." He shakes his head. What a weird question. He doesn't know any guys his age who have tattoos. That's the mark of old military guys and winos.

"How's your eyesight?"

"Excellent."

"Any distinguishing marks on your body?"

"Distinguishing marks? Like what?"

"Scars, moles, anything like that?"

Mark thinks. "A few freckles on my chest. Oh, and the scar from my smallpox vaccination from when I was a kid." He looks down at his left arm. "Like most people have."

"So you've had all your childhood vaccinations?"

"Yes. I can get a copy of my medical records if it's required."

"That won't be necessary," Roy says. "Your word is good enough."

"My health is excellent."

"Yes, so Beverly said." Roy nods his head. "Anything else about your physical condition we should know? Are you bowlegged or knock-kneed? Any problems with your spine?"

"No," Mark assures him. "None of that. The last time I saw the doctor he said I was the picture of health. I'm strong too."

Roy presses on. "What about the elderly men in your family? Do they go deaf or blind? Lose their hair? Have heart problems?" He raises one quivering finger and taps it to his chest.

"The elderly men in my family?"

"Your grandfathers and great-grandfathers. I'm wondering how long they lived and if they had health problems."

Mark makes a show of thinking. "I don't know too much about my great-grandparents, but both of my grandfathers are alive and doing great." He adds, "All of my grandparents are very religious and go to church every week." Mark knows this is likely to score points with them. "Otherwise, one of my grandfathers plays golf, and the other is in a card club. Poker." They appear to be waiting for more, so he adds, "They both wear glasses, but their hearing is perfect."

"So they've retained their mental acuity?" Roy asks. "No signs of senility?"

"Look, I'm not sure what this has to do with the job," Mark says, perplexed. "Were you thinking you might meet my grandparents at some point? Because I gotta tell you, that's not going to happen." He flashes a convincing smile. "I'll have to be enough."

"We won't need to meet anyone in your family, so don't worry about that," Roy says smoothly. "I know these are odd questions, but we're just trying to get a feel for you and your family. You'll be in our house, so it's not like working in a store or office. This is a very personal job."

That makes sense. "Of course. I understand."

Roy holds up one bony finger and gives him a smile. "To get back to the question—has anyone in your family ever gone senile?"

"No."

The old man's expression is hard to read, and Mark wonders if he's given the right response. *Do they want me to have experience with confused old people?*

"If you're wondering about my capability, I'm prepared to handle anything the job entails," Mark says. Beverly coached him to act confident, and he played along with her instructions, but what she didn't know was that Mark could have taught a course on confidence. He was born confident. His biggest challenge in life so far has been learning to tone it down. People don't always appreciate his personality. They say he is cocky, arrogant, full of it. He sees no reason to change. So what if he appears capable? There's no point in going around doubting yourself.

"I'm sure you can handle anything we'd ask you to do," Roy says, his tone pleasant. "You seem like a smart and savvy young man."

"Thank you." Mark grins; this interview is going well.

The doors to the room open. Lisa is back. "I'm sorry to interrupt, but Dr. Cross is on the telephone. Do you want to take the call?" Mark meets her glance, and she gives him a perfunctory nod. She strikes him as being a little bit guarded. If Mark gets the job, his first order of business will be to crack through that shell.

Roy says, "Please tell the doctor I'll call him back when we're done interviewing Mark."

"I'll let him know," she says, backing out of the room and pulling the doors shut behind her.

"She seems nice." Mark turns back to face them.

"Lisa is nice," Alma agrees, speaking for the first time.

"This is a gorgeous home. Have you lived here long?" Mark asks, remembering Beverly's advice about asking questions during interviews. *Employers like it when you take an interest. If you can slide in a compliment, all the better.* He glances around the room in a show of admiration.

Roy answers, "We've been here for many years. Inherited it from a friend."

Nice friend, Mark thinks. "I see."

Alma sits forward in her chair and frowns. "Why is your hair so long and shaggy?"

Mark is used to reading between the lines, translating what is really being said, and he knows that old ladies hate long hair on men. They think Hollywood stars like Robert Mitchum and John Wayne are emblematic of true men. Well, times have changed. He gives her a grin. "I've been told it looks good this way."

Her head bobs from side to side. "No," she says, her eyebrows knitting together in disapproval. "It will not do. I can't be staring at that all day."

Mark says, "Most women tell me they like my hair." Actually, what he hears are compliments from women saying they wished they had his hair. Thick, wavy, healthy hair. They run their hands through it and say it's wasted on a man. He also hears commentary on his long, dark eyelashes, but it's the hair they notice first.

Roy says, "Would you consider cutting it? For the job?"

Mark vacillates for a second. If this is a deal breaker, then he'll break the deal and get a different job. "No. Absolutely not. There's no way I'm cutting my hair."

"You won't cut it?" Alma says.

Mark gives her his sweetest smile. "If I was going to do it for anyone, it would be for you, ma'am, but my hair is part of who I am. I think it would be easier for you to adjust." She doesn't look convinced. He tries again. "What if I combed it differently?"

"What if I gave you two hundred dollars to cut your hair?" Roy asks abruptly.

Incredulous, Mark sucks in a breath. "You'd give me two hundred dollars to cut my hair?"

"Yes, on the condition that you come work for us and commit to staying on for at least six months."

"Two hundred dollars?"

"Cash. We'd go to the barber shop together, and I'd pay you immediately afterward."

"Why would you give someone that much money to cut their hair? The job can be done either way." He looks at them, puzzled. His hair barely touches his shoulders. "My hair isn't even that long."

"It's important to Alma," Roy says simply. "And I like it when she's happy."

"He needs new clothes too," she says, pointing a crooked finger in Mark's direction.

Roy gives her a fleeting smile. "All in due time, dear. Let's get this squared away first." He turns his attention back to Mark.

"If we hire you, we pay ten dollars an hour. That's in addition to the money for the haircut."

Ten dollars an hour. Nearly five times the minimum wage, and more than most recent college graduates make. Added to the initial two hundred dollars, he'd be caught up on his rent in no time.

"What do you say, young man?"

Mark suppresses the surge of excitement that flutters in his stomach. Cautiously he says, "For two hundred dollars, I'd cut my hair. But that's only if I'm guaranteed the job. Are you offering it to me?" Lisa advised against asking questions. Beverly, too, said it was better to let the employer take the lead, but screw it—Mark wants to know where this is going.

Roy reaches over and gives Alma's hand a squeeze. "What do you think, dear?"

She peers over her glasses and beckons. "Can you come here, young man?"

Mark gets up out of his chair and stands in front of her. She puts out both hands, and he takes them, pulling her to her feet. She says, "I need to get a better look," then reaches up and puts her hands on either side of his face. While it seems an affectionate gesture, everything in him wants to push her away. She smells musty, like clothes stored in a basement. Up close he sees through her thin hair to her pink scalp and notices that one of her eyes has a milky film to it. Her face is grotesque, covered with wrinkles like beaten leather. A little spittle gathers in the corner of one side of her cracked lips. He presses his lips together, quelling the impulse to gag. She puts her hands on his shoulders and gives them a squeeze, then runs her fingers down his arms. "Oh, how strong!" she says, sounding delighted.

"I told you," Mark says, looking past her. "Strong like an ox." This is something dorky his stepfather sometimes says. It seems appropriate at the moment.

"I can tell." She releases him from her grasp. "Turn around for me." He hesitates, and she says, "Come on. Turn around." He turns around slowly, and she says, "Stop!" A second later, he feels her hands on his back, tracing the line of his spine all the way down before grabbing a handful of his buttocks and giving a squeeze.

"Hey! Is that really necessary?" he asks sharply, taking a step away. If he isn't hired after enduring this, he's coming back tomorrow with a flamethrower.

Alma sits down and speaks to her brother. "He's just right."

"This isn't part of the job, is it? Getting groped?" The words are out before he's even thought them, and he is surprised at his own level of indignity. He's been felt up at discos and bars, mainly by drunk women, some of them not even remotely attractive, and he laughed it off, was flattered, even, knowing that ultimately he holds the power. This, though, is an entirely different thing. A violation.

"Not at all," Roy says. "Won't happen again."

"I hope not." Reseating himself, Mark smooths the front of his shirt.

"You have to forgive Alma. She can be a bit much at times, but she means well." He winks at Mark as if to say, *Just between us, my sister is losing her mind. Please indulge her.* Maybe this is why the topic of senility came up earlier in the interview.

"So, I'm hired?"

"I think you're just the right man for the job," Roy says. "You can start tomorrow. Come around the same time as today."

"Will it be full time? I'm going to need full-time hours."

"Full time," Alma echoes.

Roy says, "Forty hours a week or more. We may need you some nights and weekends. Is that a problem?"

That had to be the around-the-clock availability Beverly mentioned. Mark isn't thrilled at the idea of working weekends, but for the pay, he'll do it. He might as well make the money while he can. "Not a problem. I can work whenever you need me."

"Excellent." Roy rubs his hands together. "I think we're going to get along fine, Mark."

"I think so too, sir." Getting up, he shakes hands with each of them, and then, grinning, he pours on the old Mark Norman charm. "I appreciate the opportunity you're giving me, and I won't let you down. Sincerely, thank you."

"Enjoy your hair tonight," Roy says. "Tomorrow we're going to the barber."

"Yes, sir. Looking forward to it."

After they exchange goodbyes, Mark says he'll let himself out. In the hallway he runs into Lisa. "Guess what?" he says. "I got the job. I start tomorrow." He gives her his best smile.

Clearly unimpressed, she flatly says, "Good for you."

He leans in conspiratorially. "I think we're going to be friends."

"Think again," she says, moving past him.

Mark smirks, seeing her words as a challenge. He sticks his hands in his pockets and whistles as he heads out the front door. With his newly acquired bus pass, he won't have to use his remaining cash for the bus fare. Tomorrow he'll be two hundred dollars richer, and he'll get another four hundred dollars after the first week of work. He has a feeling he's going to see even more money on top of his weekly wage. He knows opportunity when he sees it, and this pair is a mine that hasn't yet been tapped.

He is, as Roy said, just the man for the job.

CHAPTER THREE

The next morning, Mark and his girlfriend engage in such wild sex that their douchebag neighbor downstairs pounds on the ceiling with a broom and yells, "Enough already," making both of them laugh. Afterward, while he gets dressed, Monica watches from the bed, laughing when he deliberately shakes his ass in her direction while pulling up his underwear.

"Sure, now you love me," he says, going over to the bed and smacking her backside.

Such a contrast from the night before when he arrived home to find her ready to kick him out, the phone bill clutched in her hand. "You're starting to feel like a weight around my neck," she said. "If you don't start bringing in your share of the money soon, we're through."

Of course, once he told her about his new job, she softened. "Their health is declining," Mark said. "Just by looking you can tell time's running out for them, especially the sister."

"Are you *hoping* they die soon?" she asked, more curious than disapproving.

"Right now it's in my best interest for them to stay alive as long as possible," he said. "I can see all kinds of opportunities in that house, and as I told you before, I'm the kind of guy who makes things happen."

"Watch, I'll have you paid back in full in the next two weeks," he said.

Monica said, "We'll see about that."

He raised one eyebrow. "Oh yes, we will."

Thinking about it the next morning on the way to the bus stop, Mark realizes that most of the women he's dated were chosen for their physical attributes, but he found that the attraction wore thin over time. So many of them turned out to be girls who expected him to be a mind reader and chattered endlessly about nothing. Total airheads. Monica, now she's a different story. Gorgeous, with dark hair and huge brown eyes, and smart as hell besides. She has ambitions, too, saving her money and planning for the future. She says that once she has enough to buy a car, her next step is to start her own business, and from there she foresees a lifetime of security and luxury. She and Mark are in agreement on so much of this. Working for other people will always be a tether that keeps them in one place. The best way to get ahead in this world is to run the show. As far as he's concerned, with Monica, he's met his match. She sees right through him and doesn't put up with any of his shit. Oddly enough, this is the biggest turn-on of all. Which doesn't mean she's perfect, just better than most.

As he finds a seat on the bus, change is in the air. Like a vibration in the atmosphere, it buzzes all around him. This new job is going to be a turning point for him.

Getting off the bus at Clarke Street, he retraces yesterday's route without a hint of yesterday's hesitation. Funny how a person gets used to things; today the condition of the neighborhood doesn't bother him at all. When he arrives at Alden Manor, the sight of a mansion tucked between two industrial buildings looks just right. Another positive? No sign of the aging hippie. He bounds up the stairs and through the arches onto the porch, so intent on arriving on time that when he steps on something small and squishy, he yelps in surprise. Backing up, he leans over to take a closer look, sickened to see it's the remains of a bird, its wing mutilated, two flies buzzing around the bloody corpse.

He is still staring at it when the door opens with Lisa on the other side. "There you are," she says. "What's the holdup?"

"A dead bird." Mark crouches. "Looks like something tore into it. Maybe a cat? Do the Walgraves have a cat?" He glances up at her.

"No, just leave it. I'll get it later," she says impatiently. "Roy is waiting for you." Lisa leads him through the house all the way back to the dining room, where Roy and Alma sit at a table, drinking from china teacups. The plates in front of them show remnants of toast and eggs.

"Good morning," he greets them.

"There's that hair again," Alma says, decidedly contentious.

"Don't worry, my dear." Roy pats her hand. "This is the last you'll be seeing of it. Are you ready to go, my boy?"

Mark hadn't imagined that going to the barber would be the first order of the day, but it doesn't matter. He'd warned Monica he would be returning home with shorter hair. He thought she might disapprove, but she was unfazed saying, "It's worth it for the kind of money you'll be getting. Besides, it's just hair. It'll grow back."

Mark answers Roy's question by saying, "I'm ready if you are."

Roy struggles to his feet and gives his sister a kiss on the cheek. "I might be gone for most of the day, but Lisa will be here for you, my dear." When he grabs his cane and hobbles away from the table and toward the door, Mark knows enough to follow.

Rather than heading to the front of the house, Roy leads the way down the hall to a door in the back of the mansion, opening it to reveal a spacious garage with one vehicle parked inside. The most glorious car Mark has ever seen. Gaping, he asks, "Is that an Excalibur?"

"You know your cars!" Roy says with approval. "Yes, it is an Excalibur. Less than a year old. I'm not up to much these days, so you'll have to help with the driving." He rustles in his pants pocket and pulls out some keys.

Mark knows about Excaliburs, replicas of a 1928 Mercedes-Benz, manufactured in Milwaukee. They are a throwback to the age of elegant motorcars, the kind 1930s movie stars drove to premieres. This one is cream with a tan top and a tan interior. The fender rolls like a wave over the back white-walled tire and continues to sweep forward up and over the front wheel. If ever a car was a piece of artwork, this is it. He takes the keys from Roy and peers into the car window. "Nice. Leather seats?" He turns to look at Roy.

Roy nods. "Of course. Nothing but the best."

Behind the wheel of the car, Mark feels his spirits soar. Zipping out of the back alley with the top down is the ultimate freedom. Roy directs him to go west on Clarke, saying it's about five miles to his preferred barber shop. Mark relishes the feel of the gas pedal beneath his foot and the smooth way the car responds when he guides it into the next lane. The responsiveness is amazing—it's like the engine anticipates his every move. He catches sight of other drivers' stares and revels in their obvious admiration and envy.

"You like this car?" Roy asks, in a way that says he already knows the answer.

"I love it." Mark grins. "I've never driven a car like this before."

Roy nods. "It puts a hex on you. Once you drive it, you never want to stop."

A hex. That's exactly right. He could drive it all day, for weeks on end. Smiling, he thinks of all the places he could go. If he were to drive on through the night, they'd be in California by morning. Hell, if he continues driving for even forty-five minutes, he'll be at his apartment. What he wouldn't give for Monica to see him driving this car. Better yet, he'd love for the neighbors in the apartment building, the ones who barely acknowledge him, to see him behind the wheel of this magnificent machine. He was born to drive an Excalibur. He just didn't know it until right now.

The rest of the day goes by in a whirl of change, all of it chipping away at Mark's usual appearance until he is a man transformed. At the barber shop, Roy instructs the barber to shave his hair short on the sides, leaving the top longer. While the barber works on Mark's hair, Roy stands alongside the chair and leans on his cane, watching.

The click of the scissors comes uncomfortably close to Mark's ears, and the buzzing of the shaver against his neck frays his nerves. He looks in the mirror as his crowning glory falls in pieces to the floor, and he resists the urge to bolt out of the chair. He's made a commitment. Besides, as Monica said, it's just hair. It will grow back once this is over.

When the barber finishes, dusting his neck with a soft brush and taking off the cape with a flourish, Roy exclaims, "Now, you're looking smart!" The old man shows his teeth in a wide grin. "You wait and see. You're going to feel so much lighter."

Mark looks at his reflection and forces a smile. When they stop at the front register, Roy pulls out a fifty-dollar bill, instructs the barber to add a tin of hair pomade to the bill, and then hands it over to Mark. "Believe me, you're going to need this."

Their next stop is a short drive to an upscale men's clothing shop called Hamilton's Men's Clothier. When Mark pulls the car to the curb, Roy rubs his hands together and says, "This is the fun part. Today, I'm buying you some decent clothing."

Inside, Roy takes charge. He pulls Mark away from a rack of sports coats and instructs the salesman that they are there to buy two suits for his grandson. He winks at Mark as he announces this. The salesman, a nattily dressed older man named Jim, has them sit down on cushioned chairs while he brings out armloads of suits for Roy to inspect. Any one of them would be fine with Mark, who isn't much for dressing formally, but Roy is quite particular. He wants a certain type of fabric, and he's also fussy about the lining. Once two suits are selected, Mark stands on a small platform, and the tailor, a short woman with frizzy hair, is summoned to measure him. By the time the session ends, two suits have been ordered, one charcoal gray and another a light tan. Roy insists on adding what he calls the *accoutrements*: matching vests, pocket squares, dress shirts, and ties. After those are chosen, Roy announces that they'll be buying two pairs of dress shoes as well. Mark has never had his feet measured with such care.

Mark notices with a shock that the ties cost thirty-eight dollars, and the suits are almost a thousand each. The old guy is clearly loaded.

When it comes time to settle up, Roy hands the salesclerk a credit card. After the card is run through the imprinter with an impressive *click-clunk*, Roy signs the top copy with a flourish. Afterward Jim rips off the perforated edge and hands Roy a carbon copy, saying, "I'm so happy to have assisted you today, sir. The alterations will take about a week. We'll call when they're ready."

"I have a better idea," Roy says. "My grandson and I are going out to lunch, and then we're going to be running a few more errands. If you have the tan suit finished by four thirty, there's an extra two hundred dollars cash in it for you."

Jim extends a hand. "Very good, sir. We'll see you at four thirty, then." After they shake on it, Mark follows Roy out of the store.

They never do get around to running errands. Instead, they spend the afternoon at a classy restaurant called Grenadier's. After a four-course lunch, they retire to the bar and drink cocktails until the place swims in front of Mark's eyes in a happy haze. Roy's drink of choice is a brandy manhattan. Mark is usually a beer guy, but in the interest of getting along, he orders the same. The old man asks question after question about Mark's life, expressing interest in every detail. He is particularly sympathetic to Mark's complete estrangement from his family, a rift that came about after Mark had won several hundred dollars playing poker with relatives and his stepfather berated him, calling him a con man. "And then he made me return their money!"

"Return the money? When you won fair and square?" Roy repeats. "And he called you a con man. Unbelievable. They should have been celebrating your cleverness instead of putting you down for it. Frankly, given that kind of treatment, I wouldn't want to associate with any of them either. You made just the right choice."

"Thank you for saying that."

"Well, of course."

Mark's family is as divided as they come. His stepfather never liked him, and gradually he'd turned Mark's brother and mom against him as well. The words his stepdad has for Mark ring in his ears. *Loser. Unreliable. Con man.* Making it worse is hearing his older brother, Brian, agree. *Brian.* The preferred

Norman brother. Outwardly, Mark shrugs it off, but inside, each word stabs his heart.

The manhattans have loosened Mark's tongue, and he blurts out the one thing that bothers him most. "My stepdad likes to say I'm never going to amount to anything." Speaking the words aloud makes him clench his jaw.

Roy clucks. "What an awful thing to say. And not true, either. I'm quite sure of that." He takes a sip of his brandy manhattan. "At least you have your brother. That must be a comfort."

"Not really. He takes their side. Not only that, but he insists on calling me Spud. He's been doing it since we were kids. He thinks it's hilarious." Mark shakes his head at the thought. As a kid he envied families where the brothers were friends, the older one looking out for his little brother. That wasn't the case in his house.

"Spud." Roy frowns, his eyes narrowing. "I don't think it's one bit funny. Family should be building you up, not knocking you down."

Mark nods in agreement and adds, "My girlfriend, Monica, doesn't see much of her family either." He drums his fingers on the bar. "Well, at least we have each other."

Roy asks, "Why doesn't Monica see much of her family?"

Because they're all drunks and assholes? Mark sighs. "A lot of them have drinking problems, which makes it difficult. Her own father and brother have stolen money from her. She finds it best to keep her distance."

Roy nods. "I see."

"Believe me, she's tried."

Roy taps the rim of his glass and speaks thoughtfully. "As you get older, you realize that some people don't deserve a place in your life, while some deserve everything. My sister, for instance. She's always been the most important person to me.

She's getting forgetful these days, and I'd be grateful if you'd indulge her. Poor thing is starting to lose her short-term memory." His expression is grim. "It's sad to watch someone you love slip away."

"I understand. I'll make a point to be patient."

"That would be appreciated."

During the pause that follows, Mark asks, "Why did you buy me the suits? Am I going to be required to wear them to work?"

"Heavens, no." Roy smiles, amused. "You can wear whatever you like when you come to work. But tomorrow night Alma and I have something special planned. We're taking you and Lisa out to dinner at a fancy restaurant to welcome you to the family. I'd like you to wear the tan suit then. Otherwise, you can just hang on to the clothing for special occasions. I firmly believe every man should have at least one well-tailored suit, and now you have two." He takes off his glasses, holds them up to the light, and then polishes the lenses with a handkerchief.

"That's extremely generous of you. Thank you."

"You're very welcome."

"I don't know when I'll get the chance to wear them." Mark takes a sip from his drink. "I don't have many special occasions."

"You will." Roy returns his glasses to his face, then tucks the handkerchief into his pocket. "Funerals, weddings, business meetings. Dress for success—that's my motto. It's how young men come to rule the world."

How young men come to rule the world. Mark likes the sound of that. Roy, a complete stranger, sees more in him than his own family does. A cause for elation.

"Besides," Roy adds, "you remind me of myself when I was a young man."

Dear God, does this mean I'm staring at my future? Not if I can help it. Mark gives him a small smile. "I do have one question: When I leave your employ, am I required to give the clothes back?"

Roy looks amused. "Day one and you're already planning your escape?"

"Oh, nothing like that," Mark assures him. "I just wanted to know what you had in mind."

"There are no strings attached. The clothes are yours. Besides, what would I do with them? They wouldn't be good to anyone else. Once they've been tailored, they'll fit you like a glove."

"I appreciate it, but you just met me yesterday. I'm grateful. I just find it hard to understand."

Roy shrugs. "Indulge me, Mark. I'm an old man, and at this age, one becomes well aware that the end is drawing near. I never married, and I have no children, but I see potential in you and want to make a difference. Your time as a home health aide will be but a brief chapter in your life, but I'd like to think my influence on you will live on. I see big things for you, Mark Norman, and I'd love to play a role in your success." Roy takes a last sip of his drink and holds a finger up to the bartender for another one. It's amazing how much liquor this old man can put away without it seeming to affect him.

"I understand. Thank you, sir. I'll try to live up to your confidence in me." Even under the haze of slight drunkenness, Mark's heart skips a beat with excitement. He's never encountered someone this free with their money, much less someone willing to spend it on him with no expectations in return. Finally, the right things are coming his way.

Near four thirty, Roy declares it's time to pick up the suit. "Jim is probably nervously watching the door right now," he says, gingerly lowering himself off the barstool. "Wondering if I'm going to show up with his money."

Mark hands Roy his cane, and they head out the door of the

restaurant to the parking lot. When they get to the car, Roy goes over to the driver's side and holds out his hand. "Better give me the keys, Mark. You're not in any condition to drive."

Mark wants to object that he's just fine, more than capable of driving them back to the shop and then home, but his tongue has gotten larger in his mouth, and the edges of his vision have become wavy. Wordlessly, he hands over the keys.

CHAPTER FOUR

The next afternoon, Mark runs the pomade through his hair and combs it in place, duplicating what the barber did the day before. He dresses with care, adjusting the knot in his tie so it's perfectly centered. Monica walks in while he's buttoning the vest. Amused, she stops to watch. "What do you think?" he asks, turning to give her the full view.

She tilts her head to one side. "You look like you're going to a party at Gatsby's house."

"Not too far off. He has money like Gatsby and seems to like spending it."

"No kidding. I can't believe your first day of work was going out to a drinking lunch and buying you expensive suits. And then you walk off with two hundred bucks in cash?" It isn't envy Mark is hearing in Monica's voice—it is suspicion. "Something about this is definitely off." She folds her arms and purses her lips, considering.

"Like what?" Mark doesn't share her propensity for doubt. Why shouldn't good things come his way?

"It's just weird, that's all. They have to have some ulterior motive. Watch, they'll want you to star in their X-rated movies or be a drug courier or something. You'll see. There's always an agenda."

Mark shakes his head, amused at the thought of the Walgraves making stag films in their home. If Monica could see how sweet and frail these two are, she'd know her suggestions are ludicrous. "They're just old and running out of time. Roy said he sees potential in me and wants to make a difference."

"Yeah, but he *just* met you."

"I guess he fell under the old Mark Norman spell."

"Or maybe *you* fell under *his* spell." She laughs. "You *did* get the hideous haircut."

He surveys his reflection. "I don't think it's too bad, actually." At the very least, having the hair away from his face accentuates his strong jaw. In another era, he would have been a leading man in the movies.

"That's just the money talking."

"Maybe so."

The previous day, when Roy dropped him off at the apartment, the old man parked at the curb and pulled a stack of twenties out of the driver's-side door pocket. Handing Mark the pile, he asked him to take out the two-hundred-dollar payment for the haircut. Holding out a trembling hand, he said, "It'll be easier for you to do it."

Mark obliged, counting out the money and surreptitiously filching two additional twenties before returning the money. Roy, who was none the wiser, shook hands with Mark before he got out of the car.

Roy said, "See you tomorrow at five?"

"Yes, sir. I'll be there."

Watching Roy drive away, he again marveled at the guy's ability to navigate the streets, given all he'd had to drink. Mark had had just as many cocktails, and he more than felt the impact.

The next morning's headache confirms it.

By the time he walks into Alden Manor that afternoon, the aspirin has done its job, and he's feeling much better. He lets himself in and walks through the house until he finds Alma and Roy, dressed up and sitting in the blue room. Side by side on the couch, the two look small and faded, like aged photos. At the sight of Mark, Alma clutches a hand to her pearl necklace and comments on his appearance. "Handsome!"

"Thank you, ma'am." He smiles down at her.

"Welcome, my boy. Have a seat." Roy motions to one of the chairs. "Our reservation is at six, so we have time. We're just waiting for Lisa to come down. She's still getting dressed." Roy tells Mark about the restaurant, a lovely place out in the country called Duke's Supper Club. "It's a historic building. Once it was an inn, but now it has a dining room on one side and a bar on the other side. On weekends, they have bands and dancing. We've been going there for more than fifty years."

"Nice."

When Lisa comes through the double doors, Alma claps her gnarled fingers together in approval. Mark turns his head to look and is stunned. Lisa hasn't just changed clothes—she's been transformed. She wears a rose-colored dress with a dropped waist, trimmed in gold. In one hand she holds a matching clutch purse. Her hair is down and falls in soft curls around her shoulders. The most striking detail is the slight smile on her face. It occurs to Mark that he's never seen her without a dour expression.

Alma says, "Didn't I tell you this was your color?"

"Yes, you did." Lisa smooths the front of the dress.

"I knew it would be." Alma turns to Mark. "Isn't she beautiful?"

"Yes, she is beautiful," he agrees. And she is gorgeous this evening, but in an old-fashioned sort of way. Personally, he would prefer to see a girl in something a little sexier. A tight pair of jeans and a midriff top. Halter tops are even better. But he has to admit that this dress is an improvement from her previous look.

Mark drives to the restaurant with Lisa in the passenger seat, while Alma and Roy sit in the back. Along the way, Lisa reads Roy's handwritten directions aloud to Mark. Once they arrive at Duke's Supper Club, Lisa helps Alma out of the back seat and guides her to the front door.

The topic of Lisa's appearance comes up again after they are seated. Alma says, "So beautiful in that dress. Just so beautiful."

Roy has requested a specific small, curved booth, and Alma insists that Mark sit next to Lisa. The atmosphere is romantic, with candles and linen tablecloths. Roy orders a bottle of wine for the table, but when the waiter comes to pour, Lisa places a hand over her glass. "No thank you," she says. "Just tonic water for me."

Alma directs her attention to Mark. "Isn't she beautiful?"

This has to be the forgetfulness Roy mentioned yesterday. Mark says, "I would have to agree with you. Lisa looks absolutely gorgeous tonight."

"Thank you, Mark. That's very nice of you." Lisa sounds vaguely detached, but then again, she's been working for the Walgraves for some time and has probably heard enough of Alma's repeated questions.

Lisa is pointedly quiet during dinner, only speaking when asked a question. Alma, too, has little to say besides commenting on the food, which is delicious, although the portions are small. Mark feels the need to fill the conversational void, so he tells some jokes, the few he knows that are clean. He also does some impressions of the other passengers on the bus. Even Lisa can't help herself and stops frowning at one point to laugh at a punch line. After dinner, they order the restaurant's specialty dessert, apple tarts topped with scoops of vanilla custard. When the waiter presents the bill along with a tray of butter cream mints, Roy pays in cash, tipping generously. Speaking to Mark and Lisa, he says, "Thank you for accompanying us this evening. We rarely get a night out, so this has been a real treat."

Alma lifts her chin and says, "But we can't go now. There has to be dancing."

"Dear, they only have bands on the weekends." Roy pats her arm.

"No." Alma shakes her head; her face transforms into that of a willful child. "After dinner there is always dancing."

Roy explains to Lisa and Mark, "We used to come here in our younger days for dinner and dancing, so of course that's what she's remembering." His voice is tinged with nostalgia. "Those were the best times."

"Can't we just see?" Alma says, her small, trembling hand clutching his arm.

Roy nods. "We'll stop and show them on our way out."

As they walk through the restaurant, Roy's cane leads the way, and Alma takes careful steps with Lisa at her side. Mark brings up the rear, painfully aware of how slowly they are walking. It's all he can do to keep his impatience in check. *Move it, move it, move it.* Around him other diners notice them for all the wrong reasons. A mustached waiter cradling a pepper mill pauses to let them pass, and Mark shoots him an apologetic look. In return, the man says, "So nice to see young people out with their grandparents."

When they get to the hostess stand, they continue on, past the door where they entered, and into a dimly lit bar area, occupied by one lone bartender. The bar top gleams, empty except for heavy glass ashtrays in front of every third barstool. Small round tables surround what would have been a dance floor on a different night, and a small platform on the opposite side waits for a band that won't be assembling tonight. "See, my dear," Roy says. "There's no band tonight. Just the weekends."

Alma's mouth furrows in confusion. She looks around the room as if expecting a band to materialize. "But there has to be dancing." Her voice quavers. "And there *is* music." She points to the ceiling, where piped-in music resonates from round speakers embedded in the ceiling. "So there has to be dancing."

Roy holds up a finger to Lisa and Mark, indicating they should wait, then steers Alma over to the closest table and helps her to sit down. He leans over her, speaking quietly, one hand on her shoulder. Mark watches in silence.

Lisa folds her arms and taps her foot. "I don't like this."

"What do you mean?"

"When Alma gets like this . . ." She narrows her eyes. "I don't know. I just get a bad feeling."

She seems like the kind of girl who often has bad feelings. From what Mark can see, there's no need to worry. Roy has it under control. "She's a confused old lady. I'm sure it will be fine."

Lisa lifts her eyebrows. "Really? Day two and you're telling me what's what?" She sighs. "You'll find out there's so much more than meets the eye."

"Like what?"

"You'll see. This is not an easy job. It can get to you sometimes." Her voice is tinged with sadness.

Mark is usually adept at sizing up women, but he finds Lisa to be a puzzle. She doesn't fall prey to his charm, for one thing. Even more baffling is her dour outlook. Frankly, she has the personality of someone being led to the gallows. A real glum Gus.

Roy makes his way back to them and asks beseechingly, "May I impose on the two of you?"

Lisa's smile is a thinly disguised grimace. "Of course. What do you need?"

Roy exhales in relief. "Would you mind dancing a song or two?" He glances back at his sister, who watches them expectantly. "It would make Alma so happy."

"The two of us?" Lisa asks, gesturing between herself and Mark.

"Please?" Roy asks, his eyes begging. "She'd love to dance herself, but obviously, that's out of the question. Poor thing can barely move anymore." He smiles at Mark. "If the two of you wouldn't mind dancing just to humor her, I would be grateful. Afterward we'll call it a night and then drop Mark off at home on the way back."

Lisa shakes her head. "No. I don't think that's—"

"We'd be happy to dance," Mark says, extending a hand. Lisa reluctantly places her hand in his, and he pulls her to him in one smooth move, then begins to sway to the rhythm of the music. Glancing back at the table, he spots Alma, her face lit up in a bright smile. He whispers into Lisa's ear, "See, it's fine. Just a dance to make an old lady happy. Not a big deal." One song ends and another starts. He presses against her, moving to the strains of the music playing softly through the overhead speakers. A Barry Manilow song that he vaguely recognizes from a cassette tape favored by a former girlfriend.

"You think that's what this is? A dance to make an old lady happy?"

Mark shrugs. "Sure. Look at that sweet face." He points with his chin. "Alma's overjoyed. She probably thinks she's started something. That now we'll fall in love and wind up getting married, having twin babies that of course we'll name Roy and Alma, and that it all began here, on the dance floor at Duke's Supper Club." He's willing to play along. Whatever it takes for him to work his way into becoming Roy's main man.

Lisa leans in closer. "You could not be more wrong. This is part of something else. Something that's . . ." She stops to think a minute, as if searching for the right word. "Brewing."

Mark raises one eyebrow. "What, exactly?"

She raises her chin defiantly. "I'm not quite sure, but the longer I'm in that house the more I feel like something terrible is going to happen. Something is wrong with that place."

"You're kidding, right?"

Lisa shakes her head. "Nope, not kidding at all. Something's definitely off. Alden Manor, it's . . ." She blinks back what looks like the start of tears, then takes a deep breath and says, "At night, sometimes it feels like the walls are breathing and putting thoughts in my head. I get the most awful dreams too."

Mark looks back at the small café table, at Alma with her head in her hands, a dreamy smile on her face, and Roy, his hands folded as if in prayer, and all he can think is that Lisa either has the weirdest sense of humor ever or is batshit crazy. He's willing to bet money on the latter. Finally, he says, "No way."

"You don't believe me? You think I'm making it up?"

As diplomatically as possible, he says, "I think it must be difficult working in an old house and interacting with two elderly people every single day."

"No," she says emphatically. "There's more to it than that. The first few months, I was fine. It's just lately that things feel different."

He has a question of his own. "If you honestly believe something terrible is going to happen, why do you keep working for them? Why not just quit?"

"I'm working on it," she says quietly. "I'm leaving as soon as I can." The hand that is draped around his shoulder goes to the gold cross hanging from her neck, as if reassuring herself it is still there. "Did you know that they don't even go to church?" Her lips press together in disapproval.

She sounds like a religious fanatic, making him wonder if she's the type who anticipates wickedness around every corner. Or maybe she's just crazy. It's also possible that this is her idea of a joke. He whirls her around the dance floor and looks to the old people for approval. When he meets Alma's eye, she sits up and blows Mark a kiss. In response, he winks, and she practically swoons. He totally has it. He, Mark Norman, is a ladies' man, even if the lady in question is barely hanging on to life. Meanwhile, the girl in his arms is not quite as enthralled with him. Lisa moves like a fifth grader being forced to slow dance with the nerdiest boy in class.

Well. If he is going to become a valued member of the Walgrave household, he needs to gain her trust. "Relax," he whispers, tightening his hold on her waist. "Just let yourself go. You've got nothing to worry about. I've got you covered."

CHAPTER FIVE

The next day after exiting the bus, Mark rounds the corner to find the side street devoid of traffic, the only sound the cawing of birds. Looking up, he counts eight of them—seven crows perched on a telephone line and another one on top of a nearby pole, wings flapping. He shakes his head. Such ugly, filthy birds, the kind that would pick at roadkill. Vermin in the sky. Their discordant squawking grates on his ears. "Shut up," he mutters under his breath.

When he reaches Alden Manor, Mark finds Lisa on her hands and knees crawling around the porch. She's wearing jeans and a plain sleeveless blouse; her hair is pulled up into a grandmotherly bun. She doesn't notice him until after he comes up the stairs and steps forward into the shade of the covered porch. "Can I help you?" he asks, a smile in his voice.

"I don't think so." She scrambles to her feet as if he caught her doing something wrong. "I was looking for my necklace. I thought it might have fallen off when I was shaking out the rugs, but it's not here." She brushes off her knees.

"Your gold cross?"

"That's the one." She puts a hand up to her throat. "It doesn't feel right not to have it on."

Mark nods. "That's how I feel when I forget to wear a watch. I find myself looking at my wrist all day."

Lisa gazes up at him with her brown eyes and nods. *There is something different about her today,* he thinks. Less guarded, perhaps? She is an odd one, with her pale skin, big eyes, and serious countenance. She has the potential to be gorgeous, but it's as if she is deliberately downplaying her looks. He's used to the women who frequent bars, the kind who toss their Farrah Fawcett hair and flirtatiously lick their glossy lips. The bar women are nearly always giddy, dancing and laughing. Lisa, on the other hand, gives off an air of unhappiness.

"After what I said last night, you must think I'm ridiculous," she says, leaning against the doorframe. "Either that or you think I'm crazy. But I assure you, I am neither."

"No. I don't think either of those things," he says, although of course he does think she's being completely ridiculous with her talk of the walls breathing and putting thoughts in her head. "We just got off on the wrong foot. Since we're going to be working together and I'll need you to help me figure things out, I'm thinking we should get along." He sticks out a hand. "Friends?"

"Sure, why not?" She shakes, her hand small in his. "We can pretend to be friends." Tilting her head to one side, she adds, "But don't get too attached to me. I won't be here much longer."

"So you said." He lets his smile fade and gestures to the door. "I should probably report for work. I don't want to be late."

"No. They're with Dr. Cross right now. When he comes, they always send me out of the room. We probably have a few minutes before we need to go inside."

"Their doctor makes house calls?"

"Every week," she says. "That's what money gets you. When you're wealthy, you don't have to go into a nursing home. The nursing home comes to you." While they're waiting, she explains that besides meal preparation and housekeeping, one of her duties is to help Alma get bathed and dressed. "I also clip their nails, and last week Roy asked me to trim his ear hair." She shudders. "He said it was driving him crazy."

Trimming ear hair is something that has to be done? "Oh God. They won't expect me to do that, will they?"

She crosses her arms. "Well, what did you expect? For ten dollars an hour you had to know it wasn't all going to be funnel cakes and Ferris wheels." A gust of wind sends some air in their direction, but it is too hot to provide any relief.

"I don't know. I guess I didn't think about it too much."

"Better start thinking about it."

"Yes, ma'am." He smirks.

"I mean it. Think seriously about why they're offering so much money. It's not because you're all that. It's because of what they expect."

There is a defiance in her voice he hasn't heard before. He doesn't mind. A woman giving him the business is easier to take than one who is depressed. Lowering his voice, he says, "Tell me more about your experience working here."

"What do you want to know?"

"Everything."

"Okay." Lisa takes a deep breath. "After I first started the job, everything was fine. It was fun, even. Roy was driving then, all the time, and Alma—well, she wasn't like she is now."

"How was she?"

She speaks softly, like she's letting Mark in on a secret. "More with it, for one thing. She and I used to have long conversations. I swear, both of them have gotten ten years older in just a few months."

Mark nods. He's heard of this before: elderly people who have health issues and age as a result, seemingly overnight. Suddenly the things they did before to stay young—exercise, dye their hair, dress smartly—is too much trouble. It's not so much that they look older; it's that they can't keep up with whatever they previously did. He had a great-aunt who had a stroke and went from being a golf-playing, peppy lady to an invalid crone. Just like that.

"You believe me?" she asks.

"Of course."

Relief washes over her face. "So, that's one thing. They've gone downhill. And around the same time, I started to hear things at night. Whispering and noises, like the walls are breathing. It's like it's trying to tell me something. You know?"

"Sure," he says, but he's really thinking that what she's describing is not all that uncommon for an old house. Even his childhood home, a suburban trilevel, made odd noises at night, especially when it was windy. Anyone with an imagination could find themselves spooked under the circumstances.

"And then one night, I went up to the second floor to look around." Lisa leans in conspiratorially and whispers, "We're not allowed up there, but I was curious." She exhales audibly. "I should have never done it. I wish I hadn't seen what I did."

In her voice, Mark hears the weight of someone who has taken on more than they can handle. "What did you see?" he asks.

"Old photos and some other things. It's hard to explain, but I'll show you sometime. You have to see it to understand how creepy it is." She continues. "After that, I started having bad dreams. Terrible, disturbing nightmares. I wake up in a cold sweat, my heart racing. One of the worst parts is that the dreams begin with me waking up in my bedroom in this house, so I feel like it's real."

Mark nods. He's had those kinds of nightmares. The dreams themselves are terrible, but equally bad is waking up the second time and not being able to discern subconscious hallucination from reality. It can feel like you're losing your mind. "This sounds really troubling. Have you thought about getting a new job?"

"Of course. But I'm trapped for now."

"But you're not. You can leave anytime you like."

She shakes her head, a look of misery crossing her face. "No, I can't. I literally have nowhere else to go."

"Your family?"

She shakes her head. "I wouldn't send my worst enemy to live with my family," she says, a bitter tinge to her voice.

"That bad?"

"Worse than you can imagine. Getting this job was a godsend. Dr. Cross knew my doctor and arranged for me to get the job. The timing couldn't have been better." She smiles ruefully, remembering. "I couldn't believe my luck. When I arrived and saw that it was such a gorgeous old house, and that I'd get my own room and bathroom, I felt like I won the lottery. Roy and Alma were a little odd, but nice. They even had all new clothes custom-made for me. Not what I would have picked out, but they meant well."

"Like the dress you wore last night?"

"Exactly. I refused to wear most of the clothes, saying I didn't want them to get ruined, and Alma was fine with that. Like it was no big deal that they spent all this money on a whole wardrobe that I'd never wear. Then I wanted to get my hair cut, but they said I could only get it trimmed. No more than half an inch."

"Why?"

"I don't know." A look of concern crosses her face, as if

something just occurred to her. "You won't repeat any of this, will you?"

"No, I promise. This is just between us." He leans against the brick facing of the building, hands in pockets.

"I've been looking at apartments for rent in the newspaper. I'm thinking I'll move in September." Lisa cocks her head to one side. "I didn't make a mistake telling you all this, did I?" She stares at him, waiting. "I don't want to hurt their feelings—I just can't keep doing this anymore."

"I promise not to say anything."

"You better not," she says.

CHAPTER SIX

The front door swings open so suddenly it takes Mark by surprise. Reflexively, he steps aside. A man carrying a leather medical bag, shirtsleeves rolled up to his elbows, steps out and joins them. "Here you are," he says, his voice mellow and warm.

"Dr. Cross." Lisa nods. "This is our new employee, Mark Norman."

Dr. Cross pulls the door shut behind him and extends a hand. "Nice to meet you, Mark."

Mark sizes him up as they shake hands. Dr. Cross is strikingly tall and younger than he anticipated, thin with sharp features, impressive sideburns, and a head of curly brown hair. His grip is firm, and he gives Mark a friendly smile.

"I'm glad to meet you, Dr. Cross," Mark says.

"Welcome aboard. I take it that Lisa's shown you the ropes?"

"Not yet."

"You will today, then?" Dr. Cross says, giving Lisa a pointed look. His voice is still friendly, but his tone gives Mark the impression that he's giving an order rather than making a suggestion.

"Of course," Lisa says.

The doctor gestures toward the door. "Lisa, why don't you go on inside and check in with Alma and Roy? I'd like to get Mark up to speed on a few things." Off in the distance a truck rumbles, and a bird lets out a distinctly angry-sounding squawk. Lisa hesitates, and Dr. Cross adds, "Just for a minute. Mark will be with you shortly."

She nods and goes inside. It isn't until the door closes that Dr. Cross addresses Mark again. "I was glad to hear you'd been hired, Mark. Roy and Alma need two home health aides, and Lisa is getting a little frayed around the edges."

From the ensuing pause, Mark senses he's waiting for a response. "I hadn't noticed. She's been helpful."

"That may be, but I've been worried about her. It's not easy caregiving for the elderly, especially when they're declining so rapidly."

"I'm sorry to hear this," Mark says, when what he really would like to know is exactly how rapidly.

"Yes," Dr. Cross says sadly. "Alma is suffering from a cognitive decline. You may notice some confusion or repetition in her speech. Her physical health isn't optimal either. She's very frail. Roy has end-stage congestive heart failure. It's being treated with medication, but it's just a matter of time for him. Of course"—and here he gives a wry smile—"it's just a matter of time for most of us."

"I understand."

"I hear that you had an outing with Roy the other day that lasted several hours?"

"Yes, sir."

Dr. Cross crosses his arms. "And last night the four of you went to dinner at Duke's Supper Club?"

"That's right." Mark senses disapproval and tries to lighten his response with a smile. "We had a delicious meal. Everyone had a nice time."

"I'm sure that's the case, but I have to tell you that these kinds of outings take their toll on older people. Today Roy is exhausted, and to be honest, I'm worried about the strain on his heart. Not your fault, of course, but if he suggests this kind of thing again, you should discourage it."

Mark says, "Of course."

"I'm also hoping that you'll be there to bolster Lisa so that she doesn't get too burned out. Alma is very fond of her, and we don't want her to quit. Lisa already knows the workings of the household. She'd be hard to replace."

"I'm happy to help."

"Older people can sometimes be odd when the end is near. He might ask you to do some things that don't seem to make sense. Just be agreeable." Dr. Cross reaches into his pocket and pulls out a white business card. "Feel free to call me for any reason. Any questions or concerns, I want to hear them. Alma and Roy are important to me."

"Yes, sir." Mark tucks the card into his pants pocket. "If anything comes up, you'll be the first to know."

After Dr. Cross leaves and is striding down the sidewalk to his parked car, Mark goes inside to find Roy and Alma at the dining room table. Lisa's there too, pouring coffee and asking if they want jelly on their toast. When Mark walks into the room, Roy greets him with a friendly smile, and Lisa nods, while Alma doesn't acknowledge his presence at all. *Why is it,* Mark wonders, *that old people so often have a vacant look about them?* It's as if the life force has leaked out of them, leaving empty shells of cloudy eyes, papery skin, and trembling limbs. Their bodies are all used up and barely functioning, and still they keep on, breathing in, breathing out, eating and dressing and bathing, a burden to everyone around them. He met these two a few days earlier, and already he can see that they are all used up. Roy acknowledged it himself—it is young men who rule the world.

Lisa directs Mark to the kitchen, where she puts him to work cutting cantaloupe into thin wedges and arranging them on two separate plates. "Like this?" he asks, and when she nods, he presents the plates to Roy and Alma as if he were an enthusiastic waiter. "Fresh fruit, just for you!" he proclaims.

After breakfast, Lisa helps Alma to her feet, brushing the crumbs off the front of her shirt as if she were a child. Mark hands Roy his cane and follows the trio down the hall to what Lisa calls the television room. A boxy TV sits on wooden legs in one corner, rabbit-ear antenna perched on top. Two recliners with plastic over the arms sit on the opposite side of the room. After getting Roy and Alma situated, Lisa kneels in front of the TV and turns the dial until she finds a game show, *The Price Is Right*. As she adjusts the antenna, Mark watches as a contestant unsuccessfully bids on a stereo. "Oh, too bad," Roy says to no one in particular.

"Mark and I are going to clean up the kitchen," Lisa announces. "We'll be back soon."

Once they are in the kitchen she begins to bustle around, gathering up the breakfast dishes and stacking them next to the sink. "What did Dr. Cross want to talk about?" she asks, handing him a dish towel.

"He's worried that you're getting frayed around the edges."

"Hmm. Frayed around the edges?" Lisa turns off the water and dips a dishcloth into the suds. "That's his take on it, huh? I'd say I'm ready to have a nervous breakdown."

"If you tell me what to do, I can take some of the load off."

"There's no real load. It's just this. What I told you about already." Her eyes dart around the room. "A big gloomy house where time stretches on endlessly and presses in on you until you feel like you want to scream."

Mark allows a small silence before saying, "So what are my chores? What's the routine?"

"Regular housework. Cleaning, food prep, getting the mail. That kind of thing. Dr. Cross comes by frequently to check on Alma and Roy." Lisa returns her attention to the sink. "Other than that, the only time they have visitors is when they have their dinner meetings."

"What kind of dinner meetings?"

She straightens, soap bubbles still clinging to her fingers. "They belong to this group. The Redevine Society. Every few weeks the group comes for dinner, and then they have some kind of meeting. Those are my favorite evenings because all I have to do is set the table and leave the front door unlocked for the guests. The society members bring the food and the wine, and I get to spend the night in my room." She wipes and rinses a plate and hands it to him. "They even help Alma and Roy with their nighttime routine, which is a nice break, let me tell you."

"What's the point of the group?"

Her mouth twists. "I don't know. It seems to be some kind of social dinner thing." She shrugs. "All I know is that I have to wash the dishes the next day."

"The Redevine Society." He lets the words roll around in his mouth. His mother once belonged to a card club of women her age who called themselves "the Posse." That name didn't make much sense either, although it definitely amused the middle-aged women in the club.

"The other members are much younger than Alma and Roy, but it doesn't seem like they do much besides eating and talking. I do know that the group has been going on for a long time, though, because I've seen pictures of them over the years."

"So you never asked about it?"

"Nope. I mind my own business." She continues soaping the plates, juice glasses, and silverware, rinsing each item before handing it to him. Letting out the water, she sighs, and the sound is heavy and dejected.

No wonder she feels time stretches on endlessly in this house, Mark thinks. *The job is drudgery because she makes it that way.* Left to his own devices, he would have the dishes done in half the time. He's new now, but once he gets the routine down, he knows he'll be taking over. It'll be better that way, and in the long run she'll be happier too.

Folding the dish towel, he turns to her and says, "Now, what about that tour?"

Lisa nods and leads the way, identifying rooms as they go. So many rooms that they soon begin to blur. The library. The drawing room. The blue room. The dining room. A powder room. The pantry. And on and on. She waits patiently while he opens doors and looks in cabinets. "I just like to know where everything is," he says, although there's more to it than that. He's scoping out the place, looking for forgotten valuables, but what he encounters is more dust, rather than items that can be easily lifted and resold. *Too bad.*

Passing the TV room, she calls out, "I'm giving Mark a tour of the first floor." When they get to the back of the house, she points out her own bedroom, letting him view it from the doorway. Across the hall are Alma and Roy's bedrooms, linked by a bathroom between the two rooms. "They share a bathroom, but I have my own," Lisa says.

"Cool." Mark gives an admiring nod.

She leans toward him, and for a moment he thinks she's going to hug him. Instead, she quietly says, "One time they slept late, so I went in to check on them, and they were both in Roy's bed. Naked."

"No way."

"Yes. I swear it's true. They were snuggled up together,

stark naked. I almost quit that day." She scrunches her nose and makes a slight gagging noise.

"Are you sure they were naked? Maybe it just looked that way."

"Trust me, I'm sure."

"What did you do?"

"What do you think I did?" Her tone is bitter. "I backed out of the room, closed the door, and knocked. Roy yelled out for me to come back in half an hour, and when I did, they were in pajamas in their own beds. I seriously wanted to quit. Right then and there. Just walk out the door." She exhales loudly. "But of course I couldn't leave. I had nowhere to go." She wanders into Roy's room, her fingers trailing across the chenille bedspread on the double bed.

Mark tries to make sense of what she's just told him. Why would a brother and sister be in bed together at all, much less naked? The image of the two old people—their bodies as bare as the day they were born, spooning in that same bed—comes to mind, and he is sickened by the thought of their tissue-paper skin laced with blue veins, the sagging folds of skin, shriveled genitals, and gray pubic hair. *If they even have pubic hair.* It occurs to him that maybe even that goes sparse with age. *Gross.*

He shakes off the mental image and walks into the shared bath, taking in the octagon-tiled floor, the pedestal sink, and claw-foot tub. A walk-in shower has been installed more recently, as has the light fixture above the mirrored medicine cabinet. The room's antiseptic appearance is heightened by the smell of Lysol. Opening the cabinet, he finds a bowl containing a bar of shaving soap and a brush, along with a razor, toothpaste, bandages, and other typical bathroom accessories. The top shelf has four vials of prescribed medication. "What are these?" he asks, taking one down and reading the label. Dr. Cross is listed as the prescribing doctor, but Mark doesn't recognize the name of the drug.

"One is for blood pressure, one's a water pill, and one is nitroglycerin for Roy's heart condition. And this one," she says, holding up the largest of the four, "contains tranquilizers. They use them when they have trouble sleeping."

"Do you have to give them their medications?"

"No, Roy keeps track of that. At least for now."

Mark nods and proceeds to Alma's room. It's nearly identical to Roy's in size, with the same chenille spread covering the bed and a dresser to match. It's plain compared to the rest of the house. "Their bedrooms aren't very big." He walks over to the window. A strip of grass separates the space between Alden Manor and the industrial building next door. "Not much of a view, either."

Lisa joins him, looking out. "These rooms weren't intended to be bedrooms, originally. The actual bedrooms are on the second floor. They just converted them as bedrooms so they don't have to go up and down."

"The stairs," he says, realizing. The staircase rising up to the second floor would be as insurmountable as Mount Everest for someone like Alma.

They step out into the hallway, and he says, "Do you think they'd notice if we went upstairs and took a quick look?"

Lisa shakes her head. "Not now." She lowers her voice. "But if you want, you can come back tonight after their bedtime and I'll take you up then."

CHAPTER SEVEN

The bus ride is completely different after dark. For one thing, getting a seat to himself is not a problem. Just a handful of riders this time of night. An old man with closed eyes, his head pressed up against the window; an older woman in a waitress uniform, her pad still sticking out of her front pocket. Most notable, though, are two attractive young women sitting up front right behind the driver. They wear clinging dresses with plunging necklines, their hair curled back from their faces. At a glance he knows they're disco girls. When he boarded the bus, he walked past them and kept going, taking a seat several rows behind them. They've made sneaky looks back at him a few times, laughing in the way of flirty girls who've had too much to drink.

He's on a bus for the third time today, not even sure why he's returning to Alden Manor except that Lisa seems to think it's the only time they can safely go upstairs. He's curious—but not expecting much. Lisa strikes him as someone who is having trouble holding it together and may be prone to exaggeration.

When the bus gets to his stop, Mark is already on his feet and making his way down the aisle. As he passes the two women, one of them says, "Bye, now," while her friend giggles. As the bus rolls away, he hears their laughter through the open windows. Walking down the block, hands in his pockets, he's on high alert after dark in this sketchy neighborhood, but he finds himself alone.

Somehow that makes it even more frightening.

The landscape has transformed after dark into something eerie; the air is cooler too. The wind has picked up, a foreshadowing of the storm front predicted for later on. He hopes to leave Alden Manor before the rain comes. He'd like to be on the bus safely heading home at that point. If the timing is right, he'll get back at the same time as Monica gets home and will join her in her after-work shower. After every shift she can't wait to take off her waitress uniform, saying it stinks of cigarette smoke and kitchen grease. She usually kicks off her shoes and sheds her pantyhose right inside the apartment door, then unzips her dress. She drops her clothing on the floor, one piece at a time, until she's at the bathroom door, deliciously nude, a trail of clothes behind her. He smiles at the thought. What he wouldn't give to be there, seeing her like that right now.

But first, he has to see what Lisa is talking about on the second floor. How did she put it? *I wish I hadn't seen what I did.* He has to admit he's curious.

When he gets to Alden Manor, he pauses for a moment on the sidewalk in front, perturbed to see it's completely dark. *Dammit.* Lisa has forgotten to leave the porch light on. When he left at five, she told him the porch would be lit and the key would be under the mat. She assured him that Roy and Alma would be sound asleep by the time he arrived.

Above the house the slimmest zigzag of lightning lights up the sky for just an instant; the flash of light makes him feel exposed. Off in the distance he hears a car honk on the main street, and overhead comes the flapping of wings of what has to be a very large bird. For a moment, Mark has an urge to turn and run before anyone sees him there, but something keeps him rooted to the spot, and he makes a sudden decision—if the key isn't where it it's supposed to be, he is going home. No way will he ring the doorbell and risk waking up Roy and Alma. At this hour, any excuse he comes up with will sound suspicious.

After Mark locates the key under the doormat, he figures he'll see it through. Waiting for his eyes to adjust, he goes to the door and locates the lock plate. With one turn of the key, he hears the satisfying click of a metallic release. Inside the house, the engulfing darkness sets loose another raft of doubts. At night, the interior feels like the haunted houses he frequented as a child at Halloween. He envisions ghoulish faces popping out and monsters grabbing at him with long claws. A large, dark mass off to the left towers over him, threatening to swallow him up. His heart gallops in his chest. *I'm in Alden Manor,* he reminds himself. *Just an old building. Nothing scary at all.*

Within a minute his pulse has slowed. Around him the dark woodwork comes into focus, and the monster rising up on his left is only the winding staircase. He's such a pansy. There's no reason to be frightened. If anything, Mark rationalizes, he is the frightening one. Anyone seeing him here at this hour, creeping in the shadows, would assume he's come to burglarize the place. Did Lisa set this whole thing up to trap him into looking bad so he would lose his job? He doubts it. Although there is something off about her, she doesn't seem that cunning.

As Mark makes his way down the hall, he notices a sliver of light under one of the doors ahead. Roy and Alma would already be in bed. It has to be Lisa in the blue room, as promised. He is painfully aware of the brush of his footsteps against the hallway runner and the rumble of thunder outside. He lifts his hand to knock on the closed door, then thinks better of it and turns the knob. Upon opening the door, he sees Lisa sitting in one of the tall-backed chairs. A tableside lamp next to her is the sole light in the room. She has a book spread open in her lap. "You're late," she says.

The admonition annoys him, but Mark brushes it off. He steps inside the room and whispers, "Take it up with the bus company."

She closes the book and sets it on the table. "I wasn't sure if you were going to show."

The implication stings. The inference is too close to his stepfather's description of him as unreliable. "I said I'd come back, and I did."

Lisa nods in resignation and gets to her feet. He sees now that she has a flashlight in her right hand. "Well, it's getting late. Let's get this over with." As if he's been pestering her and she's doing him the favor.

He follows her out of the room and down the corridor. The flashlight is their only light now, a beam that leads them through the house to the staircase. Without even pausing, she takes the steps two at a time, and he trails her up the flight of stairs, running his hand along the smooth banister for guidance. At the top, she stops on the large landing and opens the double doors. A whiff of dust tickles his nose, the musty smell of a place that has been closed off for a long time.

She continues on down a long, expansive corridor, past closed doors on either side. The walls are lined with framed paintings. Some of them are landscapes, while others are portraits of people from long ago, but he can't get a decent look while still keeping pace with Lisa. The hallway ends at another set of double doors. She opens one and steps inside, beckoning him to follow.

Once inside, she shines the light in all directions, giving him a sense of the space. Mark wasn't sure what to expect, but it sure wasn't this. This room is enormous, ballroom-sized, the ceiling rising at least eight feet higher than in the hallway. The floor is made up of multicolored mosaic tile. "Is there some reason we can't turn on the lights?" he asks, whispering.

"They don't work up here," she says. "Believe me, I checked. I even went down in the basement to check the fuse box. There are no fuses in place for the second or third floor. Someone took them out."

"Oh." As she waves the light in a wide circle, Mark takes it all in. The room is oddly naked, unfurnished except for a plain wooden table in the middle of the room. On the far end is a platform with a huge desk-sized podium facing outward, as if this was once a hall where speeches were given. Behind the podium, sitting farther back on the platform, is a large black box, the same size as the box that held the punching bag his brother got one year as a Christmas present.

The walls on each side are lined with dozens of pictures, crowding the spaces between the windows. This ballroom, if that's what it is, is interesting in its own way, but nothing about it is disturbing, unless you count the fact that he's standing here in the near-dark with this odd girl. "So what specifically did you find so upsetting?"

Lisa says, "Just take a look around first. I want to see if you have the same reaction."

Guessing games are not usually something he enjoys, but he is willing to play along. He holds out a hand. "Flashlight, please." She hands it over, and methodically he begins to assess the room, starting with the black-and-white photographs hanging on the left wall. The first photograph, closest to the door, shows a group of eight people sitting around a dining room table, lifting champagne flutes. The caption underneath reads, *1902, The Redevine Society*.

He focuses the beam of light on the group and peers at those in the picture, four men and four women, all of them middle-aged, each one smiling with delight. "The Redevine Society?" He turns to Lisa. "Isn't that the club you said Alma and Roy belong to?"

"That's the one."

The photos seem to be arranged by year, and each one is of the Redevine Society. As he walks, he reads the dates aloud. "1908. 1912. 1919." In every picture, the members who are posing are clothed in what has to be the formal wear of the time. Mark scans the faces. No one looks familiar, but of course, that was a given. It wasn't as if Theodore Roosevelt or Harry Houdini would have attended a soiree in Wisconsin.

Ever since Lisa handed over the flashlight, she's been at his elbow encroaching on his space. *She's afraid,* he thinks. If he were with any other woman, he'd be tempted to tease a scare out of her, but he senses that Lisa isn't the type to take that kind of thing well. "I guess the Redevine Society has been going on for a while, then."

He stares at the photo. Happy rich people, dressed up and eating delicious food and drinking champagne. Not a care in the world. *Must be nice,* he thinks. Maybe someday that would be him. *No, nix that.* Someday that *will* be him. He will order the finest bottle of champagne and order from the menu without even looking at the prices. Mark can envision it—now all he has to do is make it happen.

A burst of lightning outside lights up the side windows and illuminates the room for a split second. Mark, suddenly aware of the claustrophobic pressure of the stifling air in the room, asks, "Can we open one of these windows?"

"They're all locked."

"Really? That's odd."

She doesn't reply. Sweat trickles down between his shoulder blades, making his T-shirt cling uncomfortably to his back. He wipes his forehead with the back of his hand. That shower with Monica is sounding better all the time.

He studies the photos again, noting the progression of the group as they age from photo to photo, getting older and older, until finally they're all senior citizens. He peers at one that is dated 1921. Though the people are still fashionably dressed, the photos time-stamp the ravages of age. The men with their thinning hair, paunchy guts, and sagging jowls; the women dressed to disguise their spreading midsections and dropped bosoms. The women come off somewhat better, probably because they can camouflage their changed appearance with hair dye and glittery jewelry. Still, to him they look like hags. "It must be hell to be old," he says. Lisa offers no response.

And then suddenly the next Redevine Society photo, dated 1922, pictures an entirely different set of people. Still four couples, but much younger, as young as Mark himself. They sit at the same table, with wide smiles, glasses raised to whoever was taking the picture. "That's weird," he says, taking a closer look.

CHAPTER EIGHT

"What's weird?" Lisa asks.

"The Redevine Society. It's like one group retired and then another bunch of people took over. That's unusual, don't you think?" He turns to Lisa, who just stares, a blank look on her face. "With clubs, aren't there usually transitions? I mean, wouldn't the new people join the former members and learn the ropes?"

She shakes her head. "I'm not a society girl, so I wouldn't know." Her voice is loud, echoing between the tile floor and the high ceiling.

Alarmed, he lowers his own voice in response. "Don't you think we should keep our voices down? Alma and Roy might wake up." He glances down at the mosaic tiles below his feet, each piece no larger than a playing card. Together the tiles create a pattern, which starts at the center of the room and radiates outward like the rays of the sun. It's possible the old people are sleeping right below where they now stand. Easy enough for one of them to be awakened by their voices or the creaking of footsteps overhead. If they call out for Lisa and she doesn't come, what next? Would they get up and phone Dr. Cross? Or would Roy feel spry enough to search the house? How would Mark explain his presence?

He feels his stomach lurch, sickened by the risk he's taking. This whole ordeal has become a fool's errand. There's nothing disturbing here. Lisa lured him back at night by promising something that turned out to be nothing, and stupidly he fell for it. His error in judgment might just lose him a good job. "Maybe I should just leave now," he says, handing her the flashlight. "I don't care how soundly they're sleeping. They're bound to hear us walking above them. I'm going to go."

"No!" She pushes the flashlight back at him. "They won't hear us—you can trust me on that."

"How can you be so sure?"

Lisa laughs, a brittle sound in the empty space. "Because I've been living here for four months. Every night after dinner, they have three or four manhattans, and after that they sleep like the dead. Alma sometimes gets up and wanders around confused, but that's usually later, around three a.m. or so. Believe me, at this point, they're out cold."

"Three or four manhattans?" Is that a lot for old people to drink? He thinks it might be, especially for Alma, who's a small woman.

"Yeah, they hit the sauce pretty hard. It's a big house," she adds, sensing his uncertainty. "And believe me, their hearing isn't all that great."

"As long as you're sure we won't get caught up here."

"I'm sure."

He turns away and resumes studying the photos. The second set of Redevine Society members carries on in much the same way as the previous group. Dressed in evening attire, they sit at elegantly set tables, imbibing champagne and enjoying various delicacies. A few of the pictures are taken in restaurants, the waitstaff standing in the background, folded linen over their arms. All of the photos are labeled with the year and the words *The Redevine Society*, and a few of them have something handwritten across the top as well. *To never growing old.* Huh. Judging by the raised glasses, that had to be their toast. He nods approvingly. It's better than toasting to world peace or good health. Given the choice, who wouldn't want to avoid the eventual slide into decrepitude?

He keeps going until he nears the end, the last photo taken in the dining room at Alden Manor showing the same eight people in 1969, but this time all of them are casually attired and not looking nearly so happy. Clearly, the years had worn them down. He's not surprised to see that two of the members are Alma and Roy. The others are elderly, with no sign of the new members, the ones who currently meet.

Backtracking, he goes from picture to picture, watching as the years photographically melt away. Amazing how age could change someone so entirely. In his youth, Roy had a full head of dark hair and a strong jawline. His smile curved slightly, as if he had a secret, while his eyes were wide and bright. His clothes had a tailored fit. It was clear that Roy had once been a man of vitality, one with a bright future. And his sister? If you could look past the dated clothing and hair, she'd been a total fox. How sad it was to see them now, needing help to do even the simplest things.

He'd die before he let that happen to him.

"There are pictures on the other side too," Lisa prompts.

He crosses the room, Lisa on his heels. The photos lining the wall on the other side feature two people, performers of some kind. The man seems to be the star of the production, while a young female stands nearby. A circus act? No. Not a circus act at all. These two are part of a magic act. The man, dressed in a tuxedo, is the magician, the woman his assistant. With a start, Mark realizes that the pictures are of Roy and

Alma in their younger days. "Holy shit," he says, tapping the glass with one finger. "It's really them."

"It's really them," Lisa repeats. "Can you believe they kept this from me? I asked Roy once what they used to do before they retired, and he said he was a salesman and that Alma kept house for him. And when I asked Alma, she told me some story about working as a seamstress."

"Weird."

"Right?" She shakes her head. "I can't believe they lied right to my face. And they didn't even get their stories straight."

"Maybe they were afraid you'd ask them to do a magic trick," Mark says, not taking his eyes off the photos. He marvels at the Walgraves' earlier youth. In the photos, Alma has on what would have been a revealing costume at the time, and from the look on her face, she is relishing her role in the show. In the photo labeled *Milwaukee, Wisconsin*, she's inside a wooden box, only her head and feet sticking out on each end while her brother saws her in half. In another she's on a different stage in Omaha, Nebraska, holding out a black top hat while Roy pulls out a white rabbit. Definite old-timey shit. Later on down the row, the photos show tricks that are more impressive, while the locales become more far-flung. New York. London. Rome. Paris. With each successive picture, the costumes become more elaborate and the venues larger.

Lisa taps a finger against the glass. "The box they used to cut her in half is over there." She gestures toward the stage at the box Mark noticed when they first entered. "It has openings for her head and feet." Shuddering, she adds, "It reminds me of a short coffin."

He stops at a photo where Roy has one arm in the air pointing at Alma, who levitates over his head. "How did he do that?" he asks incredulously.

Lisa says, "I don't know, but you see that kind of thing all the time in professional shows. People appear and disappear and float and all that stuff. If you ask me, there's something unnatural about it. It's not what people should be doing if they want to live a righteous life." Her voice is disapproving.

So that's it. She sees a magic show as something wrong. Sinful, even. "They're just tricks done for entertainment purposes," Mark says. "If we knew how they were done, we could re-create these tricks ourselves. It's not any different than working as an acrobat or a singer. Pretty standard stuff."

"If it's all so innocent, why keep it a secret? They obviously did this magic act for years and years."

She's right about that. The photos of the two of them progress to show Roy and Alma as they got older and the tricks more complicated. In one of them, Alma's headless body sits primly on a wooden chair, her hands folded in her lap, while Roy holds her head under one arm like a basketball. Eerily, her tongue hangs out and her eyes pop out of their sockets. In another, she has inexplicably become triplets, two versions of herself standing on either side of her brother, while a third sits on the floor looking up at him with a huge smile on her face. All three Almas look delighted.

"I'd love to know how that was done." Mark leans in to take a closer look.

"I don't know. Mirrors? Some kind of projector?"

"I can't even imagine."

At the halfway point he comes to two small framed posters, both illustrated in color: *Walgrave's Astounding Wonders—Performing daily at three and eight.* The first one shows a drawing of a mustached Roy shooting a bolt of electricity out of his palm and aiming it right at Alma. Mark reads the caption at the bottom. *Prepare to be amazed! You won't believe your eyes!* He grins at the hyperbole. The second poster shows a simulated time lapse of Roy deteriorating from a man into a skeleton. The caption at the bottom says, *The amazing Roy Walgrave manipulates time right before your very eyes. Watch as flesh decays right off his bones!*

Mark pokes a finger at the glass. "Now that had to be impressive."

"I wouldn't call it impressive. I'd say it's evil." Her voice quavers, on the edge of crying.

"You okay?"

She exhales. "Not really."

"You know that he didn't actually decay in front of an audience, right? It was just a trick. I'm sure they used a fake skeleton."

"Even so, who thinks up a trick like that?" Her grimace conveys her disgust. "It's just wrong. It goes against God to do something like that."

It's clear to him that she's being overly dramatic. Not wanting to prolong the discussion, though, he nods and continues on. Beside the two posters is a series of photographs. He shines the flashlight on each one until he gets to the last one, dated 1954. This one is different. Roy and Alma are older, not performing but sitting at a linen-topped table at some kind of banquet or fancy restaurant. The caption on the bottom of the photo lacks a location or date. It simply says, *Until we meet again*. They look to be much older—not ancient, but certainly well past their prime. It strikes him as sad. "What was it all for?" he murmurs under his breath. They traveled and performed their act all over the world. From the looks of it, they had the time of their life and then it just ground to a halt.

"What?" Lisa's voice rises to a high pitch. "What did you say?"

For a moment he considers telling her it was nothing, but it's just as easy to repeat the question. "I was asking what it was all for. I mean, what's the point?"

"The point of what?"

"Of all of it. You're born, you live, and then it's over. What does any of it matter?" He gestures down the row of photos. "At one time they probably thought they were hot shit, traveling all over the place, amazing people with their act. And now they live in a run-down old house and need help with everything. Who even remembers what they did or who they were? It's just over."

"But that happens to everyone," Lisa says quietly. "That's life."

"I guess." Mark walks around the edges of the room, aiming the light as he goes. Overhead three different chandeliers, each one the size of a VW Bug, hang equidistant from the ceiling's center, creating the points of a triangle. The front wall is centered by the platform and massive podium. Behind him is the double-door entrance, while the two side walls are covered by the photographs he just examined. In the center of the room stands the wooden table, a basic rectangle the size of a family's dinner table, nothing fancy about it. This space, this ballroom—if that's what it was intended to be—has an odd setup, but nothing about it strikes him as disturbing. He imagines that Alma and Roy once used this room for parties or presentations, maybe even doing their act for guests. He turns to Lisa and says, "I'm sorry, but I don't see anything upsetting here. I mean, the pictures are a little unconventional, and their magic act had some weird stuff in it . . ." He wipes his forehead with the back of his hand.

She folds her arms. "I can't believe you missed it." Grabbing the flashlight out of his hands, she walks briskly to the center of the room and stops in front of the table. "What do you make of this?" She reaches underneath the table and pulls out a length of leather, a buckle on the end.

"What is it?" Mark comes up beside her to look.

"I have no idea. There are four in all."

He crouches down to take a look, and Lisa joins him, obligingly shining the light so he can see underneath. Just as she said, on one end of the table there are four separate leather straps, each one tucked away on its own little shelf, not visible from the top. He glances her way. "One of their props for their magic act, maybe? If they kept the box for cutting Alma in half, it makes sense that this would be something like that."

"Maybe." She sounds doubtful. "I just can't figure out what this would be used for."

Mark says, "Houdini used to demonstrate how he escaped from a straitjacket. Maybe it's something like that?"

"But trying to escape from *a table*?"

"Why not a table?"

"It doesn't seem like it would be easy for an audience to see if it was up on a stage."

"You never know. Maybe they angled it." He gestures with curved fingers. "Can I have the flashlight for a minute?" She hands it over, and he sweeps the beam across the floor. The outward-radiating tiles that start at the edge of the room meet underneath the table, ending in a series of loops unfolding in a circular pattern. The symbol reminds him of a Spirograph drawing. "What do you suppose this means?" he asks, directing the flashlight's glow under the table.

Lisa leans over to take a closer look. She tilts her head to one side, considering, and says, "I don't know. Some kind of black magic?"

Hearing the fear in her voice, Mark says, "You don't need to worry about anything like that. It's clearly just decorative."

"I don't need to worry?" Lisa repeats, her tone incredulous. "How can you say that? Those photos are bizarre. And why would they lie about what they used to do for a living? No." She shakes her head defiantly. "This is not right. Normal people do not do these kinds of things." She waves a hand. "Flying through the air, decaying flesh, strapping people to tables? Who does that?"

But it was a magic act. He almost says the words, but it seems beside the point, and besides, she is on a tear now.

"Knowing they lied to me makes me wonder what else is going on. It's giving me bad dreams, and you tell me there's nothing to worry about?" She's hyperventilating now, choked sobs threatening to come out full force. "I thought you'd help me through this, not give me the brush-off."

"Hey, hey, hey." Despite the stifling heat of the room, Mark gives her shoulders a squeeze and pulls her close, leaning down so their faces are aligned. He still has the flashlight tucked under his arm, aimed at the floor. Lisa is lucky he's had a lot of practice in dealing with distraught females. How many times has he consoled women after giving them bad news? More times than he can count. If it were a sport, he could go pro. "Lisa, when you put it that way, I understand why you're upset. But you're not alone here anymore, okay? I'm here now. And when I'm not here you can call me anytime, even in the middle of the night, and if you need me, I'll come right away. We're in this together."

Judging by her reaction, his performance was even better than he thought. She sighs, leans in, and tells him, "It's not for too much longer. I have money saved. I'll be getting my own place soon." As if she is trying to convince herself.

"Of course you will," he says soothingly. "Just relax. Not too much longer now. It's all going to be fine."

CHAPTER NINE

Getting Lisa calmed down takes at least ten minutes. She rests her head on his chest; her arms wrap around his neck. His shirt gets wet with her tears. Admirably, he pretends not to care. "It's all going to be fine," he murmurs, hoping it won't go much longer. "Things are going to get better. You're doing great."

"It's just . . ." She pauses to take a gulp of air. "Sometimes I think I'm totally losing it. What am I doing here? How is this even my life?"

Mark understands the feeling. So many times he's wondered why he hasn't made it to the big time yet. How can it be that he's still the underling at every job he's ever worked at, when he is clearly smarter, stronger, and better looking than those around him? Lisa has no reason to feel that way, of course, but he doesn't tell her that. He just lets her cry.

Judging from the way she clings to him, he knows he has a shot at steering her into one of the bedrooms for some consolation sex, but even if he wasn't worried about Roy and Alma hearing, she seems too uptight to be much fun. Besides, Monica awaits, and she is a sure thing.

Once Lisa pulls herself together, she offers an excuse for not continuing on to the third floor. "It's just the old servants' quarters anyway," she says, wiping her eyes. "The rooms are mostly empty now, except for some boxes." She explains that because of the ballroom ceiling, the servants' area is half the size of the two lower floors. "There's not much up there to see," she says.

Even though he knows the way, she leads him to the front door, where they say good night. He's more than ready to leave. He's seen enough.

Stepping outside, Mark sucks in a grateful breath of the balmy air, aware of his shirt sticking uncomfortably to his body and the sweat stains circling his armpits. He can even smell himself, it's that bad. When he gets home, he'll have to peel off his clothing. If Monica isn't there yet, he'll shower without her.

A bolt of lightning flares across the sky, but it isn't raining just yet, thank God. With any luck, he'll be on the bus before it begins pouring.

Mark steps from the dark porch onto the front walkway and surveys the empty street. Shadows fall between the streetlights. The rush of cars off in the distance is vibratory, like hearing a sound underwater. He continues down the block, his gaze on the cracked pavement. *Step on a crack and break your mother's back.* The childhood refrain wavers through his mind, haunting, singsong. *If only.* A broken spine would be small justice for all the times his mom stood by and let his stepfather berate and physically abuse him. She just stood and watched as he manhandled Mark, shaking him so hard his teeth rattled. *Loser. Never going to amount to anything.* Yes, Mark did a few things wrong—notably he cheated on tests at school, took the car without permission, and stole money from his brother's bank account—but he was just a kid. Abuse is no way to teach a child how to do better. Besides, what kind of mother doesn't stand up for her own child? He clearly got the dregs when it came to parents.

He blames his stepdad for dominating the household, especially for targeting Mark. The guy is an asshole with a capital *A*. His mother's biggest failing is lack of a backbone. If she said something even once, Mark would start coming around again, dropping by on her birthday with a gift, taking her out to dinner for Mother's Day. Mark isn't a bad son at heart. An outsider came into the family and *made* him an outsider. What's fair about that?

They say living well is the best revenge. Now that he has this new job, the money will be flowing, and his life is going to change. Who's the loser now?

His mind is so occupied that when he turns the corner, he almost walks right into a tall figure silhouetted by the streetlight beyond. "Oh my God," he says, his heart thudding in his chest.

"You again." A man's voice. As Mark stares, the looming presence of the aging hippie who confronted him the day of his interview takes shape. *What is his name? Doug? Yes, it's Doug.* A stupid name, perfect for a whack job. Lightning flashes again, this time closer. The air crackles with electricity, revealing a grimacing face resembling something like skin stretched over a skull. "I warned you, didn't I? And now they have you coming at night. That's how it starts." He lifts a cigarette to his lips. It glows as he takes a drag.

This man makes him nervous, so Mark lifts his chin to a confident angle. "You have it all wrong. I came here tonight on my own."

"So you think." He leans against the side of the building, one leg propped up flamingo-like. "But who comes down here on their own at night?" He gestures around the street with its graffiti-covered buildings and deteriorating sidewalks. "No one smart. Not if you have a nice place to live. Rich boy like you should know better."

"I came down to help a friend." It wasn't exactly a lie, and anyway, what he did or didn't do was none of this hippie's business.

The man shakes his head. "I told ya—when people go in that house, they come out different. Sooner or later, they're gonna get you."

Mark glances down the street. No bus in sight. *Shit.* "Okay, I'll play. Different how?"

Shadows flicker over the man's face. Thunder rumbles in the distance. "Body and soul, man. Body and soul." It comes out like a taunt. "That's how it's played, rich boy. Always remember —it's better to take action than to be a victim."

This conversation is going nowhere. *Fucking druggie.* Mark has known guys like this from previous jobs. The dishwashers who went out in the parking lot to smoke some weed. (*Primo shit, man!*) The maintenance men who drank from paper bags. And the most hard-core addicts, the ones who shot up behind dumpsters in back alleyways. Yeah, he's had a lot of dead-end jobs and has met some real quality people. This guy is obviously molded from the same clay. Nothing but a waste of time.

"You mark my words. Someday you'll be thinking back on this and know that I'm right."

Mark brushes by him, muttering, "Asshole." Glancing ahead, he is relieved to see the bus off in the distance, heading his way. He turns to tell Doug to piss off, but inexplicably, the man is gone. Mark blinks, then takes a few steps and peers around the corner, relieved to see Doug loping down the sidewalk toward Alden Manor. Odd that he moved so quickly and quietly, but Mark is happy to have sighted him, glad to know he hasn't vanished into thin air. The man's words spooked him more than he'd like to admit.

Mark breathes deeply and mentally recites his childhood mantra. *Just words. Shake 'em off. Just shake 'em off. They're only words, and words can't hurt me.*

When he climbs up the steps to the bus, it begins to rain. All the way home rain pelts the roof of the bus. The storm is in full force now, which means his timing was excellent. By the time he arrives at his stop, his mind is on Monica, and the conversation with the aging hippie has been completely forgotten.

CHAPTER TEN

The next day, when Mark rounds the corner onto Bartleby Street, he is surprised to see the Excalibur parked in front of Alden Manor. Even more surprising is the sight of Lisa sitting on the porch steps, an empty, distracted look on her face. Spotting him, she raises a hand half-heartedly in acknowledgment. As he turns onto the walkway, he calls out, "What's up?"

In answer, she holds up a ring of keys. "We're getting kicked out." Her voice has an air of despondency.

Mark jogs up the steps and takes a seat next to her. "Kicked out *how*?"

"The Redevine Society decided to *convene* today at the last minute." She puts the word *convene* in finger quotes. "And they don't want us hanging around, I guess. Roy wants you to drive me to run a bunch of errands." She reaches into her jeans pocket, pulls out a piece of lined paper, and unfolds it. "Pick up two prescriptions at the pharmacy. Drive all the way to Westfall to pick up a pocket watch that's being repaired at Goodman's Clock Shop. Go to the grocery store. There's a whole list of food items." She rolls her eyes. "The delivery guy just brought our order three days ago, and the fridge and cabinets are full, so I don't quite get it. Why the sudden need for pickled herring and canned peaches?"

Mark shrugs. "Maybe you're right and they just want us out of the way." He isn't about to complain about an opportunity to drive the Excalibur. Getting paid to do it makes it even better.

"He gave me a bunch of money and said we should go out to lunch and not to hurry back. It's so weird. This has never happened before, not in all the time I've worked for them. The few times I've run errands for them, they had me take the bus and told me to hurry." She shakes her head. "I have a bad feeling. Something's going down."

Mark smiles. *Something's going down.* Clearly, Lisa has been watching too many detective shows on television. He says, "I'm sure it will be fine." Maybe the Walgraves want to visit with their friends without Lisa lurking around. Perfectly reasonable.

"I hate leaving them." She purses her lips.

"What could happen? Besides, they'll be with friends."

Her face becomes more than serious. "Sometimes friends are the ones to worry about." And in that one statement, she reveals so much. Mark knows now that life has treated Lisa very badly. She is a wounded soul, something he has experience with.

"Even if you're right, there's not too much we can do about it." He gestures to the car. "You want to get going?"

"They want to meet you first."

"Who does?"

"The other members of the Redevine Society. They want to meet the new guy."

"Me?"

"Yeah, Mark. Who else?" When he doesn't move from his

spot, she adds, "They wanted to meet me too when I was first hired. Trust me, it's not a big deal. Just go in and say hi, and then we can go."

Wordlessly, he gets up and goes inside, shutting the door behind him. By now he is accustomed to the transition on the other side of the door, the shift from bright to dark, hot to cool dampness, but he still stands for a few seconds, letting his eyes adjust, before following the sounds of conversation at the end of the hall.

Voices float out from the blue room. He makes his way down the hall. Stopping short of the door, he flexes his fingers as if he's about to play the piano, which isn't too far from the truth. If Roy and Alma's guests need reassurance that he is an okay guy, his performance has to be spot-on.

He's taking a deep breath when the voices inside hush, almost as if they know someone might be listening. He hears a female softly saying, "If that doesn't work . . . ," followed by something he can't quite make out. Neither can he identify the speaker. It certainly isn't Alma, whose voice has a more childlike cadence.

A man answers, loudly enough so that the words are clear. "This has taken too long already."

Mark raises his knuckles to the doorframe and raps twice before stepping into the room. He walks in to see two couples sitting opposite Roy and Alma. "Lisa said I should check in with you before we head out?"

Roy's face lights up when Mark enters the room. He struggles to his feet, pushing off the arm of the chair. "Come in, my boy! I was just telling our friends all about you. Everyone, this is Mark Norman."

"Hello, Mark."

"Nice to meet you, Mark."

"We've heard good things."

"Hey there, Mark."

The comments come all at once and overlap one another, making it hard for him to know how to respond. The four newcomers, two guys and two women, are a marked contrast to Roy and Alma. For one thing, they are young, nearly as young as Mark himself; secondly, they are all strikingly attractive and dressed smartly. Mark raises a hand in greeting, waiting for introductions that never come. Finally, he walks over to shake their hands, saying, "I'm Mark Norman. Pleased to meet you."

The first woman takes his hand and gives him an appreciative once-over before winking suggestively. "I'm Lara Whitlock," she says. "And I am so glad to meet you. I hope to see a lot of you in the future, Mark." The words come out in a purr, making him grin. Women could be so obvious.

The man next to her is a hulk of a guy—big shoulders, barrel-chested, and strong jaw. If he notices the flirting, it doesn't appear to bother him. He stands and grips Mark's hand. "Baird Whitlock. Welcome aboard. I'm glad Roy and Alma have found a good man to help carry the load. Both of them are very important to us."

"The Redevine Society, right?" Mark says. The group exchanges glances, and for a second, he wonders if he's somehow blundered. Did he hear about the society from Lisa, or did he only read about it on the photos upstairs? No, he's sure she's referenced it several times. To cover himself, he says, "That's what Lisa said, anyway."

They all nod, and Baird says, "Of course. That's exactly right."

Mark moves on to the next guy, a slender man with dark hair who says his name is Sam Burman. His wife, Neela, has a soft voice and shy manner. They both shake hands curtly, as if not wanting to prolong things. He takes a step back and says, "It's so nice to meet all of you." Then addressing Roy, he adds, "Unless you have something you need me to do, I'll let you get back to your meeting. Lisa says we're to run errands today?"

Roy bobs his head up and down. "Yes, my boy. I gave her a list and told her not to hurry back. I hope the two of you find a nice place to have lunch."

"That's so generous of you. I'm sure we will."

Roy grabs the cane leaning against the side of his chair. "If you'll wait just a moment for this old man, I'll walk you out."

The group is quiet as the two slowly leave the room, but once they are out in the hallway, Mark hears the murmur of voices as they resume their conversation. He thinks they might be talking about him, although he can't say for certain. With Mark at his side, Roy hobbles down the hallway. When they are out of earshot of the blue room, he pauses and grabs Mark's arm. "You might have guessed that I wanted to speak with you alone."

"Yes, sir."

Roy's brow furrows. "I'm concerned about Lisa. Alma's health has been getting worse, and I know it's made her job more difficult. That's why I orchestrated a day out of the house for her. I would like the two of you to enjoy yourselves. Take your time. It would be nice if Lisa could have a break until dinnertime. Don't worry about us. Our friends will ensure we're covered for lunch and dinner."

"I understand."

Roy takes off his glasses and holds them up to the light, then pulls a handkerchief out of his pocket to polish the lenses. "If Lisa talks about quitting, please encourage her to stay. Alma won't last much longer, and we need Lisa here. And you too, of course."

He says it so calmly. *Alma won't last much longer.* What do people say to such things? Mark comes out with, "I'm sorry to hear your sister isn't doing well. Lisa hasn't mentioned wanting to quit. I know she's fond of both of you." All lies, but what's the difference? Anything to ease the old coot's mind.

"I'm glad to hear it," Roy says. "But if she does get discouraged and wants to leave . . ."

"Trust me, I'll do everything I can to convince her to stay. I can be very persuasive." Mark claps a reassuring hand on Roy's shoulder.

Roy pushes his glasses up the bridge of his nose and looks up appreciatively at Mark. "I'm counting on it."

"You can rely on me, sir. That's a promise."

When Mark gets outside, Lisa asks, "How'd it go?"

"They're all members of my fan club now." He plucks the keys out of her hand. "What do you say we blow this pop stand?"

After Mark slides in behind the wheel of the car, he lets out a whistle of appreciation.

"What?" Lisa fastens her seat belt.

"This car. It's magnificent." He runs a hand over the dashboard. "I'd give my left nut to have an Excalibur. All this power in a beautiful body. And here it belongs to an old guy about to kick the bucket."

Lisa says, "Tell him you want it and maybe he'll leave it to you in his will."

"You think so?"

She shrugs. "Sure. I mean, they don't have any relatives—not that I know of, anyway—and their friends seem pretty well-off. Someone's going to get the car when they're gone. Why not you? Roy's already promised me all of Alma's jewelry and clothing, and believe me, I didn't ask."

Interesting. Mark files this information away.

On the way to their first destination, Lisa asks, "So what did you think of the Whitlocks?"

Mark thinks. "The big guy and his wife? They seem . . . friendly?"

"But too friendly, right?"

Not particularly. The wife winked at him, which was a little surprising, but it wasn't too out-there, considering what Mark has experienced in the past. When he was a teenager bagging groceries, housewives sometimes flirted with him. At discos, women routinely buy him drinks. And once he was at a family wedding and one of the bridesmaids propositioned him when he was on his way back from the men's room. One quickie in the coatroom later and he was on the dance floor, no one the wiser. Mrs. Whitlock's wink is tame by comparison. "Just friendly," he answers.

"And what's with their names? Baird and Lara. I hate that." She shudders as if biting into something sour.

"Why do you hate their names?" Noticing a yellow traffic light ahead, Mark slows to a stop.

"Baird. Lara. So hard to pronounce. I keep wanting to say *Brad* and *Laura*."

Lisa is really something with her obsessive fretting. It's as if she creates things to worry about. He says, "You can always call them Mr. and Mrs. Whitlock, if it's that much of a problem."

"It's just the point of it," she says, setting her hand on the dashboard to steady herself. "Why make things so complicated?"

The morning continues as planned. At the pharmacy, Lisa double-checks the typed labels on the pill vials before paying with the cash Roy gave her. At Goodman's Clock Shop, Mark stands idly by while Lisa chats with the owner of the store. As Mr. Goodman brings out a pocket watch and sets it on a velvet-lined tray, explaining what he did to repair it, Mark finds his interest waning. He wanders the store, drawn to the men's wristwatches displayed in the glass cases. Funny how they keep the time the same as his Timex yet cost ten times more. Better quality, he guesses, although how that helps a person in his day-to-day life he isn't certain. Time passes either way.

He glances over at Lisa, who is commenting on the timepiece's newly polished finish. "I know Mr. Walgrave will be happy to see it looking like new," she says, fishing money out of her purse.

"I'm sorry Roy wasn't able to make it today," Mr. Goodman says, looking over his wire-rim glasses. "I always enjoy our talks."

As they leave the store, Lisa clutches her purse to her side and says to Mark, "I know we're supposed to go out to lunch, but maybe we should just skip it, get the groceries, and go back right away?"

Cut the day short? Sit and talk to old people all afternoon when he could be eating at a restaurant and continue driving this fine car? Not if Mark has anything to say about it. He shakes his head while jangling the car keys. "No way, Lisa. Roy made a point to say we should have a nice lunch and that we shouldn't hurry back. I'm not going against his wishes."

She flattens her lips into a disapproving line but doesn't voice an objection. When Mark suggests going to an Italian restaurant nearby, she says, "Whatever you want." Her tone is so glum he almost laughs. She makes it seem like going out to eat on Roy's dime is such a burden.

Once they are inside the restaurant and have ordered, he makes an effort to cheer her up with small talk. "I've heard the food here is great, totally authentic," he says, looking around at the décor, which is, as far as he can tell, also authentic. Round tables with red-checked tablecloths. Chianti bottles serving as candleholders with the wax dripping down the sides. Stained-glass panels on the walls depicting grape clusters still on the vine.

Lisa nods, seemingly preoccupied. "I hope this doesn't take too long." She taps her fingers on the linen tablecloth. "I'm sorry. I have a lot on my mind."

"No problem. I get it."

"If I tell you something, can you keep a secret?"

"Of course. You can trust me. I won't breathe a word." Mark gives her a reassuring smile. "I keep telling you, I'm here for you, Lisa."

She glances around to make sure she can't be overheard. "This morning, before you arrived, I had a talk with Roy. Dr. Cross says Alma is failing both mentally and physically and that she won't be around much longer."

"He said as much to me as well. It's a shame, but everyone dies sooner or later."

"Yes, well . . ." A pained expression crosses her face. "So he told you about Alma, but did he tell you he asked me to sign some legally binding paperwork and have it notarized?" She raises an eyebrow questioningly.

The waitress, Sandra, arrives with their drinks. She sets down the cocktail napkins first, then places the drinks before them with a flourish. "A cranberry juice for the lady, and a Sprite for the gentleman." She flashes a smile in Mark's direction.

"Thank you." Mark picks up his glass and takes a sip, appreciatively watching the waitress's backside as she walks away. "To answer your question, no he didn't say anything about signing paperwork. What's that all about?"

"Get this. Dr. Cross is coming over tonight with Sam and Neela Burman. Sam is an attorney, and Neela is a notary." She moves the candleholder and her drink to one side and leans across the table. She speaks so quietly he can barely make out the words over the clatter of a table being cleared, the chatter of conversations, the piped-in Frank Sinatra tunes coming through the speakers overhead. "They want me to be the executor of their will, and they also said something about me inheriting the estate."

"And you *don't* want to do this?" Is she crazy? To Mark this sounds like one sweet deal.

"Well, no. I'm going to be quitting, remember? I'm trying my best to leave that house, but if I agree to their plan that goes out the window." Her face tightens. "I think they can sense I'm ready to quit, and they're trying to pull me back in."

For the first time, Mark notices the haunted circles around her eyes, giving her the look of someone who hasn't had a good night's sleep in a long, long time.

She says, "Now I'll never get out of there."

"Are you feeling pressured?" he asks. "Because it's okay if you don't want to do it. Tell them you aren't up to the responsibility. They'll find someone else."

"But they say they don't have anyone else." She looks like she's about to cry.

Mark waves a hand. "That's what they say, but they have their friends from the Redevine Society, right? And Dr. Cross?" He ticks off his fingers. "So that's five people right there. Trust me, they'll figure something out." He leans forward and places a reassuring hand over hers, nearly flinching at the coldness of her fingers. "Don't worry, Lisa. They can't force you. Just tell them you're honored, but no thanks."

She nods as the waitress comes to serve their salads.

Mark gives a sympathetic smile, but inwardly he wants to rejoice at this turn of events. Lisa might choose to say no to this opportunity, but if and when it's laid at his feet, he's going to pick it up and claim it as his own. He will ingratiate himself to Roy and flatter Alma, and before long they'll start to think of him as the grandson they've always wanted, and soon enough they'll give him the same deal Lisa doesn't want. And if that happens, he will be rich. The house, the Excalibur, and everything else, all of it his. The idea is intoxicating. He'll sell the house, of course. There is no way he'll want to live in that monstrosity in the worst part of town. Someone will buy it, if only to tear it down and build a warehouse or factory.

Once he is wealthy, everything will change. He'll get a better girlfriend than Monica, for one. She's been fine, for now, but money brings opportunities, and he'd be foolish not to explore all his options. He'll buy his mother a new car. Not that she deserves it, but it would be the perfect way to stick it to his stepfather. The man's words still ring in Mark's head. *Unreliable. Loser. Never going to amount to anything.* The asshole got it all wrong. It isn't so much that Mark tries to game the system. It's more that he looks for opportunities others have overlooked. How is it fair that some people have so much more than others? It isn't. Well, that could be rectified. Mark is more cunning than most, and in the end he is going to come out on top.

Lisa interrupts his thoughts, saying, "I hope you're right."

Mark thinks of Alma and Roy and how frail they are. A strong wind could knock them off their feet, and here Lisa is worried that they could somehow control her. The thought is ludicrous. "It's going to be fine."

Lisa gives him a thankful smile. "Thanks for listening, Mark. I appreciate it." She tucks a stray lock of hair behind her ear. "Lately I feel like if I stay in that house one minute longer, I'll totally lose my mind. I can't sleep. I can't eat. I have all these bizarre thoughts. Sometimes I wonder if I'm going crazy."

"We all have those days. It might just be time to move on. No shame in that." He says the words knowing full well that he's breaking his promise to Roy. He is supposed to convince

Lisa to continue on at Alden Manor. Instead, he's doing the opposite.

He shrugs. A guy needs to look out for himself. Besides, Lisa's mental health is at stake, and it's not like the old man will know any different.

CHAPTER ELEVEN

At the end of the workday, Roy suggests that Mark cut the day short and take the Excalibur rather than ride the bus. "No need for you to walk in the rain when we have a perfectly good vehicle just sitting there."

"Are you sure?" It's the polite thing to ask, but Mark isn't really objecting. He tightens his fingers around the ring of keys in his palm. Already he can see himself pulling into a space in the back of his apartment building. When Monica comes home, they'll go out, no matter how late it is. He can't wait to see the reactions they get driving the Excalibur in his neighborhood.

The next morning, as he drives back to Alden Manor, he is still thinking about the stares of envy he and Monica got when cruising down Highway 57 the evening before. Cars on either side of the road honked, their drivers giving him the thumbs-up as he went by. Monica was in her glory, basking in the attention and giving Mark well-deserved looks of appreciation. Driving an Excalibur speaks volumes about the man behind the wheel. It says he is a man of means with a penchant for luxury. Monica jokingly called him a show-off, but why not? He sees nothing wrong with standing out from the crowd.

When Mark arrives, Dr. Cross's car is parked in front of Alden Manor, so he pulls in right behind him. He whistles as he makes his way up the walkway. Inside, when he pauses in the entryway to let his eyes adjust, he hears a woman's distressed voice drifting from the other end of the hallway. "No, no, please no." He listens intently, tipping his head forward, as if that would somehow help him to understand what is going on. Loud sobbing rises into a wail that sounds more animal than human. *Good God, what the hell is going on?* He's unable to move and remains rooted to the rug, fearful of walking in on some kind of terrible medical emergency. He can only imagine what would precipitate such a horrific noise. Glancing at his watch, he sees he's arrived ten minutes early. If he slips out onto the porch for a few minutes, maybe he can avoid the crisis altogether. Just as his hand is on the doorknob, he hears a scrabbling of footsteps and Dr. Cross's voice calling out, "Lisa, stop. Come back!"

Mark freezes. There is no escaping now; the problem is headed right at him in the shape of Lisa, who's running toward him, breathlessly panting, hair a mess, eyes wild. Dr. Cross is on her heels. She runs right to Mark and throws herself into his arms, clinging as if he is her sole salvation. The motion gives him such a jolt that his backside slams up against the door. "Help me, Mark!" Her eyes are wide with terror, her voice raw and guttural. "They're trying to kill me!" Her eyes dart back and forth, first to Mark and then behind her to Dr. Cross. "You need to do something. Please! Please!"

Mark wraps a protective arm around her and calls out, "What's going on?"

Dr. Cross ignores his question, instead addressing Lisa. "Just take a breath, Lisa. It's all going to be fine. You're among friends here." He has a hypodermic needle in one hand, held casually in the way of an unlit cigarette. "No one is going to hurt you. I'm trying to help."

She screams at the doctor, "Don't come any closer!"

Dr. Cross halts in his tracks.

With Lisa trembling in his arms, Mark says, "Just a minute. What's happening?"

"They want me dead," she whispers. "Make him stop." She buries her head against Mark's chest. "Please. Don't let him hurt me."

Dr. Cross holds up the needle but doesn't move. "Lisa has had a psychotic break. I'm trying to give her a light sedative, just to calm her down. She's worked herself into hysterics."

Lisa grips the front of Mark's shirt, words spilling out in quick succession. "I need to go right now. Can I come live with you, Mark? I have money. I'll pay rent. It won't be for long." Her eyes well up with tears. "I can sleep on your couch or on the floor. I don't need much space. I'll be no trouble at all."

Mark imagines Monica's reaction if he brings home a random chick to live with them and shakes his head. "I don't think that would work out."

Defeated, she lets out a whimper.

Dr. Cross takes a step closer. "You'll feel better after you get some rest, Lisa. You haven't been sleeping lately, have you?"

She gulps and sucks in a deep breath. "I haven't been sleeping at all."

"Why don't you let me give you this shot? I promise that you'll feel better after a nap. You're just sleep-deprived," he says soothingly. "You've been working so hard. You deserve a rest."

"I am tired." Lisa wipes at her eyes with her fingertips and sniffs.

Mark looks from Dr. Cross to Lisa, trying to make sense of the hypodermic needle in his hand and the overall situation.

Does he always keep sedatives in his medical bag? Or was he anticipating a need? Something Lisa said yesterday comes to him. *Sometimes I wonder if I'm going crazy.* What else did she say? Something about having thoughts she didn't think came from her. Is that connected to having a psychotic break? He doesn't know.

The doctor smiles kindly. "I know. I know. It's been hard, but you've done an excellent job. Alma and Roy are so happy to have you here."

At the sound of their names, Mark feels Lisa stiffen in his arms. She turns to face him and whispers, "Please help me."

Dr. Cross continues. "Won't you let me walk you down to your room for a rest? We can decide then if you want the shot or not. It'll be up to you."

"No." Lisa shakes her head and meets Mark's eyes. "I need to get out of here. Drive me to the bus station?" She has a tight grip on his arm. "Please! I have money. I can pay you!"

Mark sees the crazed fear in her eyes. In the dim light of the hallway, her skin looks even paler and her eyes more sunken. He glances over at Dr. Cross, who has an earnest expression, the way any doctor would in treating a troubled patient. Behind Lisa's back, Dr. Cross shakes his head, signaling his advice to Mark. *Don't let her leave.*

Mark keeps his voice low and steady. "Lisa, I don't have a car, so I can't take you anywhere. Why don't we all sit down and talk about this?" Off in the distance, he hears Alma coughing, a phlegmy, choking sound. A fly buzzes around Lisa's head. Mark whisks it away with his free hand. "We can talk it over and come up with a solution, something that will make you happy. Maybe Roy would let me use his car? Why don't we go ask him?"

She straightens, her eyes widening as if she's reaching a conclusion. "You're one of them." Glancing back at Dr. Cross, she says, "All of you are in on it."

Mark says, "I don't know what you mean. Lisa, I just got here. I'm trying to figure out what's going on." His mind races, trying to make sense of things. Yesterday Lisa seemed fine, if a little down. Today she's had a psychotic break and needs sedation? Something is seriously wrong here.

Tears fill her eyes. "If you're not one of them, then help me." Her voice is thick with emotion. "Please." Her body shakes with fear; she hyperventilates audibly.

Hysteria, Mark thinks, pulling her into an embrace. Is the pounding in his ears the racing of his own heart, or is it coming from her? Her anxiety feels contagious. *Time to slow things down.* "Lisa, I want to help you. Let's just take a walk around the block and we can talk, okay?" He lowers his chin to speak to her. Mutely she nods, just as Dr. Cross comes up behind her and sticks the needle into her arm.

As Dr. Cross presses down on the plunger, Mark makes a split-second decision and presses his elbow down, holding her arm in place. Realizing what is happening, she opens her mouth. The sound that comes out shakes Mark to his core. More than a scream, it is a horrible, heartbroken keening, the kind mothers make when they come to identify their child's body at the morgue. Mark releases his grip, and when he does, she stops her wailing and turns to see Dr. Cross standing right behind her, the now-empty syringe in his hand.

The doctor says, "It's all going to be fine, Lisa. You'll see."

"No." The word comes out in a guttural sob. She stumbles to the staircase and grabs on to the newel post. With her other hand, she wipes her eyes and turns to look accusingly at Mark. He thinks she's going to say something, but she just shakes her head, then dashes up the steps, her footsteps clattering on the wooden stair treads.

Mark asks Dr. Cross, "Should I go after her?"

Dr. Cross glances upward. "Let's give her a few minutes.

Once the sedative kicks in, it'll be easier for us to guide her back down."

Mark watches as she rounds the second landing and continues on, heading up to the third floor. "Where is she going?"

Dr. Cross says, "When in pain or upset, humans often seek seclusion. It happens with animals too. She just needs a moment to herself. Just leave her be."

"What happened, exactly? When I saw her yesterday, she was fine." *More than fine,* he thinks. She was fed up and stressed out, but not even close to having a nervous breakdown.

Dr. Cross shakes his head. "It came out of nowhere. She just snapped. I suspect her mental state was not that strong to begin with. I take the blame. I should have picked up on it sooner."

They stand quietly for a few minutes. Overhead Mark hears the quick *clip-clip* of Lisa's footsteps as she rounds the landing on the second floor and continues on to the third. He thinks about the expression on Lisa's face, how terrified and distraught she seemed, and the way Dr. Cross plunged a needle into her arm without her permission. True, he is a doctor, but is this ethical? Mark wants to believe the doctor has her best interests at heart, but he has a sinking feeling he should not have helped Dr. Cross give her a shot against her will, that somehow it's made him liable for whatever happens to her going forward. Could he be sued or charged with a crime? Lisa is right. This is a weird, weird house, but being here is still better than the tedious tasks he's done at other jobs: folding turtlenecks, flipping burgers, and trying to sell stereo systems at Radio Shack. Nothing at Alden Manor is tedious.

Dr. Cross clears his throat. "I'm going to tell Roy and Alma what's happening. I know they've been worried about her." He heads down the hall.

"I'll go check on Lisa," Mark calls out after him, and without waiting for an answer, he bounds up the stairs. The air around him changes with each step. Warmer, certainly, but denser and more oppressive too, making him aware of his breathing. If the windows and doors were open, it would be different, but of course, these floors are not in use. When he gets to the third floor, he calls out Lisa's name, listening as his own voice echoes back at him. No other sound can be heard. All the doors in the corridor are shut, and it's dark, too dark to see clearly. If only he had a flashlight. Making his way down the hall into the dark, he opens one door at a time and steps into each room, leaving them open afterward to let some light into the hallway.

With every step he calls out her name, waiting a few seconds for a response before moving on. He turns knob after knob and finds nothing but empty rooms.

When Mark gets to the last door, he finds it slightly ajar. He's certain she's in the room, so it's surprising to fling open the door and find it empty. He checks behind the drapes and calls out, "Lisa?" No answer. He opens the closet door, and instead of finding a rod and some shelves, he discovers it's an empty walk-in storage area. Inside is another door, slightly open, leading to wooden steps. The attic? With his hand on the doorknob, he tries again, yelling, "Lisa!" then charges up the steps. The stairs turn on a landing and keep going, narrow wooden steps going so far up that he realizes the attic space must run the length of the house, above the ballroom ceiling on the second floor and over the bedrooms on the third.

As he rises, the air becomes claustrophobically hot and heavy, and he has the sensation of walking through cobwebs. When he gets to the top, he finds himself in an open space with tall windows on each end. Mark squints. In one of the front windows, there's a form blocking the light. It's Lisa. On the ledge. *Oh God.* He runs toward her, trying to make sense of what he's seeing.

But before he gets there, she shimmies along the ledge, away from the open window and almost out of reach. Her splayed fingers frame her anguished face; her nose is a spot of white pressed against the glass. A slight breeze lifts her hair off her shoulders.

Mark reaches out the open window and extends a hand, but he doesn't touch her. His heart pounds in his chest and sweat beads his forehead, but he tries to sound reassuring. "Lisa, come back inside. Let's talk about this." He keeps his voice measured and even, as if it's perfectly normal for someone to be perched on a narrow ledge three stories above street level.

She does not react, is frozen in place. From the expression on her face, she's seen something traumatic, but he can't imagine what that would be. They spent yesterday together, and she was worried, but she was essentially fine. What happened between then and now? He can't even imagine what would drive her to think this is a good option.

It's possible, he surmises, that nothing happened. Perhaps the doctor is right and she's emotionally fragile. Maybe all it took was a misinterpreted word or one more added chore for her delicate outer shell to crack. "Lisa, please?" He resists the urge to grab her, knowing that the slightest movement might throw her off-balance. Glancing down, he's shocked at the distance between them and the ground. From street level, the house doesn't look that tall, but from this angle, the tiled overhang of the porch and the front walkway appear far away. If she falls now, will the overhang break her fall? No, it's a solid surface, not a canopy, and this isn't a movie. No one could survive a drop like that.

"Lisa," he urges. "Please don't do this. Whatever it is, we'll get through it. Together." He curls his fingers, beckoning, and keeps talking, telling her that sometimes things at Alden Manor weird him out as well, that what's she's going through is normal.

That she's done an incredible job taking care of two elderly people, and no one would fault her for walking out the door. He adds that he admires and respects her. "I don't want to see you hurt, Lisa. If you want, I can ask my girlfriend if you can sleep on the couch." Monica probably won't go for it, but Lisa doesn't know that. It's not a lie if it saves a life. And if need be, he can always insist. It's his apartment too.

Her face softens, making him think his words are registering with her. With a glimmer of hope, he keeps going. "We can leave right now if you want and head over to my place. It's an apartment over on Alcott Avenue. It's not very big, but it's a safe place for you to stay until you find something else." Mark wonders what's going on downstairs. Doesn't Dr. Cross wonder what's taking so long? A little assistance would be nice. He considers leaving and going for help, but he doesn't dare. Her perch is precarious, her state of mind frighteningly muddled. He wonders how much longer he has until the sedative takes effect. Dr. Cross made it sound fairly imminent. Once that happens, he fears the worst.

He continues. "Just take my hand and come inside. We can talk about what's troubling you." Slowly, she slides one hand down the glass before stretching it out to him. Her gaze is still straightforward, as if her hand is operating independently of the rest of her body. He breathes a sigh of relief. Progress is being made. "That's right," he says. "You're doing great. Just take my hand."

A Buick drives past, stereo blaring with the strains of Aerosmith's "Dream On." The driver is clearly oblivious to the drama three floors above street level. Birds caw, and he notices a gathering of crows lined up on the telephone wire, a raucous avian audience flapping their wings and randomly croaking. *Such ugly creatures.*

"That's it," he says to Lisa. "Just a little more." Her fingertips brush against his, and he's stunned by the chilliness of her touch. Both of them are perspiring profusely—in fact, his palms are slick with sweat, yet her skin feels cold. A disturbing image comes to mind as he imagines her body on a slab. Mentally he shakes it aside. "That's it." He allows himself to relax just a little when his fingers wrap around her hand, and he sticks his head out the window to get closer. He slides his thumb up to her wrist, but he stops when he feels her start to pull back. *She's spooked,* he thinks. "It's okay, I'm not going to hurt you. I just want to see you safe."

"Not safe." Her voice, loud and guttural, startles him. Mark tries to make eye contact, without success. When she does glance in his direction, her eyes are swimming, not seeming to focus at all. He's seen this before, in the disco girls who've had too much to drink. It has to be a side effect of Dr. Cross's injection.

"I can keep you safe." Mark smiles encouragingly.

She shakes her head. "It's them and this house. I should have left when I could." Behind her, one of the crows hops sideways on the telephone wire, forcing another bird to move down the line.

"You can still leave." He strokes her wrist with his thumb. If he gives a slight pull, will she move close enough that he can grab her? He can't support her for long, he knows. He continues with the tactic he's heard on cop shows. Keep the person engaged, take their mind off jumping. Talking them off a ledge—that's what it's called. "You don't want to die, do you, Lisa? You have so much to live for."

"It's too late." The anguish in her voice is heartbreaking.

"It's not too late. I'm going to grab hold of your arm, okay? Move this way, and I'll help you get inside. Nice and easy, one inch at a time."

"No."

"Please? For me?"

Lisa gives a slight shake of her head and blurts out, "This is the only way to stop it."

"Stop what?"

"It's either them or me. I tried to do it, but God help me, I just couldn't."

He watches in horror as Lisa leans back, all her weight pulling against his grip. He tightens his hold on her, but it's not enough, and a second later she pulls loose, falling backward. The descent happens both immediately and in slow motion. When she lands, slamming against the tile overhang with a sickening thud, she ends up on her back. He leans forward, his mouth open, staring at the sight of her body, arms and legs splayed out, eyes wide open and staring up at him.

Mark just saw it happen, and yet he still can't believe it.

One of the crows sails down from the telephone wire and struts around her body. Another comes to join it, hopping right onto her torso and pecking at her midsection as if she were roadkill. A second later, a halo of blood forms around her head.

Even as Mark screams her name, he knows she's gone.

CHAPTER TWELVE

Mark walks right past the hospital information desk. No need for directions—he knows the way. The hallways are strangely empty, but through open doorways he sees patients propped up in bed. He hears the beeping of machinery and the intro to the soap opera *Days of Our Lives* emanating from multiple television sets. The floors gleam, smelling of disinfectant, as if they've been recently washed. When he gets to Lisa's room, the door is slightly ajar. He raps twice before entering. As expected, she's flat on her back in bed, and also as expected, she's not fully conscious. A snow-white sheet is pulled up to her chin. Her pale face is perfect, and her hair fans out on the pillow; the sole reminder of the suicide attempt is the wide bandage wrapped around her head, putting him in mind of wounded soldiers in war movies.

Suddenly, remembering the roses in his hand, he sets the vase on the ledge near the window. He walks back to the bed and stands over her, watching her breathe in and out, her eyelids fluttering. He debates whether or not to disturb her. She's been through such an ordeal, it would be a shame to interrupt her sleep, but then again, he did come all the way here on the bus. Or did he? His forehead furrows as he tries to remember the events leading up to his arrival at the hospital. It's possible he drove Roy's car. Or maybe Monica dropped him off? No, that can't be right. Monica doesn't own a car. The details are fuzzy, but ultimately it's unimportant. The main thing is that he is here now and has an opportunity to talk to Lisa.

Mark needs to make things right between them. God knows he hasn't always been the best person, but he's certainly not the worst either. And now a girl is dead, or almost died—he's not really sure—because he didn't handle things well. A better man would have saved her. He failed, which is not surprising. Despite his attempts to get past the flaws stamped into his psyche at a young age, he is still a loser. Maybe this is something he'll never overcome. A flush of shame washes over him as he thinks of how he's fallen short once again. At the very least, he can apologize to this girl in the bed. Words have power, he knows, but at the same time words can never be enough. Right now, though, they're all he has.

"Lisa?" He leans over and whispers, "How are you doing? I brought you some flowers." He gestures to the vase and notices the flowers are no longer roses. Somehow they've morphed into tulips. A big improvement, he thinks. Tulips remind him of springtime and fresh starts. And God knows he needs a fresh start.

With a sigh, she opens her eyes and then says his name so faintly he can barely hear it.

"Yes," he says. "It's me. Mark. I came to see you to tell you I'm sorry."

"Mark," she whispers. Her hands come out from under the sheet and grip the front of his shirt.

He nods. "Yes, it's me." She pulls with such force that he's nearly on top of her now. His ear is just over her mouth; she's trying to tell him something important. "What is it, Lisa?" He holds his breath and listens but can catch only a few sounds. "I'm sorry. I don't understand."

She tries again, but he still can't make sense of what she's saying.

Out in the hallway a cart rattles as it goes past. He wishes for silence so he can hear better. Finally, he speaks his piece. "I came to tell you I'm sorry, Lisa. I shouldn't have let Dr. Cross give you that injection. I should have gotten you off the ledge. You're dead now because of me. I hope you can forgive me." The words don't sound much like something he'd say, but getting them out makes him feel better. "Do you understand what I'm saying, Lisa?"

With a shove, she pushes him backward, and with a shaking hand, she points. He turns to see Alma and Roy in the doorway. He knows it's Alma and Roy, even though they look different. Roy's flesh is decaying off his bones just like in the poster. Bits of skin stick to his skull, but his friar's fringe of gray hair is still evident. He wears his usual baggy old-man pants and button-up shirt, but the fingers gripping his cane are skeletal. His sister's fingers wrap around his bent elbow. She looks much the same, except for the fact that she's missing her head. A surge of disgust rises in his throat when he spots Alma's disembodied head on the floor near her feet, tongue out, eyeballs dangling out of the sockets.

Lisa's voice rises from the bed behind him. "*Run!*"

Every fiber of his being wants to flee.

But in the way of dreams, he is rooted to the spot, watching in terror as Alma and Roy move closer and closer. As they step forward, Alma kicks her head like a soccer ball so it rolls toward him. Roy's skull-face leers at him, his tongue flicking snakelike in and out of his mouth.

Mark knows they're going to get him and there's not a damn thing he can do about it. When Alma's rolling head lands next to his foot, the tongue stretches out grotesquely and licks his shoe with loud slurping noises. Roy, meantime, has extended his skeletal fingers so that they're brushing the front of Mark's shirt. His skull-face grins.

In a flash, Roy has a grip on his shirt and is pulling him closer. He licks his teeth as if about to bite into something delicious. His mouth is so close to Mark's face that he can smell the rancid meat on his breath.

Mark remembers he is in a dream. With a huge effort, he wills himself toward consciousness. *Wake up! Wake up! Wake up!*

And like being shot out of a cannon, he finds himself thrust into a completely different atmosphere, wide awake in the darkness of his own bedroom. He sits up, his pulse racing. A sob rises in his dry throat. He's in bed with Monica, who slumbers next to him. Somehow, while he slept, the covers became untucked from the end of the bed and are now awkwardly wrapped around his legs.

As he's untangling himself from the sheet and blanket, he mutters, "Oh my God, oh my God, oh my God," the words echoing the pounding of his heart. It was only a dream, he tells himself, but it felt so dangerous. His breathing turns to wheezing.

Next to him, Monica rolls over and extends an arm in his direction. "What's wrong?" Even half-asleep she manages to sound concerned.

How to explain? "Nightmare," Mark says. "It was terrible. Lisa was there, and Alma and Roy . . ." He trails off, having to catch his breath.

She sits up, rubs her eyes, and gives him a hug. "It's okay. It was just a dream." Monica is not usually a nurturer, but then again, he has never been vulnerable around her. He lets her pat his back while the words spill out.

By the time he's finished, he's related the whole thing, starting with his walk down the halls of the hospital. He ends with, "It seemed so real." His heart is just now beginning to slow. "You know how usually dreams are little bits and pieces and they don't make sense? This one was different." Different in how it felt, certainly, but also in how he experienced it. The sights, the sounds, the smells. The feel of the flower petals. The antiseptic odor of freshly mopped hospital floors. The rattle of a cart in the hallway.

"Some dreams are like that," she says soothingly. "You had a horrible experience, and your mind is trying to make sense of it."

He did have a horrible day, the worst of his life. After Lisa fell, slamming against the tile roof, he rushed downstairs to alert the others. The police were called, and before long the place was swarming with men in uniforms. The fact that Mark had been the last one to see Lisa alive made him the one everyone wanted to talk to. He gave his version of the events leading up to the fall many times, and Dr. Cross and the Walgraves were questioned as well. He left out the part about the injection, not knowing if this would somehow get Dr. Cross in trouble, but then later he wondered if the omission would wind up getting *him* in trouble. He rationalized that if the subject came up at some point, he could always say he'd forgotten, which wouldn't be unusual given all that had happened.

The fire department lowered Lisa's body from the roof. She was declared dead at the scene and carried away in a black body bag. Mark watched as they zipped up the bag, and all he could think was that she might not be able to breathe inside the bag, which didn't make sense, of course, because she was dead, but his mind wasn't functioning well. All the while, the black birds cawed and danced on the telephone line up above. Watching this sequence of events was unreal. He had *just* talked to Lisa. He'd felt her hand in his. The two of them had made eye contact. They'd spoken. How could she be dead? How could it be that he was the last one to see her alive?

This kind of thing only happened in movies. And yet, it had happened to him.

When he told the police, he had to sit down because he felt dizzy and light-headed. One of the paramedics said he could be in shock, so they had him lie down on a gurney right on the porch and elevated his legs. And then he felt like a fucking idiot because a girl was dead and they were treating him as if he were the patient, checking his temperature, covering him with a blanket, urging him to drink water. The other four members of the Redevine Society showed up around that time, dashing down the sidewalk to Alden Manor. Neela and Sam Burman were in the lead, with Baird and Lara Whitlock walking right behind them. As they hurried toward Alden Manor, Mark remembered Lisa talking about their names. Baird. Lara. She was right, he realized. The names were too close to Brad and Laura, and now he would always think of that and have to mentally correct for the difference.

When the four came up the walkway, Mark, who was getting his blood pressure checked, became self-conscious about being treated as a patient, so he looked in the other direction. No matter. They paid no attention to him, but went right into the house to see Roy and Alma.

For the first time he wondered what these people did for a living that allowed them so much free time during the day. Independently wealthy, maybe?

Must be nice.

But why was he thinking about such things? A girl was dead.

When everything died down and Mark had been medically

cleared, Dr. Cross offered to drive him home. While the doctor went back inside to get his medical bag, Mark waited on the front walk. He was biding his time, his gaze toward the ground, when he heard a familiar voice. "I told you so. I told you!" It was the hippie, Doug, standing by the curb, hands at his waist like he was Superman. "What did I say? People go in that house—they don't come out the same."

Mark narrowed his eyes at him. *Asshole.* What kind of man crowed like that when a young woman had just died? Mark tried to think of a response, something that would shut him up permanently, but nothing came to mind. He was usually fairly quick-witted. Maybe he was still reeling from witnessing Lisa's death.

"I seen it with my own eyes." Doug leaned down and scratched at the section of his foot between the straps of his sandal. "Bad things happen to folks who go in there." He straightened and pointed a long finger at Alden Manor. "You better watch yourself, mister, or you'll be next. I always say it's better to take action than to be a victim."

Mark turned away from him, relieved to see Dr. Cross had arrived, bag in hand, ready to drive him home. After they were in the car and buckled up, Mark pointed to Doug, who was now leaning against the industrial building next door, and said, "What do you know about that guy?"

Dr. Cross followed Mark's gesture, but Doug chose that moment to step into a shadow. "What guy?" The doctor donned a pair of mirrored aviator sunglasses.

"There, in front of that building. The old hippie guy. He's always hanging around here telling me there's something screwy going on at Alden Manor."

Dr. Cross started up the car and pulled away from the curb. At that instant, Doug darted between the buildings and was gone from view. The doctor said, "There are a lot of vagrants in this neighborhood. If you're afraid . . . ?" The question hung in the air.

"No, I'm not afraid. He's just weird."

"I'd ignore him if I were you," Dr. Cross said, changing the subject. "Just for the record, all of us know that you did the best you could. You have no reason to feel guilty about Lisa's death."

"I'm glad to hear you say that. It eases my mind," Mark said, without conviction.

"I hope this doesn't cause you to reconsider your position at Alden Manor." He glanced his way, and Mark saw his own face reflected in the lenses of the doctor's sunglasses. "Alma and Roy are going to need you now more than ever."

"I don't think I can handle all of Lisa's tasks," Mark admitted. He thought about cooking meals and clipping the old people's toenails and trimming Roy's ear hair, not to mention, worst of all, Alma's bathing needs. He couldn't imagine having to do that. The idea of touching her body sickened him. The skin he could see was grotesque—the rest, the part under her clothing, had to be even worse. Could he actually help her take a shower and wash her hair? Maybe, but there was a definite possibility he might throw up. He thought of what Lisa had told him. *You signed on as a home health aide. Did you think you'd make ten dollars an hour and it would all be funnel cakes and Ferris wheels?* What he'd actually expected was that he'd be cutting up meat and doling out pills. Maybe doing some laundry and unpacking groceries. He'd been completely ignorant in knowing what the job actually entailed.

"Don't worry," Dr. Cross said, flicking on the turn signal. *Tick-tick, tick-tick, tick-tick.* "We're going to have a group meeting tonight and figure it all out. You won't have to do anything you're not comfortable with. I'll make certain of it."

Mark nodded, relieved. This was great news. He didn't know who was involved in the group meeting, but most likely it consisted of the Redevine Society and Dr. Cross, along with Roy and Alma. He wondered if Baird, Lara, Neela, and Sam found this new obligation to be a chore. They had thought they were joining a fine-dining group and now were involved in elder care. But it wasn't as if they had no choice. They wouldn't do it unless they were fond of the Walgraves. They could walk away anytime.

Dr. Cross added, "If you need to take tomorrow off, call in the morning to let us know. We'll understand."

"No, that's not necessary. I'll be there," Mark promised him. On some level, he was afraid that if he took a day off, he'd never go back. He needed to keep busy, and working at Alden Manor was preferable to sitting at home with nothing to do, replaying Lisa's last moments —the tortured look on her face and her anguished words. *No one is safe. It's too late. This is the only way to stop them.* Even thinking about it made him shudder. And the way she fell backward, resigned to dying, as if there were no other way. Horrendous. One minute, alive. The next, dead.

He didn't know anything about psychotic breaks, but judging from what this experience had looked like, going through one was hell on earth. Poor Lisa.

Monica was still at work when he arrived at the apartment, so he had to wait to tell her what happened. When she walked in the door, he gave her time to drop her purse and kick off her shoes before he related what had happened at work that day. His telling was matter-of-fact: a troubled girl had killed herself right in front of him. He'd tried to help her but couldn't. It was awful and sad. Monica listened, fascinated and sympathetic, then asked how he was doing. He took a deep breath and said, "I'm fine."

That's how he'd felt late that afternoon. But the nightmare he just had says otherwise. Clearly, Lisa's death affected him.

Monica continues to console him, patting his back and

speaking soothingly. "Poor sweet baby," she says. "You had quite a day. It's not surprising that this ordeal has intruded on your subconscious." She wraps her arms around him, and he's suddenly grateful that she has a large enough vocabulary to use the words *ordeal* and *subconscious*. Not too long ago he didn't care who he slept with as long as they had an hourglass figure and a beautiful face. Monica has both, although she's not at the top end of the range. She's attractive, there's no doubt about that, but she's not Playboy Bunny material or anything. Still, now that he needs some emotional comfort, she's proving more than up to the task. That alone is worth a lot.

Monica is the more objective one, he knows, and she has figured it out. The dream is nothing but his mind toying with him. Emotionally, he has regrets about not being able to stop Lisa's death, and he would like to be able to tell her so. The part about Alma and Roy coming after him was just dream nonsense—no doubt his brain picked it up from the posters depicting their magic act.

He shudders. "You're right. It was awful, though." He's too macho to use the words *terrifying* or *frightening*, but she seems to understand.

"Do you want to quit this job?" she asks. "I would understand if you do. I wouldn't even give you any crap about the rent." When he doesn't answer right away, she adds, "They need busboys at work. I know that's beneath you, but you could do it for a while until you find something better."

The thought of working as a busboy is even more appalling than going back to Alden Manor. She means well, but clearing tables is not an option for him. "No," he assures her. "I'm not going to quit. I promised Roy I'd stay six months, and I will." He will get through it, and once he does, if it works out the way he hopes, he'll come out ahead financially and move on to better prospects. The fact that Lisa is gone is terrible—no one can argue that—but there is one positive. Her absence clears the way for him, giving him an automatic promotion.

If only going back to that house didn't fill him with such dread. He pushes the feeling aside. Best not to dwell on it. He can do this.

Just a few more months.

CHAPTER THIRTEEN

The next morning, Mark arrives at Alden Manor and is greeted at the door by a tall woman wearing a starched white uniform, tan nylons, and polished white shoes. She can't be more than five years older than him, and yet she has an imperious air about her. "I am Nurse Darby," she says with a frown. "And you are Mark Norman?" She has an odd melodic accent that sounds vaguely Eastern European.

"Yes," he says. "I've been working here for . . ."

But she has already turned and is heading down the hallway. "There is much to do," she says. "No time to waste."

He follows her to the dining room, where Alma and Roy are eating breakfast. Today's feast is oatmeal with bits of chopped banana sprinkled on top. Alma has a large child's bib around her neck and a spoon in her hand. Both of the elderly folks brighten when he walks in the room. "Mark!" Roy says. "So glad you're here. We were afraid you might not show up."

"Of course I'm here." He smiles.

Roy adds, "You just missed Dr. Cross. He stayed the night to make sure the transition went smoothly." He gestures to

Nurse Darby with a tilt of his head. The mood of the room is different. With Lisa, Mark always felt a quiet sense of gloom. Today, there is something else, some emotional state he can't quite place.

"You can count on me," Mark says. "I'm reliable."

"Reliable is only good when the work is done," Nurse Darby says, out of nowhere. "And so our day begins." She turns to Mark. "I am the one with the training and credentials, so I am in charge. You will do what I say, understand?"

Mark bristles. This woman just shows up and thinks she can order him around? He has seniority, and besides, he's nobody's servant. Time to turn on his always reliable charm. "I think we can divide up the chores in a way that's fair," he says. "Of course, anything medical and all of Alma's personal needs would fall to you."

Nurse Darby imperiously lifts her chin and folds her arms. "Oh, so this is how we start? You have your own ideas? Well, that will not do. I will run things, and it will go smoothly. You will see. A ship cannot have two captains."

Mark chuckles reflexively and then makes a quick decision. Let her be in charge if it's that important to her. He'll play along. Eventually, with time and some strategizing on his part, it will shake out in his direction. For now, it's best not to make a scene. He bows in her direction. "Whatever you want."

The next few hours go by quickly. Under Nurse Darby's direction, he is busy every minute: folding clothing, mopping floors, and doing dishes. He barely sees Roy and Alma. Nurse Darby has taken their care upon herself. He is on his knees scrubbing out the toilet in Alma and Roy's bathroom when he hears the squeak of rubber-soled shoes. A second later, Nurse Darby appears in the doorway. With a crooked finger, she beckons. "You will come with me."

After putting the toilet brush back in the holder under the sink, he quickly washes his hands while she waits. Without a word, she leads him to Roy's bed. "We will strip off the old sheets and put on fresh ones," she says. "This must be done at least twice a week."

Her condescending tone pisses him off. He's not some idiot who needs constant direction. Besides, who decided twice a week is the rule for bedding? Is this something she learned in nursing school? He would guess it's just her random preference. He says nothing, just continues helping. With both of them working together, it goes quickly, and a few minutes later, they are in Alma's room repeating the process.

As he tucks the sheet in between Alma's mattress and box spring, his fingers brush against something solid that doesn't belong there. It feels like a chain. He pulls it out and examines it. It's a necklace—Lisa's gold cross. He sneaks a peek in Nurse Darby's direction, but she is busy creating hospital corners and is not paying any attention to him. Surreptitiously, he slips it into his pants pocket. *How did it wind up in Alma's room?* He has no idea. Alma seems too addlebrained to have found it and secreted it away, but it doesn't make sense for Lisa to have put it there either.

Before he can give it much thought, Nurse Darby orders him to put the sheets in the washing machine and to meet her in the kitchen afterward. "We will be making the lunch," she says.

While he's cutting up apples and she's making sandwiches, the nurse attempts small talk for the first time since they met. "Mr. Walgrave says you are like a grandson to them." Her eyebrows rise questioningly.

Hearing this, Mark feels a weird, elated glow, but he is careful to give a neutral response. "I am very fond of both of them." A satisfactory comment.

"And he says that you will be put in charge of everything very soon."

"I'm not sure what you're referring to."

She gestures around the kitchen. "He says all decisions will be up to you. About the house, their care, their finances."

Mark concentrates on the apples, careful to separate the seeds from the slices. From outward appearances, he's busy and calm, but inwardly he's rejoicing at the news. This is, he thinks, a step toward the deal that Lisa turned down. He holds back a smile. "I will gladly take on whatever responsibilities they would like me to have."

She nods. "Then I have a favor to ask of you."

"Shoot." He arranges the apples on each plate in a crescent pattern.

"They will need more nursing care as they reach the end, which will be soon, I think." She pauses, and Mark waits. "If you are in charge of arranging for care, I would be happy to be the full-time nurse. Around the clock, I mean. At my last job, I was the charge nurse at St. Mark's. I am more than qualified to make their last days pleasant and pain-free."

He stands upright and stares at her. She was once a charge nurse? And now she's doing personal care nursing in someone's home? Kind of a come-down in status. Why? He has a hunch. "Why did you leave St. Mark's?"

"I . . ." She looks stricken. He's caught her off guard. She smooths the front of her dress. "I had a personal conflict with another staff member. We could not work together."

"I see. Well, I'll definitely keep you in mind when it comes time to make that decision."

"Thank you. I would appreciate it."

But he knows that when the time comes there's no way in hell he'll choose Nurse Darby. Working with her is like having a sharp pebble in his shoe. One day in and already he would like to wring her scrawny neck. He imagines that with enough pressure her eyes would pop out, like the novelty squeeze toy he had as a kid. His next mission is to have her gone, by whatever means possible.

In the afternoon, Nurse Darby brings out two garbage bags and orders him to clean out Lisa's room. "We will be using it soon, so all the personal items must go." She sweeps her hand. *All the personal items must go.* As if Lisa is being erased. "You must also strip off the old bedding and bring it to me. I will make it fresh."

Mark takes the bags, not saying a word, but his thoughts are vicious. *Who do you think you're ordering around? Die, you hag.* He takes some comfort in the fact that Roy is planning to put him in charge. Before the day is over, he will try to wrangle some alone time with the old man and firm up the details. All of this is happening quickly, but Roy and Alma's health is declining fast, so he has no time to waste.

Nurse Darby points to one bag. "In this bag, you will put the things that are garbage. They must be disposed of." Indicating the second bag, she says, "And in this one, clothing and anything else that can be donated. If you come across any valuables, you must set them aside and then give them to me. I will decide what will be done with them."

So patronizing. He nods as if in agreement.

Once he's alone in Lisa's room, he takes the necklace out of his pocket and sees for the first time that although the clasp is intact, the chain is broken. Perhaps it fell from her neck just as she was making the bed? He tries to imagine how likely it would be that she didn't see it and then accidentally tucked it in with the sheets. Not likely, but not impossible either. It's the only explanation. He shrugs and tucks it into his wallet for safekeeping. Monica is friendly with a jeweler who might know if the cross is real gold. Maybe they can get a little something for it.

Turning his attention to the room, he is struck by how little is left behind. The closet has a few clothing items on hangers. A purse containing a comb, compact, makeup bag, mirror, checkbook, and wallet sits on the floor. Mark opens the wallet and finds a library card, a prayer card, and a driver's license, along with some cash. He pulls out the paper money, transferring it to his pocket. He will give the wallet to Dr. Cross or Roy instead of the nurse.

The dresser drawers contain carefully folded jeans, underwear, and socks. Would she have taken the time to arrange them so neatly if she knew the end was near? Probably not. He wonders if people ever know when it's the last time they'll be doing something. It's a sad thought. All of life is temporary.

On top of the dresser is a cigar box holding a few pairs of earrings and a charm bracelet. None of the jewelry looks valuable, but one set of hoop earrings, still in the box it was purchased in, looks like a style Monica might like, so he filches them for a future birthday present. It's not as if Lisa needs them anymore, and why should Nurse Darby get any of it? She didn't even know Lisa.

He takes the clothing and unceremoniously stuffs it into the bags. Yes, it will get wrinkled, but that's the next person's problem. When he's done, he stands back to survey the empty closet and dresser drawers, then shuts the drawers and closet door with a rush of melancholy. How is it that a person can live for more than twenty years, and all of her possessions can fit in two garbage bags? Tragic. When he dies, it will be different. He'll have a veritable estate—property, investments, a business. So much will be left behind that he'll never be forgotten. Mark Norman's name will be known far and wide. He intends to put his stamp on the world.

Mark sets the bags next to the door and goes to the double bed with one lonely pillow in the middle of it. After taking off the pillowcase and the zippered cover, he notices that the naked pillow is water-stained. He imagines Lisa at night crying into her pillow, and the full weight of her misery presses upon him. With an audible exhale, he shakes the feeling aside, then folds the bedding into a loose pile so that Nurse Darby can make it fresh.

CHAPTER FOURTEEN

Three days later, Mark finds himself gritting his teeth at the sound of Nurse Darby's voice. The squeak of her white shoes gives him the urge to stab her with a fork. He knows it's not just him. No one on the planet would enjoy working with this woman. He should get an award for remaining polite under these circumstances.

Besides being bossy, she keeps him endlessly busy and apart from the Walgraves. He is now limited to greeting them in the morning, serving their food, and saying goodbye before he leaves. One positive—Alden Manor is now cleaner than it's ever been. At least on the first floor, there's not a cobweb or bit of dust anywhere. Nurse Darby makes sure of that. She makes a point to double-check his work, making him stand there as she does inspection. Worse yet, she has him redo the chore when his efforts don't meet her standards. "Cleanliness is next to godliness," she says, with a knowing smile. Mark has no idea what that means, and he doesn't care either.

While he cleans on the first floor, she is upstairs doing the same. He hears the vacuum cleaner overhead and wonders if she's noticed the creepy posters of Alma and Roy's magic act.

She seems lacking in imagination. The very thing that Lisa found disturbing might barely register with Nurse Darby. Somehow, he can't imagine her becoming unhinged.

As he was leaving on the first day after Lisa's death, Baird and Lara arrived, carrying overnight bags, to cover the night shift. The second day, the night hours were covered by Neela and Sam. Each time, the bedding in Lisa's room had to be washed, to be made fresh for the visitors.

By the third day, Mark wonders if this is something they intend to do indefinitely.

Without a doubt, this is the weirdest job he's ever had. Best pay, though, so that's something.

He finally gets an opportunity to talk to Roy when the old man catches sight of him heading down the hall and waves him into the blue room. "Mark, my boy!" he calls out. "Come visit with us."

Mark, who'd been instructed to go to the kitchen to wash dishes, gladly abandons the plan. "Certainly, sir," he says, taking a seat opposite them. Alma looks vaguely distracted, but she does not seem unwell. She sits straight-backed on the sofa, hands on her knees. Frail in appearance, but certainly not at death's door. He wonders how Dr. Cross knows her time is reaching an end.

"Tell me, Mark," Roy says. "Are you enjoying working with Nurse Darby?"

Mark hesitates for a second. "Not particularly." He gives Roy his famous smile, the one that has always gotten him compliments from every girl he's ever dated. "I don't mind doing more of the housework, but I miss interacting with the two of you." He lets the statement lie there, watching as Roy presses his lips together thoughtfully. "I don't think Nurse Darby understands that I can be of more value serving you directly."

Roy says, "Alma and I were just saying the same thing."

Alma doesn't react at all. Mark suspects that Alma doesn't contribute much to their conversations and that what Roy attributes to her is mostly wishful thinking. "Both of us enjoy your presence here, and we thought you and Lisa worked well together. Obviously, we didn't know the extent of her troubles."

"Of course not," Mark interjects. "How could you?"

"But Miss Darby is not quite what we had in mind either." Not *Nurse Darby*, Mark notices, but *Miss Darby*, as if she's been demoted. Roy reaches over and takes his sister's hand. "And we still need nighttime coverage. Our friends have been helping us out, but that can't go on."

There's a long pause, as if he's waiting for a response, so Mark says, "I see."

"So we have a proposition for you, one we're hoping you'll seriously consider. How would you like to move in and be our round-the-clock helper?"

The question catches him off-balance. "Round-the-clock helper?" he repeats.

"Yes. You can move into Lisa's old room and live here. Your pay would be raised to account for the additional hours, and we'd still give you time off, of course."

Mark makes a point to look as if he's thoughtfully considering this offer. So many guys his age would balk at this idea, but he's smarter than that. He knows it's a perfect opportunity, the likes of which he may never see again. The contemplative pause is intentional. He knows the one who holds back a little is always at an advantage. "Can I give you an answer tomorrow? I'm not sure how this will work with my girlfriend. I want to be fair to her."

"Your girlfriend. Monica, right?"

"Yes, sir."

Roy leans over and spreads his bony fingers over his knees.

"I'm glad you mentioned her, because this brings me to another question." He clears his throat, a gargling sound. "Alma and I have discussed it, and since we still need coverage of the female persuasion, we were wondering if Monica would like to come aboard?"

Mark blinks. "Come aboard?"

"Come to work for us. Around the clock."

"Work here," he answers slowly. "Doing what?"

"Why, the same as you, of course! Just stay here and help us out as need be."

He looks so hopeful that Mark feels terrible saying, "That doesn't sound like something Monica would be interested in. I mean, she has an excellent job that she enjoys." The truth is that Monica makes pretty decent money as a banquet waitress and bartender. Besides the legitimate tips and wages, she's also skimming off bar sales and pocketing cash from drunk patrons. "Compensation for what I have to put up with," she said the first time she told Mark about this tactic. But besides the money, she likes her coworkers, and they often go out together on nights off. Mark went with them once, but he quickly became bored when he realized most of the conversation involved trashing the idiotic management at the banquet hall.

"Could you ask her?" Roy asks with a tilt of his head. Next to him, Alma even seems to be paying attention, fixing Mark with a penetrating stare. "Maybe she could stop in today or tomorrow and we could meet her? If income is the problem, she should know that money is not an issue with us. We would compensate her quite well for her trouble."

Money is not an issue with us? Someday Mark hopes to be able to say those exact words. Right now his mindset regarding money is completely different. Every dollar is accounted for. Every expense tabulated. He considers each grocery item before putting it into the cart. What would it be like not to have to mentally calculate the total? It must be like heaven. "I can ask," Mark says, "but I can't promise anything. I doubt she'll be interested. And honestly, she's probably not the right person for the job. For one thing, she doesn't have any experience as a home health aide." He also can't imagine Monica locked up inside someone else's house all day. She is a party girl, a real people person, and Alma and Roy, nice as they are, aren't her type of people.

Roy points a finger to the ceiling. "But that's exactly why she'd be perfect for the job. You didn't have any experience, and you've been wonderful to us. We appreciate that you don't try to take over our lives. You're just here to help. Both of us feel that you fit right in." He leans forward and lowers his voice. "Someone like Nurse Darby treats us like invalids, and we know she's a bit totalitarian in her dealings with you. We're not happy with her. Please, can't you convince Monica to join us? We're so fond of you already. If she's your girlfriend, I have a feeling she'll be perfect."

"I'm glad you're happy with my work."

"You're like family," Alma blurts out, almost as if she's following the conversation.

Mark smiles. "Thank you. You've made me feel welcome in your home. I'll certainly do my best to persuade Monica, but like I said, I can't guarantee she'll go for it. Maybe Beverly at the agency can line up some possibilities for you?"

"Perhaps," Roy says smoothly. "But Monica would be our first choice. Since you already know each other, I'm sure that would be an ideal coupling."

Ideal coupling. Such an odd choice of words, Mark thinks, but then again, old people have their weird expressions. Mark remembers all the inane things his grandparents have said over the years. *As full as Fibber McGee's closet. Pardon my French.*

I'll be there with bells on. They brought their own weird language with them from the past. He smiles. "Yes, sir."

"You know, Mark, it's not easy to get old."

"I would imagine it's difficult at times." He nods in a sympathetic way.

"It happens before you know it," Roy says. "Everyone knows about the gray hair and wrinkles. The ear hair, the liver spots. You hear people mention the aches and pains, the knees that don't cooperate, the extra pounds that creep up when you aren't looking." He stares off into the distance. "But no one seems to talk about the dreams that were never realized. The regrets for things said or done, or not said or done. At some point you weigh the time wasted, time that you can't get back, and the thought crushes your spirit. And there's a moment in your life when you realize, with absolute certainty, that you'll never again know the joy of breaking into a run or bounding up the stairs. Simple things that you took for granted at one time are no longer possible. Your own body has betrayed you. Worse yet is when it becomes apparent that you'll never know the thrill of falling in love ever again. That feeling of connecting with someone new, discovering each other body and soul. The rush you get in looking forward to all the moments ahead. The places you'll go, the things you'll do. When you're old, those days are behind you. There will be no new love, no exciting future. Your best years are behind you. And that," he says with sad finality, "is the worst thing of all."

What a bummer. Mark asks, "Does it help to think back on all you've done?"

"Not really." Roy shakes his head. "No matter how much you've accomplished, it's never enough."

This strikes Mark as a little greedy. Roy has had his day in the sun. Yes, it's sad when things end, but that's the way of the world. Nothing lasts forever. Mark tries to look thoughtful and asks, "So do you have any advice for someone my age?" Old people, he knows, love to pass on their wisdom.

"Don't take it for granted. Enjoy this stage in your life. Your good looks and your youthful physicality will be gone before you know it."

"Yes, sir." Mark thinks of something he actually wants to know. "Do you have any advice for becoming successful?"

"Successful in what way?"

Mark has a ready answer. "Making your mark on the world. Achieving what everyone wants: power, money, influence."

"Ah." Roy tips his chin in understanding. "Each person finds their own path to success, but there is one thing I've found to be crucial."

"Yes?" Mark leans forward, eager for this insider tip.

"Envy is not a productive emotion. You can spend your whole life wishing you were someone else, or you could just become that person."

Mark exhales, disappointed. "I see." This is the type of psychobabble nonsense espoused by his insurance salesman stepfather. *Work smarter, not harder. Make a plan, then work the plan.* He was hoping to be given a blueprint for success, something he could actually use. Instead, all he gets are bullshit platitudes.

"Maybe you see, maybe you don't," Roy says. "So much of insight comes with age."

Nurse Darby chooses that moment to come to the door. "So there you are, Mark! I have found you at last." As if he's been in hiding. "You come with me now. You are needed in the kitchen."

He really, really hates her. When Roy and Alma don't intercede on his behalf, he reluctantly stands. "I better get back to work."

Alma stares at her lap while Roy nods. "We appreciate your

hard work. Don't forget to talk to Monica on our behalf. We'd love to have both of you here."

"I won't forget." From the corner of his eye, he sees Nurse Darby frown. "It's been nice talking to you." He directs this to Roy before leaving to follow Nurse Darby and her squeaky shoes down the dark hallway to the kitchen.

CHAPTER FIFTEEN

Mark comes home to find Monica curled up on the couch, watching a rerun of *Happy Days* and drinking a rum and Coke. Mostly rum, by the looks of it. Usually she's a motion machine, but on occasion she goes into sloth mode, and luckily for him this is one of those times. When he asks if they can talk, she raises her eyebrows and answers with a simple nod, then sets her glass on the coffee table. He goes over to the TV and turns down the volume, knowing he'll never be able to compete with the show's canned laughter.

He takes a seat on the other end of the couch and begins his prepared speech. He thinks he's doing fairly well at putting a happy spin on the subject of them both moving to Alden Manor, but Monica is having none of it. "You've got to be fucking kidding me," she says when he's halfway through his pitch.

Shifting closer to her, he tries again, this time making it a plea. "Won't you please consider it?" He gives her the puppy-dog eyes, but she doesn't seem to notice.

"I'm still recovering from the fact that you just announced you're moving out," she says, her face showing the storm clouds of her thoughts. "What the hell! You're bailing on me with absolutely zero notice? And what about the rent, Mark? Have you even considered what a bind you're putting me in?"

He's not crazy about the way she contemptuously spits out his name, but he is trying to stay on her good side, so he remains calm. "I gave this a lot of thought on the bus ride home, Monica. Can you at least hear me out?"

She cocks her head to one side and narrows her eyes. Everything about her says she won't be yielding, but begrudgingly she says, "Okay, I'm listening."

"We work for the Walgraves for as long as we can, save the money, and start our own business. We'll do it together." Mark hadn't actually planned on having their lives become entangled to this extent, but for the sake of convincing her, he's throwing out the idea. Whether or not it happens is a matter for another day. "We're talking about a lot of money, Monica. Way more than you make now."

She scoffs. "You have no idea how much I make now, Mark Norman. I do very well for myself. And who says I want to go into business with you? Do you even remember my business idea?"

He remembers hearing her talk about starting her own business, but he never paid attention enough to be able to bring anything to mind at the moment. Still, he has an answer. "I'm sure that whatever you've got in mind is absolutely brilliant."

"It is brilliant," she says. "I want to start a commercial cleaning service. Offices and stores. That way I can start small and then hire other employees as I get more accounts. The added bonus is that the work is at night, so everyone is gone and I won't have to deal with the customer being on site."

"As I said, absolutely brilliant."

She starts to smile, then gets serious again. "Your charm is not going to work on me this time, not when I think you've lost your mind."

"It's not just the pay. Nurse Darby told me Roy is planning on putting me in charge of everything—the house, their care, their finances."

"People talk shit all the time." Monica waves her hand as if shooing away a pesky mosquito. She has a general distrust of people and promises. "That doesn't mean anything. Maybe she was trying to get a rise out of you."

"No," he says, shaking his head. "I believe that he told her that and that he means it. She said that Roy feels like I'm like a grandson to him."

"Oh, Mark." Her tone is pitying. "You think you've got it all figured out."

"Monica, I'm telling you, this is a great opportunity for both of us."

"Have you even given a thought to this apartment?" As she gestures around the room, he takes in the mismatched, shabby furniture: chair, loveseat, couch, and a beat-up coffee table. On the walls are cheap framed pictures, one of sailboats on turbulent waters, the other a farmhouse surrounded by autumn foliage. They exist solely to break up the white space. Neither one reflects Monica's life or interests.

"What about this apartment?"

She says, "Am I supposed to break my lease and just walk away from all this? And what about everything I own here? I started with nothing, and it took me a long time to get set up. Every piece of furniture, every pot and pan. It all belongs to me, and I'm not about to toss it aside for some crazy scheme of yours."

Mark knows that everything in the apartment belongs to her, but he hardly thinks secondhand furniture and framed department store prints should be a deterrent to a better life. He says, "I know, babe. You've accomplished a lot."

Monica has more to say, however. "And what would you have me do, quit a steady job to take another one, one I may not even like? Then I'll be living with geezers in the worst part of the city, probably doing God knows what." She shudders. "What if they die in two months and we're out on the street? I bet you didn't think of that."

Mark walks around to the back of the couch and begins to rub her shoulders. "I did think of that. Here's my thought—we leave the apartment the way it is and sublet it to your friend Brenda." Brenda works with Monica and is currently living unhappily with her parents. From what Monica has told him, she'd jump at the chance to move into an already furnished apartment. And if she can't afford the whole amount, Mark and Monica could always make up the difference in the rent and still come out way ahead. "We tell her that it will be a month-to-month arrangement, so if you don't like the job or the Walgraves die suddenly, we can move back in. Tell your job you want a leave of absence. That you're going to take care of a dying grandparent."

"I don't think they'll go for it."

"They will. It's easier to take someone back than to train a new person."

"They'd need to train two people. I don't just waitress—I also bartend," she reminds him.

"Making you all the more valuable."

"They'll replace me, and when I want to go back they'll say, *Too bad, so sad.*"

He shakes his head and says, "No, that won't happen. How many times have you told me someone didn't show up or that some waitress quit unexpectedly? So much turnover there. They'll let you have a leave of absence, believe me." He feels the tightness in her shoulders loosen, and he knows he's making some headway. He croons, "Come on, baby. You and me. We go live at Alden Manor and rake in the money. It will be an adventure. What do you say?" He thinks he comes off as both convincing and endearing. How can she say no?

She stretches like a cat and motions to her back. "I say to go a little lower, right between my shoulder blades."

Mark accommodates her request. "Answer the question." He shifts his thumbs lower and makes circular motions against her back. "What do you say about my plan?" She stretches again and sighs with pleasure. He leans in and whispers. "Come on. Say yes."

After a long silence, she says, "No."

"No, you won't do it?" He stops massaging her back.

"No, I won't do it. And I still expect your half of the rent until the end of October when the lease is up. I never would have rented this apartment on my own." She turns to face him and shakes her head. "You're putting me in a bad position."

He can tell she's dead serious, but he also knows she has no way to enforce this. Her name is the one on the lease, which means Mark Norman is a nonentity to the building management. He could slip away like a shadow in the night. Still, he wants to keep things positive between them, at least for now. "Of course. We'll still be seeing each other from time to time, and I'll send you a check every month. You know I wouldn't leave you high and dry."

She eyes him suspiciously. "You agreed to that awfully fast."

"Because it's the honorable thing to do." He is proud of the way he manages to pull out the right words.

"Hmm."

Mark can tell that Monica knows he's feeding her a line of bullshit. He doesn't have an honorable bone in his body. She's got his number.

"So I take it that we're breaking up?" she asks.

"Not breaking up, exactly, but I'll be pretty busy, so I won't be able to see you that often." Even to his ears this sounds a lot like breaking up. It will be sad to be alone again, but he reminds himself that eventually there will be another Monica to take her place.

"You do know this whole thing is bizarre, right? It was weird enough when they hired you, and now they want *me*, sight unseen? They don't know anything about me, and neither of us has any experience taking care of old people. They don't need me. I'm sure they can find any number of qualified candidates for the job."

"They want regular people. Nurse Darby treats them like invalids. Roy told me he *hates* that."

From the expression on her face, he's not making any headway. She says, "So they prefer to have you as opposed to a medical professional? Sorry, Mark, not buying it."

Mark takes offense at the notion that he somehow falls short. If Monica spent even one minute with Nurse Darby, she'd understand why he's the better choice. His personality, for one thing. And Roy did say that Mark reminds him of his younger self. That counts for a lot. He walks around the couch and sits down on the end, one cushion between them. Monica gets up to turn up the volume and begins to watch her show again. Mark knows that this is the episode where Fonzie rents a room above the Cunninghams' garage, and he also knows Monica has seen it already. Nevertheless, they watch together in silence.

Maybe, he thinks, Monica just needs some time to get used to the idea. He hopes that she'll reconsider his proposal after a full night's sleep.

The rest of the evening is spent without a word, each of them respectful of each other's space. Once they are in bed in the dark, he reaches over to stroke her hair, and she pushes his hand away. He knows then not to try for sex. Sadly, he realizes he's already had sex with Monica for the last time and hadn't even known it. In the morning, Mark tries once again to convince her to take the job at Alden Manor. As she watches him pack up his things, he says, "Won't you at least come down and talk to them? If nothing else, it will make an interesting story to tell your friends." He has a full suitcase and a duffel bag. He'll come back later for the custom suits Roy purchased for him.

"Why would I bother?" she asks. "Really, Mark, it's such a long bus ride to end up talking to old people. Honestly, how interesting could it be?"

"If Roy lets me pick you up in the Excalibur, then would you do it?"

"Maybe."

His heart sinks. When Monica says *maybe*, she actually means *no*. Sleeping on the subject hasn't changed her mind. When he leans in to give her one last kiss, she lets him, so he makes it a good one, a passionate, lingering connection of the lips. Always leave them wanting more.

CHAPTER SIXTEEN

By the time Mark rounds the corner to Alden Manor, the duffel bag hangs like dead weight off his shoulder and he is half dragging, half carrying the suitcase. He knows that he's scuffing the bottom of the leather suitcase, but some part of him doesn't care. The damn thing is heavy.

He's not happy to catch sight of Doug, who stands with one leg bent, his back against the industrial building next door. As he gets closer, Doug calls out a greeting. "Good morning!"

"Morning," Mark says, not meeting his eyes.

"Moving in, huh? Right on schedule. Don't say I didn't warn you!" He throws his head back and laughs.

Mark chooses to ignore him. Climbing the steps to the porch, he spots another dead crow lying feet-up in front of the mat. With a swing of his leg, he kicks it off the porch and watches as it lands on the lawn. He is no longer shocked by the sight of a bird corpse, even this one, which appears to be disemboweled. If a predator doesn't eat the rest of it, it will stay on the grass until the next scheduled visit by the gardener. He imagines it being sliced and diced by large lawn mower blades and winces only slightly at the mental image. Not his problem anymore.

Inside, he greets Nurse Darby, who is wiping down the woodwork in the front hall. For once she does not bark orders at him, but just says, "Morning," and continues her work. Next, he drops his things off in what used to be Lisa's room and takes a look around. The furniture— double bed, dresser, nightstand—is comprised of plain maple wood. The headboard is a solid rectangle. The room is small and cozy, with adequate storage space in the drawers and closets. He gives the bed a try, sitting down and giving it a bounce. It seems fairly comfortable, and the mirror above the dresser gives back a flattering reflection. Overall, the room is similar in size and shape to the bedroom he had as a child. In general, it's fine, but he can't shake the feeling it's not really his room. He feels as if he's stolen it from Lisa, which is ridiculous because she has no use for it anymore.

When he gets to the blue room, he finds Roy and Alma visiting with Dr. Cross. After he gives them the bad news about Monica, Dr. Cross nods and says, "Well, that's it, then. I'll get in touch with Beverly at the agency and have her send some female candidates. In the meantime, we still have Nurse Darby to cover the daytime, and Mark will be here at night." He gestures to Mark. "Once we hire the new girl, we won't need Nurse Darby anymore."

They talk among themselves as if Mark isn't there, with the men discussing how likely they are to find someone willing to move in right away.

"But we need a new Lisa," Alma says, whimpering.

"Yes, my dear," Roy says, putting a reassuring arm around his sister's shoulders. "Never fear. Calvin is taking care of everything."

With a start, Mark realizes that *Calvin* must be Dr. Cross's first name. The good doctor has to be a close personal friend.

How else to explain his constant visits and how he dotes on them? After they wrap up the chat, Dr. Cross reaches into a leather satchel at his feet and pulls out a slim binder, which he hands to Mark. "Everything you need to know is right here," he says. "Any questions, call me, day or night. My numbers, home and office, are listed under *Important Phone Numbers*."

"Yes, sir." Mark leafs through the binder and finds topics on everything from the daily schedule, to household services (cleaning, snow shoveling, mechanic, grocery delivery, lawn care), and where things are located in the house. That particular page is topped with a warning in capital letters: THE FIRST FLOOR IS THE ONLY FLOOR IN USE. DO NOT GO UPSTAIRS UNDER ANY CIRCUMSTANCES. *Interesting.* He guesses that at one time Lisa was also given this binder, but she disregarded that particular caution. At their first meeting, he pegged her as a good girl, a complete rule-follower, but like everyone else, it turned out there were two sides to her. It is true what they say: you never really know a person.

According to one of the binder notes, Dr. Cross would take care of all medical and dental appointments for the Walgraves, including transportation and serving as their advocate. *Thank God for that.* One less thing for him to do.

True to his word, Dr. Cross calls Beverly at the agency, and candidates start arriving that afternoon. There are five in all, and they arrive one after the other. Mark is tasked with greeting them at the door and taking them back to the blue room, where they are questioned by Roy and Dr. Cross, with Alma sitting silently nearby. After each one leaves, Mark is asked what he thinks. It's hard to know what to say. Although they are attractive and in his age group, none of them do much for him personally. He uses the words *satisfactory* and *nice* to describe most of them, and when he does, Roy and Dr. Cross exchange troubled glances, as if he's said the wrong thing. Collectively, all of these young women blur together in his mind, but even so, any one of them would be better than Nurse Darby. And isn't replacing her the objective?

After the fifth one leaves, Dr. Cross sighs and says he'll have Beverly send a few more applicants the next day. "We were lucky in getting Mark," he says, gathering up his things to leave. "Maybe we'll get lucky again."

Once they're through eating dinner, Roy takes Mark over to the drink cart and shows him his preferred method of mixing a brandy manhattan, dry and neat in a martini glass. Mark is surprised by the lack of ice, but he has to admit it does make it easier.

"Like this?" he says, setting the glasses down in front of them.

"Perfect!" Roy exclaims, taking a sip, his face rapturous. "Lisa would never mix cocktails for us," he chuckles. "She disapproved. But when you get older, you have so few pleasures left." Mark assures him he is happy to serve as bartender. After a few rounds and an evening of television watching, Mark helps both Roy and Alma make their way to the bedrooms. It is nine o'clock, but it feels like midnight. Before she left, Nurse Darby helped Alma get undressed and into her nightgown, so at least that part is done. Roy assists his sister in washing up and brushing her teeth while Mark stands by. He watches as they both climb into bed, and then Mark adjusts the covers for Alma like she's a child. He shuts off the lights but leaves their bedroom doors ajar as instructed in the binder. He still has the dinner dishes to wash, but then the rest of the evening belongs to him.

In the kitchen, he has time to think. Time crawls by in Alden Manor. Roy and Alma move so slowly that he finds his own heart rate and breathing slowing. How can it be so exhausting doing almost nothing? So much of today was spent helping them do the most basic tasks. Hoisting Alma to her feet from the chair, handing the cane to Roy, walking to the refrigerator to get the ketchup. He's done nothing physically taxing, and yet he feels dead on his feet. Maybe once he gets into a routine it will be better. Tomorrow he'll suggest they all go for a drive in the Excalibur. Mark knows that being at the wheel of that car will give him an adrenaline spike certain to counteract his current lethargy.

The dinner dishes are done in fifteen minutes. Reluctantly, he heads to his room, feeling like a child with an early bedtime. He's never been in the house alone and so late at night. The light switches in the hallway are not conveniently located, so there are moments when he has to grope his way through the suffocating dark. He walks carefully, and when his foot lands on a thick softness, he gasps, thinking that he's stepped on another bird, but then he realizes it's the edge of the narrow carpet runner. *Keep calm, Mark. The house is the same at night as during the day. Nothing scary here.*

When he reaches his bedroom, he proceeds with caution until he finds the lamp on the nightstand, right behind the clock radio, the way he remembers. He's relieved once he's turned on the switch and light fills the room. Although there are shadows in the corners, nothing appears odd. Had he really been afraid a few minutes ago? He hates to admit that he was, but only a little. Being in an old house at night is disquieting. He just needs to get used to being here.

Mark sits on the bed, his back against the headboard. He opens the binder and reads over all the information one more time. It seems rudimentary enough. He hopes that the new Lisa will be the one doing the cooking, because the baked chicken he made that evening pretty much exhausted his kitchen skills. Until the new hire comes on board, they'll be getting carryout or grilled cheese sandwiches.

After reading over all the directions, he can tell that his new job is not all that complicated. Tedious, but easy. Mentally, he calculates his pay over the course of the next three months and rejoices at the amount. He's always wanted to run his own business, to be in charge, but he never had the money to get started. Now that it could be a reality, he just has to decide what kind of business would work best.

Monica's idea is not the worst he's ever heard. Maybe, once she gets past her anger at him, she'd be open to running a cleaning business with him. Or if not, he has another thought. He once heard of a guy buying vending machines, then convincing business owners to allow him to place them in highly trafficked areas of their buildings. All the guy had to do then was periodically stock them and empty out the money. This sounds exactly like what Mark has in mind. Profitable but not too arduous. He makes a mental note to look into this.

He flips through the pages again and then shuts the binder. As he sets it down on the nightstand in front of the clock radio, he spots something on the floor wedged between the furniture and the wall. A book of some kind. The space is too narrow for his hand, so he gets up and slides the nightstand to one side and finds a leather-bound journal, the kind with an elastic strap running top to bottom. A quote stamped on the front cover says, *Be on your guard; stand firm in the faith; be courageous; be strong. 1 Corinthians 16:13.*

After moving the nightstand back and sitting on the bed, he opens it. The first page has a handwritten inscription. *Lisa, the staff and I would like to present you with this journal so you can document your thoughts and feelings as you move forward in your new life. We're very proud of all you've accomplished and wish you well. Sincerely, Dr. John Bauer.*

Well, that's definitely weird.

The handwriting on the next page is decidedly more feminine and definitely Lisa's. She began writing on the bus ride down to Alden Manor. She talks about being an inpatient at a facility and mentions how fragile she'd been when she arrived. *With the help of God, the staff at Emerson Mental Health Clinic, and a lot of hard work, I feel renewed and ready to face the world!*

The cylinders in Mark's brain turn and then click into place as he remembers something Lisa said. She said she'd gotten the job at Alden Manor because her doctor knew Dr. Cross. Her doctor must have worked at this mental health clinic. Knowing that she was mentally delicate to begin with makes complete sense. She wasn't up to the job, and in the end, the stress got to her. He continues reading.

I'm cautiously optimistic about my new job. I hope it works out and the Walgraves are happy with my work.

Mark finds the next few pages boring. The first entry gives her thoughts on the pair (Roy is very attentive to his sister, while Alma is sweet) and her impressions of the house (so fancy, but worn and needing some refreshing). "You can say that again," Mark mutters. He continues reading, noting that she tops each entry with the date. Some of them are short, just a few sentences, and only reveal her mood or a list of the mundane tasks she's performed that day. Mark sits up in surprise to read that a week after her start date, Dr. Cross brings in a new hire, a young man named Ted. Lisa takes an immediate dislike to Ted. The next few weeks are filled with entries about how Ted gets on her nerves. *A sanctimonious know-it-all,* she says. *Not as good-looking or smart as he thinks he is. Why does he think he can order me around? I was here first.*

Mark's interest picks up. Ted sounds like a complete asshole. No wonder Lisa never talked about him. He continues reading. The next entry almost makes him laugh.

Alma and Roy keep trying to set us up. Tonight they gave us time off and instructed us to go to dinner and a movie. We went out and had dinner at a steak house (Roy's treat), but it was awful. Away from the house, Ted is even worse. He has two modes of conversation—bragging and complaining. So obnoxious. And he kept pushing me to drink wine, which is rude. I don't want to lose this job, but I will tell them I don't enjoy his company and do not want to see him outside of work. Thank God he goes home in the evening and has Sundays off. At least I get a break from him.

"Ted," Mark says, "you don't know this, but you're on your way out." He flips through the next few pages to read more complaints about Ted. Lisa says Ted tries to order her around, and when she ignores him, he gets in her face. Whoever this Ted is, he knows nothing about how to treat a lady. Mark is not surprised to see that one day when Ted doesn't show up, Lisa is told that Ted's time at Alden Manor has come to a close and he won't be coming back. Lisa is relieved and happy. *I have to be honest here and say that I'm glad he's gone.*

In spite of his best efforts, Mark's eyelids are getting heavy. He wants to keep reading, but he's running out of steam, and he still has to get ready for bed. He flips through the rest of the journal, noticing that Lisa's handwriting gets worse as she goes along and that some of the passages are short. A few sentences jump out at him.

I don't know how much more of this I can take.

Had the same nightmare again last night. I'm exhausted but can't let on. I need to just soldier through and do my job.

I told Mark some of my concerns. He seemed sympathetic, but I can tell that he doesn't understand.

On the top of the last page, it says, *It's all getting to be too much. I'm losing my mind.* And below that is written a whole column:

Losing my mind.

Losing my mind.

Losing my mind.
Losing my mind.
Losing my mind.
Losing my mind.
Losing my mind.
Losing my mind.

Mark closes the journal. He has enough morbid curiosity to want to read the book all the way through, every word from where he left off to the end. This journal chronicles Lisa's life at Alden Manor as she lost her grip on sanity, and how fascinating is that? He should hand the book over to Dr. Cross, but he knows that he won't. Tomorrow, first chance he gets, he'll read it more thoroughly.

He opens the nightstand drawer and finds it empty except for a flashlight, the same one Lisa used to show him the ballroom on the second floor. Pushing the flashlight to one side, he puts the journal next to it and closes the drawer.

Poor Lisa. He pictures her all alone in this room, writing in this book, her worry and fear building and building, weighing upon her, until she can't bear it anymore. All of it leading up to her thinking the only way out of her misery was to throw herself off the top of a building.

What a tragic ending. Lisa checked out of life before she even found out what happened next. How does someone get to that place?

CHAPTER SEVENTEEN

As Dr. Cross promised, more applicants come the next morning. Again, Mark is put in charge of greeting them and walking them in to talk with Roy, Alma, and Dr. Cross. This time, though, Roy and Dr. Cross insist Mark stay in the room during the interview process, because they say it will make the young women more comfortable. Mark doesn't know about that, but it keeps him out of the clutches of Nurse Darby, so he's pleased to go along with this decision.

There are six applicants in all, each of them attractive, and they're scheduled in close succession. One in particular, Debra, seems nervous, but the rest are poised and confident. The candidates usually start the interview by listing off their qualifications. A few of them have done elder care for years, usually in nursing homes. Roy asks each one, "So why do you want to work in a private home instead?" He gets a variety of reasons. One woman says she wants more one-on-one time with her patients (Mark notices Roy wince at the word *patients*), another says she's tired of the management at her last job, and yet another says it's simply time for a change. There's a story there, not that Mark will ever hear it.

Only one of them seems excited at the prospect of living there full time: Debra, the nervous one. She primly says, "I believe my heavenly Father put me here on earth to serve the elderly." She makes a point of smiling at Mark as if he will concur. "I have a God-given talent for anticipating the needs of the infirm. I would love to be a member of your household."

From the look on Roy's face, Debra will not be getting the position.

After each woman leaves, Dr. Cross asks Mark to weigh in with his opinion. Each time he tries to be helpful, mentioning specifics about the applicant's answers. The last question that is always asked of him, either by Roy or Dr. Cross, is something along the lines of, "What do you think of her as a person? Is she someone you'd like to be friends with or date?" Each time he's honest and tells them no, but he is careful to add that he would be able to work well with any of them. It's not his decision to make.

By noon the last applicant has left, and the group has not made a decision. Alma twists her hands and says, "What will we do? We have no time."

No time? Alma must have a cement mixer for a brain because Mark can never quite figure her out.

Roy takes on a reassuring tone. "Don't you worry, Alma. Dr. Cross and I will come up with something." He nods at Mark. "Thanks for your help, Mark."

Nurse Darby walks in then and says, "Mark, there is a man on the front porch who is asking for you. He says he is your brother, Brian?" She raises her eyebrows questioningly.

Not Brian. There's no one he wants showing up at Alden Manor less than his family. Mark turns to the Walgraves, mortified at getting an unannounced visitor during working hours. "I'm so sorry. I'll tell him not to come here again."

Roy waves his hand. "Not to worry, my boy. You're allowed to have guests, if you like."

But Mark doesn't want guests, especially his older brother. When he opens the door to find Brian waiting on the porch, he immediately asks, "What are you doing here?"

Brian folds his arms and laughs. "Is that any way to greet your brother?"

"Fuck off, Brian. I'm working. How did you know I was here?"

Brian leans against the house as if he's not going anywhere soon. "Stopped by your place. I have to say your girlfriend, Monica, is easy on the eyes." He gives Mark a tight-lipped smile. "Anyway, she gave me the inside scoop on where you were and what you're doing." Glancing around the porch, he comments, "I have to say that this is different, even for you. Monica wasn't too thrilled about you moving out, but I guess you knew that already."

Good thing Mark already warned Monica about his brother. It wouldn't be the first time Brian has hit on one of his girlfriends. The infuriating thing is that on two occasions the girls fell for him. One of them came crawling back begging forgiveness, but sadly for her, that was a foregone conclusion. Mark doesn't take Brian's castoffs. "Yeah, well, she knows all about you, so you can just forget any ideas you might have." His voice is impatient. "Listen, I have to get back to work, so—"

Brian grabs hold of the door before he can close it. "Hold off there, Spud. I came to give you a message. Dad said to tell you there's an opening at his company. It's entry level and doesn't pay much, but if you apply yourself, in a few years it could lead to some great opportunities. If you're interested, he'll get you an interview. What do you say?"

What does he think of being an underling at the insurance company his stepdad works for? Yeah, that's never going to happen. And how typical of his stepfather to send Brian to do his bidding. "I'd say, no thanks, I already have a job."

"As a home health aide?" Brian laughs.

"That's right. I'm a home health aide. What's wrong with that?"

"It's a woman's job, for one. And secondly, there's no future here. It's a loser job. Mark, even you can do better than this."

Mark feels his face redden in anger. "We're done here," he says.

"Oh, Spud, there's no need to be that way. I'm just trying to help you out."

As if. This is one of Brian's games—pretending to act in his brother's best interests while subtly putting him down. Mark says, "Brian, don't ever come back here again." He's about to slam the door when Brian holds up a sealed envelope.

"Wait!" he says. "I have a letter from Mom."

Reluctantly, Mark takes it from him. "What's this?"

"Mom misses you. She wants you to come for dinner tonight." He gestures to his car, parked at the curb. "I can drive you there right now." Mark is ready to tell him off, but then his brother adds, "Grandma is coming too, and she'll have your birthday check."

His grandmother's birthday checks are usually generous, but that's not enough to compel him to attend a family gathering. "Tell Mom no thanks. I have to work." Before Brian can get in another word, Mark slams the door and locks it. When Mark turns, he sees Roy standing a few feet behind him. He mumbles, "Sorry for the interruption."

Roy says, "Your brother didn't come bearing good news?"

"No, he never does."

"Ah, well, families are complicated." Roy exhales.

Mark feels a battle within, anger conflicting with shame.

"You can say that again. He wants me to come to dinner at my folks' house tonight. My grandmother will be there, he said."

"And you don't want to go?"

"No. There's no way it can go well. Everything is always on their terms."

Roy leans on his cane, a thoughtful expression on his face. "It seems to me," he says slowly, "that you would like a separation from your family, at least for the time being. Am I right?"

"That's right."

"You can do what you want, but I would think telling them that in person would be immensely satisfying. It would put you in the driver's seat, so to speak."

"Maybe." Mark can see the sense in what Roy is saying, but he doesn't relish the thought of sitting in his mother's living room completely outnumbered, while his stepfather criticizes everything about him. "I told him I had to work."

"I think we could spare you for a few hours if you want to spend time with your family. Believe me, there's something enormously satisfying about meeting when you have the upper hand. Take the Excalibur, and if they don't behave appropriately, tell them off and leave."

A minute ago, Mark had no intention of eating dinner with his family, but the idea of showing up in the Excalibur is tempting. And knowing he can leave at any time would put him at a distinct advantage. "You wouldn't mind me taking the car?"

"Of course not! I wouldn't have offered otherwise." Roy grins. "Imagine their faces when they see you behind the wheel of a luxury automobile. They'll have a whole new respect for you."

Mark can picture himself pulling up in the driveway, parking the Excalibur right over the oil stain left behind from Brian's first car, a rusty Plymouth Duster. The Duster was a complete piece of junk. Of course, at the time, Mark's transportation had been a ten-speed bike, so Brian had lorded his car ownership over him, offering him rides in exchange for cash and chores done on his behalf. Brian has a better car now, but it still looks like a heap next to Roy's car. Even if Mark stays for just five minutes, it will be worth it to see their reaction. "I'll do it," he says at last. "I won't stay long, though."

"Take all the time you need," Roy says. "And if they give you any guff, make sure you tell them they've seen the last of you. People get divorced. Friendships break up. Couples stop dating. Just because they're family doesn't mean you need to put up with abuse. You're an adult man, and you're entitled to your own life."

Mark walks with Roy back to the blue room, where Alma sits alone, picking imaginary lint off the front of her shirt. When the two men walk in, she doesn't even acknowledge their presence. Mark pauses inside the doorway to open the envelope his brother gave him and reads over his mother's message. Most people would interpret her words differently, but Mark knows it's a lure disguised as love. He frowns as he folds the paper and sticks it back into the envelope. They're always trying to reel him back in.

Roy gestures for Mark to take a seat and says, "I've found that when I have to confront a contentious situation, it's best to be prepared."

"What do you mean by prepared?"

"Just this—if you practice ahead of time, you'll always have a contingency plan. Would you like some help running your lines?"

Mark starts to laugh, then realizes the old man is completely serious. "I'm not sure what lines you mean." Down the hall, he hears Nurse Darby and Dr. Cross having their own conversation. Although he can't make out the words, Nurse Darby's voice is louder than the doctor's, and she sounds decidedly cross. He doesn't know what Roy is talking about, but if it keeps him away from Nurse Darby, he's glad to go along. "Maybe you could give me an example?"

Roy's eyes light up, and his back straightens. "I'd be happy to." As vacuous as Alma looks, her brother is just the opposite. He gestures animatedly while he gives Mark a lecture on not letting other people dominate and ends with, "You must be in charge!"

"Got it," Mark says agreeably.

"Just like in magic, the trick is misdirection. Always misdirection." He holds one finger up. "Tell me something your parents might say that would upset you, and we'll come up with an appropriate response."

Mark considers all the arguments he's had with his parents over the years. "They like to bring up all the things I've done wrong in the past and how they know I'm not going anywhere in life." His mom frames her concerns as motherly love, while his stepfather prefers to list all of Mark's faults. At least once in his teenage years, the man had said Mark was destined for prison.

Roy smiles. "Oh, this is an easy one. It won't be a conversation if you don't respond. If they provoke you, don't answer. Instead, you write a different script, and your words will create the reality. Tell them that you're not the same person anymore. That you've moved on from your past and don't want to discuss your life choices. If they can't respect that, you're going to have to go your separate ways."

"Do you think that will work?"

"I do. Just don't let them get a rise out of you."

They spend the next hour practicing hypothetical exchanges between Mark and his family. At one point, Dr. Cross comes to say goodbye, and Roy acknowledges him with a nod but never takes his eyes off Mark's face. When Nurse

Darby fires up the vacuum cleaner in the back of the house, Mark is still throwing out responses.

"I'm not that person anymore."

Roy nods approvingly and spurs him on. "Keep going."

Mark says, "I've moved on and don't wish to discuss it."

"That's the spirit!" Roy says with a grin.

"If you can't respect my decisions, I'll have no choice but to cut you out of my life." This last one Mark says so emphatically that the words are practically shouted.

"Bravo!" Roy says, struggling to his feet and applauding. Next to him Alma raises her eyes, startled, and gently begins to clap. Roy adds, "Now you sound like a man to be reckoned with." He takes off his glasses and wipes his eyes. "I'm proud of you, my boy."

"Thank you," Mark says, a slow grin crossing his face. Getting the old man's approval gives him a boost like he's never had before. Why couldn't he have a grandfather like Roy? Even Alma appears to approve, smiling in his direction. Mark no longer dreads seeing his family today. Instead, he feels ready. Ready to take on any bit of disapproval or attempt to control him. It's as if Roy has outfitted him with a coating of armor, a shell that will deflect anything negative tossed his way. "Is there anything else to keep in mind?"

"Just one thing." Roy fumbles in his back pocket, pulls out his battered wallet, and rummages around for what seems like ages before pulling out a twenty. "If the car needs gas, go ahead and stop on your way. And if it doesn't, keep this for yourself."

Mark nods. "Thanks, Roy."

CHAPTER EIGHTEEN

The note from Mark's mother is the usual:

Dear Mark,

I love you and miss you. We would love to have you join us for dinner this evening at five o'clock. Grandma Norman is coming and is eager to give you your birthday card. Hope to see you there!

Love,

Mom

It doesn't escape him that she used the word *love* twice. His mom has always been prone to theatrics. When his dad (his real dad) died in the car accident, she wept and wailed for months, carrying on as if it were the end of the world. Mark was eight at the time, and Brian ten, almost eleven. Like a big weakling, Brian cried as well, turning to their mother for consolation. This annoyed the hell out of Mark, who actually knew how to control his emotions. A year later his mom married the new guy, replacing his dad, so obviously the whole thing had been for show.

For years now the three of them have ganged up on him, something that rankles him to this day. And now he's going to face all of them at once, but with his new strategy, he will finally be the man in charge.

After their practice session, Roy urges Mark to call his parents. For the sake of privacy, Mark calls from the kitchen, cradling the telephone receiver between his shoulder and ear. When he gets the family answering machine, he breathes a sigh of relief. After the beep, he speaks into the mouthpiece, saying, "I'm able to come for dinner tonight after all, but I can't stay late." He ends with, "See you at five," then hangs up the phone. Why his parents insist on eating so early is beyond him. At least he'll get it over with and have the rest of the night to spare. And it will be nice not having them tracking him down and popping up in his life unannounced after this. Roy is right. He is ready to be done with them.

Good riddance.

Stopping at a traffic light on the way to their house, he rolls down the window. When a teenage girl in an adjacent car calls out, "Nice wheels!" he gives her a thumbs-up. When the light turns green, he stamps on the accelerator and flies right past her.

The trip from Alden Manor to the family's boring trilevel in the suburbs goes quickly. As he turns down the street, he's struck by the sameness of the houses, with their aluminum siding, asphalt-shingled roofs, and black shutters. One leafy maple tree stands sentry in front of each home. Some of the residents make an attempt to stand out with lawn ornaments: old-fashioned wagon wheels, reflecting balls on pedestals, garden gnomes. Tacky crap. These people are oblivious to the fact they're leading sad, cookie-cutter lives.

Mark parks the car in the driveway, strides confidently to the front door, and presses the doorbell. His mom opens the door wearing a striped apron she's had since he was a kid. "Mark?" she says, her tone uncertain. "Your hair is so different. I almost didn't recognize you."

"It's me." He grins broadly. "Can I come in?"

She ushers him in, saying, "You don't have to ring the doorbell. You're family." Taking a step back, she studies him with a long, measuring look. "I'm so glad you came. I made your favorite for dinner. Roast beef."

Already he feels his throat tightening. Roast beef is not his favorite dish. It's Brian's. Normally Mark would correct her, but Roy's voice rings in his ear. *If they provoke you, don't answer.* "Smells great."

She wipes her hands on her apron. "Come on in. Your dad will be happy to see you."

Mark follows her into the living room, where his stepfather and Brian sit waiting for him. Both of them greet him with tight smiles and false pleasantries, Brian saying, "Glad you could make it, little bro."

His stepdad adds, "It's been a long time. I'm glad to see you, Mark. I like your haircut."

Mark doesn't need his approval, so he just nods and takes a seat across from them on the couch. The living room is for company—that's always been the rule. Normally, family members are restricted to the family room, with its plaid furniture and orange shag carpeting. His mother heavily dosed the carpeting with Scotchgard when it was first installed to make it stain resistant. The house stank of it for days.

This room has a tightly woven beige rug. Porcelain figurines of small children fill the curio cabinet in the corner. A family portrait, taken shortly after his mom and stepfather's wedding, hangs above the couch. All of them smile broadly in the photo, except for Mark, who had taken a stand and refused to say *cheese*. Mark has been in this room a dozen times in his entire life.

Still in her apron, his mother sits on the opposite end of the couch. She says, "We've been worried about you, Mark."

And so it begins. Luckily, he's prepared. "I'm doing well—thanks for your concern."

"Of course." She twists her hands and shoots a look at his stepfather, who doesn't react. After a long silence, she says, "Did you know that Brian has a new job? He's the nighttime manager at the car dealership now."

"Good for you, Brian!" Mark exclaims. "I always knew you had it in you."

"If you ever want to buy a vehicle, I can get you a deal." Brian leans forward eagerly. "Help with financing too."

"That's kind of you, but that won't be necessary." Mark keeps his voice deliberately light. "I drive an Excalibur right now. It's one of the benefits of my current job. A company car."

He expects them to react, to leap up and look out the front window at the car parked in the driveway, but they're strangely mute. "We saw you pull into the driveway," his stepdad says, by way of explanation. His eyebrows furrow. "Does your boss know you're using his car for a personal outing?"

"Yes, he's aware." Mark surveys the room, suddenly remembering. "Where's Grandma?"

His mom and stepdad exchange uneasy glances. She scoots closer and rests her hand on his elbow. "Oh, honey. She wanted to come, she really did."

"Is she okay?"

"Oh, she's fine," his mother reassures him, drawing back. "She still misses Grandpa, of course, but she's in great health and keeping active."

"So why isn't she here?"

His stepdad clears his throat. "After much thought, she chose not to come." He speaks slowly, each word precise. "To be completely honest, the last time your grandmother saw you, your outburst scared her. It scared all of us, if you want to know the truth. We're concerned about you and your temper."

Mark swallows to tamp down the emotion raging through his body. The last time he saw his grandmother was months ago at a gathering for his brother's birthday. Brian had taunted him about something in his past. He wouldn't let it go, even after Mark repeatedly told him to knock it off. The evening ended with Mark throwing a lamp. He intended to hit Brian, but the edge of the shade collided with his grandmother's shoulder on its way across the room. She wasn't hurt, and besides, it was a long time ago. He can't believe they're bringing it up now. He takes a breath and counts to five. "I'm not that person anymore. I've moved on, and I don't wish to discuss it." To change the subject, he says, "Did she drop off my birthday check?"

"That's what you're concerned about?" his stepdad says, incredulous.

Before Mark can answer, the doorbell rings. "I'll get that," his mom says. When she returns a moment later, she's followed by a woman Mark hasn't seen for years, but even so, he'd know her anywhere. She looks much the same, right down to her silk bow-tied blouse, pencil skirt, and short haircut. Mark's mom says, "Look who was in the neighborhood and decided to drop by!"

Dr. Temple slants a smile in Mark's direction before taking the spot on the couch previously occupied by his mother. "Good evening, Mark. How have you been?"

Mark knows the score and chooses his words with care. "Never better, Dr. Temple. What brings you here tonight?"

Instead of answering his question, she repeats, "Never better?" Her eyes doubt Mark's sincerity.

Mark still remembers his first appointment with Dr. Temple. He was in eighth grade when she told him that her specialty as a psychiatrist made her uniquely qualified to treat children like him and that she would never betray a confidence, which was a lie, because eventually he suspected everything he said during his sessions was relayed to his parents. He caught sight of the doctor's notes a few appointments later when she was making small talk with his mother. It was only for a second but long enough for him to read the words, *Prevaricates when asked pointed questions, and lacks impulse control.*

After that, he spun tales of top grades and outstanding behavior. All of it lies, but if she thought he prevaricated, that's what he would give her. She called him on it, but he never broke. That was then. As a kid, he had to talk to her, but now his welfare is none of her business.

"That's right. Never better. I have a well-paying job, a beautiful girlfriend, and I'm happy and healthy. All is fine in my world."

"You're a home health aide, I understand? Does your employer know about your legal history?"

Mark knows now that this whole evening is a charade. There might be beef roast in the oven, but his grandmother was never going to come. His parents set up this ambush with Dr. Temple to try to exert control over him again. He stands and says, "I think we're through here."

"Wait!" Dr. Temple stands. "Do you think working with the elderly is a good fit for you, given your history of violence? I ask as someone who cares about you, Mark. I want to help you." She holds out a business card. "I have a colleague who would love to work with you. He's exceptional. I think you two would get on well."

Through a sudden swell of anger, Mark turns away from the psychiatrist and addresses his family. "I don't appreciate that I was invited here under false pretenses. I'm not the same person anymore. I've moved beyond my difficult past. Since you can't respect me as an adult, I have no choice but to cut you out of my life. Please don't contact me again." Wheeling, he heads to the front door, his mother on his heels.

"Mark, don't do this! Please, just stay and listen. We're trying to help you." His mother follows him outside. "I want the best for you, and I don't want anyone else to get hurt." The reference to others getting hurt is painful. In junior high, he once broke a girl's arm, but it was a complete accident. He got into a fight with a kid who'd been bullying him, and she happened to get in the way. Another time, when he was twenty, one of the lowlifes at the restaurant he worked at made fun of him in the parking lot after his shift. That time, Mark's temper *had* gotten the best of him; he threw the guy against the side of the brick building, and his injuries required a trip to the hospital for stitches. That one didn't count, either, because the asshole had it coming, and everyone knows that head wounds cause excessive bleeding.

None of this qualifies him as dangerous. Under the circumstances, most guys would react the same way.

Mark climbs into the Excalibur and starts the engine. As he's backing up, his mom is moving alongside the car, crying and pleading for him to stay. "Mark, I love you. Please don't do this!" She slaps at the windshield and says, "Just come back inside for dinner. I promise we won't bring it up again."

Mark believes her, but it doesn't matter. He's done with all of them.

CHAPTER NINETEEN

When Mark returns to Alden Manor, he discovers Nurse Darby is still there. She's made dinner, some kind of pasta dish, which Alma and Roy have eaten in his absence. When she finds out Mark hasn't eaten yet, she offers to reheat some for him.

"Thanks. I appreciate it." He suspects Nurse Darby knows she's on her way out and is trying to accrue points. A real Hail Mary pass on her part. While he eats dinner, she gets Alma ready for bed. Mentally, Mark gives her credit—not that it helps. Once the new person is hired, she's history.

While he's sitting at the kitchen table, eating his pasta and green beans, Roy comes in, eager to hear about his visit home. When Mark is done relating the tale, conveniently leaving out the parts that don't put him in a good light, the old man's face softens, and he exhales an exasperated sigh. "I'm sorry to hear that, Mark, but I think you've made the right decision. You're a fine young man, and you don't need that kind of aggravation in your life."

After dinner, the evening, complete with brandy manhattans, is a repeat of the night before. This time, though, Roy encourages Mark to make a drink for himself. "After all you've been through, you deserve it, my boy." Wanting to be agreeable, Mark goes ahead and mixes himself a strong one and then another. As he feels the warmth of the drink coursing through his veins, he has to agree that the sensation does put the evening in a better light. When Roy announces that it's time for bed, Mark is happy to get them settled in for the night. He's eager to get back to reading Lisa's journal.

Once inside his room, he wastes no time in getting the book from the nightstand drawer and opening it. Starting from the beginning, he reads each word, carefully weighing her frame of mind. At the start, Lisa is guarded but hopeful. Eventually, she's wary and anxious, but not entirely certain why she feels that way. Something about the house troubles her. She hears odd noises at night, has trouble sleeping. On one occasion, she tries to diagnose the problem: *Too much time in this house is screwing with my head.*

After Ted is fired, Lisa is relieved, but the nightmares begin. She makes a point to write about them. Normally, Mark hates it when people talk about their dreams, but given her suicide, these take on some importance. The dreams always take place in the house at night, and they involve Alma and Roy and the large ballroom upstairs. Sometimes the people from the Redevine Society are there as well. To add to the horror, in the dreams she is sleeping, then awakened by noises in the hallway. Whispering and the shuffling of feet. When she goes to investigate, the terror begins. Most of the descriptions of the nightmares are brief.

Another bad dream. Trapped in the ballroom. Pounded on the door but no one heard me. Woke up with my heart pounding.

And another night: *Woke up gasping for air. Had a nightmare where I was chased through the house.* He keeps reading. More passages about taking care of Alma and Roy's needs and her restless nights and troubling dreams. He notices a trend. She is either chased or trapped. Classic nightmares.

Mark gets closer to the end of the journal and reads a longer descriptive passage, one that makes him sit up in shock. *Tonight I had the most disgusting dream. I dreamt that I heard Alma crying in the ballroom. When I went to find her, she was with Roy, who was a living corpse with bits of skin sticking to his bones. Alma's headless body was alive, and her head was rolling around on the floor. Her tongue was long like a snake's and flicked around, and her eyes bugged out when I walked into the room. They were dead but still living. Repulsive. I feel like throwing up. If I live to be a hundred, I will never forget how they looked. I dread seeing them today.*

Mark's heart is pounding in shock.

He had nearly the same dream the night after Lisa's death, back when he was still in the apartment with Monica. He reads her description of the nightmare again and compares it to his own. Virtually identical. How is that possible?

She hadn't told him about her dream, but they'd both seen the photo of the headless Alma from the magic act. Besides that, one of the posters talked about Roy manipulating time and said something about watching as flesh decayed off his bones. Both he and Lisa must have combined the two concepts to create any person's worst nightmare. It's odd that both of their brains came up with the same horrible images, but not impossible. It is, he decides, just a weird coincidence.

He looks at the date. She had that nightmare four nights before her death. He reads on, anxious to get to the end. The night before she jumped from the third floor, she woke up during the night, convinced she needed to return to the ballroom. This wasn't a dream, she said. Feeling compelled, Lisa got out of bed and climbed the stairs, flashlight in hand, looking for some answers. She was spooked before she even reached the room, writing: *The air up there was thicker, and the walls of the hallway were closing in on me, like they didn't want me to be there. I could feel them pulling me down the hallway to the ballroom. I had no choice.*

She'd become totally unhinged.

After reaching the ballroom, she had a revelation: *I can't believe I never thought to look inside the podium before. What I found! My skin crawls thinking of it. And those sounds! They will haunt me forever. How can this even be? I can't make sense of this, but in my bones I know it's evil. Tomorrow, first thing, I'm confronting Roy. Then I'm calling Dr. Cross, and I will make him take me away from here. I can't stay another night. I'd rather sleep on the street. This house is not safe.*

The next page has just one sentence, but the letters fill half a page, and she'd underlined the words three times, the last time so forcefully that the pen tore through the paper. It says: *The Redevine Society is a cipher!*

A cipher? Like a code? He shakes his head, unsure what she's getting at, then turns the page again to see the words he saw earlier, but now they have more meaning: *It's all getting to be too much. I'm losing my mind.*

Mark scans the column with the repeating words: *Losing my mind. Losing my mind. Losing my mind.* Then he flips back to read the previous page once again. What could she have found? And what sounds? He's aggravated at how vague this is compared to previous entries. Earlier in the journal, she wrote extensive posts about what she made for breakfast, right down to how many eggs were in the omelet, and *now* she bails on giving details? He flips through the pages, double-checking to see there is nothing he missed. If Mark had to summarize what happened, he'd say she started off fine, then became anxious about something vague and indefinable. That, coupled with nightmares and lack of sleep, messed with her head. The final straw was her last visit to the ballroom upstairs.

Could she have been delusional or sleepwalking? Possibly. Or maybe she had a mental breakdown. Somehow, though, he doesn't think that was the case. He'd worked with her every day, and although she was anxious on occasion, her demeanor was normal. All was fine until that last day, when she came running to him in the hallway, completely crazed, trembling with fear. Neither Dr. Cross nor Roy mentioned that she'd asked to be taken away from the house or that she'd confronted them about something she saw on the second floor. Instead, Dr. Cross said she'd had a psychotic break. He said it so confidently.

But is Dr. Cross even qualified to make that kind of diagnosis? He isn't a psychiatrist—or at least Mark doesn't think so.

Mark suddenly realizes that he has no idea what kind of doctor Dr. Cross is or where he works. He's never mentioned an office or a hospital, and he seems to be available to Roy and Alma on extremely short notice. Odd. Aren't doctors usually busy professionals with jam-packed schedules?

Things that seemed ordinary enough earlier are starting to strike him as suspicious. It's as if Lisa's anxiety has been transferred from the page through his fingertips and into his own body. Was she unhinged, or was she onto something? At the very least, she found something horrifying behind the podium on the second floor. He can't even begin to guess what it could be, but he knows a way to find out. Without hesitating, Mark opens the nightstand drawer and puts the journal back inside, then pulls out the flashlight.

There's no other way around it. If Mark wants to know what spooked Lisa, he needs to go upstairs and see for himself.

CHAPTER TWENTY

Once he's in the hallway, flashlight in hand, it occurs to Mark that he should check on Roy and Alma before heading upstairs. The door to Roy's bedroom is open slightly, so he pushes it wider, wincing as it creaks. Holding his breath, he listens, and when he doesn't hear any signs of Roy stirring, he walks into the room and stands over the bed. No need for the flashlight here—the light seeping in from the hall is enough. Roy is sleeping on his back, mouth open, gums on display. His dentures sit in a glass of water on the nightstand next to the bed. His snoring is a guttural, back-of-the-throat gargling noise, slow and steady.

From there, Mark passes through the bathroom into Alma's room, using his flashlight as a guide. Unlike her brother, the old woman sleeps on her side, one arm raised as if she's in grade school and knows the answer. Her snoring makes a whistling noise as she exhales through her nose. With her face mashed against the pillow and her mouth open like a hooked fish, she looks half-dead. Mark shakes his head at the sight. In movies, sleeping people, even the elderly, are always pictured as beautiful and serene, but in real life nothing could be further from the truth.

At least there's one good thing: Lisa was right about the brandy manhattans. Neither one looks likely to wake up anytime soon.

He backs out of Alma's room, goes through the bathroom, and passes Roy once again. He thinks about the stories of old people going to bed and never waking up. How must it be to go to sleep not knowing if you'll be opening your eyes in the morning?

After he leaves the room, Mark flicks off the overhead light in the hallway and uses the flashlight to move down the hall. Alone, in the dark, he might as well be in a different house. Or maybe it's not the lack of light, but the liquor kicking in? In any case, his sense of space is off. The distance to the front of the house stretches forward endlessly in the dark.

When he reaches the front entryway, he is surprised to hear the howling of the wind outside. He doesn't remember hearing that there would be a storm, but of course, now that he's living in Alden Manor, he's cut off from news of the outside world. Curious, he turns off the flashlight and pulls the sidelight curtain aside to peek outside. Spotting a figure on the sidewalk directly in front of the house, a cold shock runs down his spine. The person stands in the slice of gloom between streetlights, making it hard to see clearly, but when Mark's eyes adjust, he can tell it's a tall man wearing something over his face. An oval mask, made of some stiff material, with cut outs for the eyes and the mouth. The openings are rough and uneven, as if the mask is made of cardboard and the holes were snipped without having been drawn or measured first. The man faces him, open stance, in a challenging way, as if he's waiting for a fight.

Mark's mouth drops open as he gets a sinking feeling. Is this guy for real? He wonders if he's a burglar, but if so, why is he standing out in the open, so close to the street? As he continues to stare, the man reaches out and points to Mark, then beckons to him, like asking him to come out of the house.

What the hell? How can he even see me?

Mark drops the curtain and steps away from the window, his heart pounding, fear and anger filling his chest cavity. Fear because a guy in a mask beckoning like he's the Grim Reaper is scary as fuck—and anger, because, really? Some asshole on the sidewalk is ruining his night with some crazy-ass behavior?

After taking a few breaths, he peeks out again, only to see that the man has moved and is closer, now halfway up the walkway to the house. Again, he waves a finger in Mark's direction, then points to the space in front of him. Accompanying the gesture, Mark's mind brings up taunts from a childhood game. *Come out, come out, wherever you are!* Like hell he will.

He weighs whether or not to call the police and then decides against it. The guy is trespassing, but he doubts they'd come out for that reason. No real crime has been committed. Mark has a feeling they'd think his call was ridiculous, and he can understand that mindset. This is trivial. It's stupid to be afraid of some idiot walking around in a mask. Probably that obnoxious hippie, Doug. Mark looks down to double-check that the door is still locked, and when he glances back through the window, he's shocked to see that the guy is gone. How did he move that quickly? If this were a horror movie, Mark would turn around to see the guy right behind him, scary mask covering his face and a butcher knife in his hand. His legs weaken at the thought. Mark closes his eyes and talks himself through his fear. He checked all the locks earlier in the evening. No one can get in, and even if they could, he'd certainly hear them first.

As he turns around, he flicks on the flashlight and scans the entry, relieved to see it empty. The wind still howls, but the sound is gentler now, more of a whimper than a wail.

Well, he decides, it's best to head upstairs before he loses his nerve altogether. He walks slowly up the steps, hand gliding along the banister. There seems to be more steps than the night he followed Lisa.

Lisa. He thinks about what he just read in her journal: *This house is not safe.*

If she'd told him what she was going through, could he have helped her? Maybe. He tries not to think about her last moments, how she looked falling away from the window and plummeting to the roof. He should have saved her, but he didn't. He failed. That's all there is to it, and there's no going back. Nothing can be done about it now.

When he gets to the second floor, he tucks the flashlight under his arm and opens the double doors that lead to the wide hallway. As before, the air upstairs is stagnant and hot. Thicker, Lisa called it, and he understands that now. It takes effort to draw a deep breath. He keeps going down the hall, which seems both longer and narrower than it did before. What did she write? *The walls of the hallway were closing in on me, like they didn't want me to be there.* There must be a plausible explanation for this. Most likely, because Lisa knew she wasn't supposed to be up here, her guilty mind played tricks on her. It's clear she was seriously losing it, and her insanity must have been contagious, because it's affecting him now.

The urge to turn around and go back is so strong that he has to talk himself out of it. He tells himself that if he just sees this through, in half an hour he'll be in his room safely tucked in his bed. Snug as a bug in a rug, as his mom used to say when he was a kid. All he needs to do is see for himself what pushed Lisa over the edge. Hell, if it winds up being too frightening, he'll stop by the drink cart afterward for a shot of brandy. If he'd thought of it sooner, he would have done it beforehand. An extra dose of liquid courage would come in handy right about now.

As he walks, he reaches out with his left hand and lets his fingertips graze the wall, just below the framed paintings, to ground himself. *Nothing scary here,* he thinks, trying to keep his heart from racing.

Reaching the double doors to the ballroom, he's surprised to see they're wide open. Lisa must have been so rattled that she fled the room without bothering to close up. His steps echo on the tile floor, making the room seem bigger than last time—and more menacing too. When he casts the light beam around the room, his imagination turns the chandeliers overhead into large spiders, waiting to swoop down on him. He swallows hard and walks forward, past the weird wooden table with the leather straps and to the podium in the front of the room.

Inside the podium. That's what she'd written.

Mark steps up onto the wooden platform and shines the light behind it. The podium has a shelf underneath, which holds a large leather-bound book, spine facing out, the size of an encyclopedia. The lower part of the podium is covered by a door. A storage cabinet. He pulls open the cabinet door, and a waft of dust flies up, causing him to step back to wipe his nose and blink his eyes. When his vision clears, he sees an old-fashioned Victrola record player sitting on a shelf near the floor. The metal horn is fluted, like a flower. The base is a wooden box, with a metal crank handle on one side. A record is on the turntable.

Maybe it was used in Alma and Roy's act back in the day? But no, he does the math and doesn't think they're quite that old. This antique would have been old even before their time. Still, it could have been part of one of their tricks. Magicians use all kinds of props.

But Lisa specifically mentioned hearing something horrifying, which fit with the Victrola. *I can't believe I never thought to look inside the podium before. What I found! My skin crawls thinking of it. And those sounds! They will haunt me forever.*

The crank is too close to the edge of the cabinet to comfortably turn, so he tucks the flashlight under his arm and picks up the whole thing. It's heavier than he would have guessed, and bulky too. He moves slowly, carrying it across the room and setting it down on the table. Now he inspects it, noticing a metal plate attached to the front with the word *Victor* next to an image of a dog, head cocked to one side, listening to a Victrola just like this one. At the bottom of the plate are the words *Victor Talking Machine Co*. He turns his attention to the record, but the label in the middle is blank. He turns the crank clockwise a dozen times, hoping he's not breaking a valuable antique, and waits. When nothing happens, he tries turning a latch located adjacent to the record. When the turntable begins revolving, he feels his heart thump in anticipation of what comes next.

And those sounds! They will haunt me forever.

Mark knows that he needs to just get it over with. He lifts the needle and lowers it onto the outside groove of the record. At first all that comes out of the horn is static, but eventually an undercurrent of conversation can be heard. It sounds as if the voices weren't intended to be recorded but are speaking in the background. He tries to make out the words, with no success. Too soft and blended. Another noise comes through. A woman sobbing? He lowers his ear to the Victrola's horn, trying to distinguish it over the voices and the static. It may be a woman, or it could be an animal. It's a whimpering, tormented sound.

Just as he's about to lift the needle to replay the beginning, a man's voice, whiskey-hued and loud, says, "Let us begin."

And then the chanting starts. The voices recite the words in unison in a language he doesn't understand. From the sound of it, the group is comprised of both men and women. Maybe fewer than ten individuals? They speak in a singsongy fashion. It reminds him of kids' nursery rhymes, the way they emphasize the syllable on the end of each line. He listens, trying to make sense of it. Each beginning line is different, followed by an identical chant. To him the repetitive part sounds like *Sursum corda.* He recognizes these words from the Catholic masses his grandparents took him to as a kid, the ones conducted by the priest entirely in Latin. The whole thing sounded like so much gibberish back then, but he must have been paying attention on some level to have this phrase stick in his head.

The chanting gets faster and faster, the voices more impassioned. The sounds are clearer, the static less noticeable. Mark feels a chill go down his spine, and he wishes they would stop. He could, in theory, lift the stylus off the record anytime, but he's caught up in the sound. It's carrying him along, holding him in its grip. The sound of the voices emanates from the horn, but it also seems to surround him, as if the people are in the room, right next to him. But that's impossible. He knows it can't be so, but some part of him is afraid to move, too frightened to turn the flashlight away from the Victrola because if there are other people there, he doesn't want to know.

As fearful as he was earlier that Alma and Roy might wake up, now he wishes they'd walk in right at this moment and relieve him of this, turn off the Victrola, tell him that it's nothing, that it was part of their magic act back in the day, save him from the chanting that all ends the same.

Sursum corda.

Sursum corda.

Sursum corda.

Mark knows he is breathing too fast. His heart is hammering, muscles trembling. His vision is affected; dancing spots like dust motes are all around him.

He swallows hard, forcing rational thoughts into his brain. *It's just a recording from a long time ago. All of the voices belong to people who are most likely dead. The house is locked up. There's nothing here. I have conjured up my own fear.*

Bile creeps into his mouth, and his stomach lurches.

His heart is going even faster now, racing crazily out of control. Just when he thinks it might explode in his chest, the chanting stops and there's the noise of a woman's scream. A high-pitched, tortured sound, it fills the ballroom and echoes off the walls. It is the exact sound of misery and impending death. There's a pause, a silence filled with static, and after that, another noise. This time it's a woman's laughter, a melodic giggling, followed by her shouting, "Praise be!"

The other voices whoop in merriment, and there's a shuffling sound as if they're now moving. Closer to her, maybe? The sound quality is poor, so he can only guess. At the end of the recording, he hears a man say, "Success."

And then it's over. The stylus goes around and around many, many times before Mark is able to lift it off the record and stop the turntable from revolving. His legs have turned to jelly, barely holding him up. He wouldn't have believed he could suffer this kind of emotional reaction listening to an old record. Lisa's doing, most likely. Leaning against the table, he wills his heart to stop racing. Once it slows, he finally gets the nerve to shine the flashlight around the room. With shaking hands, he turns.

Of course, no one is there.

Wedging the flashlight under his arm, he picks up the Victrola and carries it back to the podium, returning it to its original spot. After he closes the cabinet door, he moves quickly, to leave the room and go downstairs.

It's after he's downed a shot of brandy and gone to bed that he remembers the book on the shelf in the podium. *Damn.* If he'd been thinking rationally, he would have brought it down with him. Too bad.

He knows one thing—he's never going up there again.

CHAPTER TWENTY-ONE

Mark wakes with a shock. The room is bright. Instinctively he knows too much of the morning has elapsed. It's his second day working as a live-in home health aide, and he's overslept. At the exact instant he looks at the clock radio, the number for the minute hand flips from six to seven, making it 9:27 a.m. *Damn.* Why didn't his alarm go off?

He planned to be up at six thirty in order to serve breakfast by seven. Nurse Darby normally arrives at eight, so in theory she should be in the house already. How is it that no one came to wake him? Although he feels sluggish and hungover, he forces himself out of bed and scrambles to find some suitable clothing. Pulling on his pants, he has a sudden explanation for the fact that no one woke him. Is it possible that both Alma and Roy died in the night, and Nurse Darby is at home with her own illness? He shakes his head. No. What are the chances disaster should befall all three of them at once? Shrugging a T-shirt over his head, he decides to skip his morning ritual. It won't kill him not to shave or brush his teeth this once. He'll work it into the day later on, after he's made his apologies.

If there's anyone to apologize to.

While he's tying his shoes, the events of the night before play through his mind. The masked man standing outside. The trip upstairs and listening to the Victrola. The vibrations of the chanting making their way through his entire body, chilling him right to the bone. And then fleeing the ballroom and going to the blue room, where he downed a shot of brandy. Afterward he took a cold shower. Actions intended to help him sleep, but obviously some overcompensation happened, and he wound up in a sleep coma instead. He can't believe that he overslept by so much. Shame washes over him, and he hears the words he's tried so hard to shake off over the years, but here they are again: *Loser. Unreliable. Never going to amount to anything.*

Mark casts off these negative thoughts and tells himself that oversleeping is not that big a deal. He hasn't done anything that can't be undone. He'll grovel if need be, beg Roy and Alma to look past his mistake, and assure them it will never happen again.

Making his way down the hall, he checks rooms as he goes, finding all of them empty. This house is entirely too large. Closer to the front of the house, he hears voices coming from the blue room, and when he enters and sees both Alma and Roy, dressed for the day and sitting comfortably on the sofa together, he is ready to throw himself at their mercy. "I'm so sorry," he says, still standing in the doorway. "I can't believe I overslept." He is ready to say more, to tell them he'll make it up to them, work harder, longer, be more attentive, whatever it takes, but Roy is already disregarding his concerns.

"My boy, don't worry yourself." Next to him, Alma is all smiles. "Moving into a new place takes some adjustment. You were obviously tired, so we decided to let you sleep in." He takes his sister's hand. "Didn't we, dear?"

She nods. "Sometimes you need to sleep." Simply stated, but definitely tuned in. Mark finds that Alma surprises him at times. He is starting to believe that her brain is like a radio that's occasionally on the fritz. Sometimes things come through clearly. Other times her mind appears to malfunction completely.

"That's kind of you," Mark says, leaning against the door-frame. "But I promise it won't happen again." He runs his fingers over his scalp. Without the benefit of the pomade, his hair seemingly has a life of its own.

"Go ahead and get yourself together, then eat some break-fast. You'll want to be at your best this morning. We have a surprise for you."

"Oh?" Mark raises his eyebrows.

Roy rubs his hands together. "Wait until you see!" His eyes sparkle with mischief, while his sister gives Mark a yellow-toothed grin. "I think you're going to be delighted."

"Sounds intriguing."

"Off you go." Roy smiles and points a finger at the door.

Mark doesn't need to be told twice. He visits his bathroom, first splashing his face with water, then getting acquainted with his toothbrush in order to alleviate his cottonmouth. When he's done, he runs pomade through his hair, sculpting it into some-thing resembling a style. A few minutes later while he's eating breakfast, Nurse Darby walks in and stands in front of him, her arms folded over the front of her white polyester dress. "I am here to say goodbye."

"You're leaving for the day?" Mark says, surprised that he was not informed of this ahead of time. He leans back in his chair to look up at her.

She nods. "For the day and for always. I have been informed that my service is no longer needed." Her face darkens with irri-tation. She lifts her chin. "They will see that I am not so easily replaced." And with that, Mark understands that her bossy demeanor is a cover for her need to feel indispensable. To him, the idea is laughable. Why does she think they won't be able to function without her? It's a universal truth that everyone is replaceable. He's known this his entire life.

Mark nods and says, "It's been nice working with you." If she were someone he cared about, he'd get up and shake her hand, look into her eyes, and say he hoped they'd cross paths again. Instead, he stays in his seat. "I wish you the best of luck in your next job."

"You have not seen the last of me." She turns and leaves the room, her white nurse's shoes squeaking as she makes her way down the hall.

From this new turn of events, Mark guesses that Roy's big surprise must involve Nurse Darby's replacement. Whoever they hire will definitely be an improvement. Knowing she's gone makes him feel lighter. He washes the dishes and wipes off the table, whistling as he goes. This will probably be his last time doing it, since he's decided to assign the new girl kitchen duty. With any luck, he can play Nurse Darby's role as the supervisor and spend more time with Roy and Alma. He hasn't forgotten how Nurse Darby quoted the old man as saying Mark would be in charge of the household and their finances. Mark intends to take a bold approach and volunteer for the position. He'd also like to ask more questions about the second floor and the record on the Victrola. He's curious to see the look on Roy's face when he broaches the subject, but he will never reveal that he's been up there himself. He'll have to say he heard about it from Lisa. If they're going to be mad at anyone, let it be the person who can't object.

It's always important to know who to blame.

When he's finished in the kitchen, he makes his way back to the blue room. He's been promised a surprise, so hearing several voices doesn't faze him. By the sounds of it, the new Lisa has arrived, accompanied by Dr. Cross. One of the voices coming from the room is decidedly familiar. He quickens his pace, and when he turns into the room, his eyes widen when he sees Monica sitting in one of the chairs opposite Roy and Alma. Dr. Cross is in the other chair, intently gazing at Monica, who is animatedly chatting with the group.

"Monica?" As he says her name, untold questions go through his head. She obviously came to deliver the suits he left behind—that's the only thing that makes sense. He didn't leave an address, but he described the place and said it was on Bartleby off of Clarke. It wouldn't take much to track down the house, seeing as it's the sole mansion in the industrial area. Or maybe she looked up the Walgraves in the phone book. Monica is known to be enterprising. "What are you doing here?" He walks into the room and is now standing center stage, all eyes on him.

"Mark!" She stands up and joins him, then kisses him on the cheek. Dr. Cross and the old people are beaming in their direction, so they must not be too disapproving of the fact that he has a female guest visiting while he's on the job. "Are you surprised to see me?" She raises her eyebrows flirtatiously.

"Very," he answers. She slips her hand around his arm, making him self-conscious. "Have you met everyone?" he asks. "Roy, Alma, Dr. Cross, this is my girlfriend, Monica." Or at least she *had* been his girlfriend.

"Mark, don't be so dense," she says, giving him a little slap. "Of course I've met them. They just hired me to work here full-time."

And she's not even kidding. Mark looks around at the others in the room, all of their faces showing barely restrained joy.

"Surprise," Alma says, smoothing her skirt across her knees.

"I do believe Mark is speechless," Roy says, chuckling. "Are you surprised, my boy?"

"More than I can say," he says, the first words that come to mind. All he can think about is how adamantly opposed Monica was to the idea of coming to work at Alden Manor. He asks, "How did this happen?"

Monica laughs. "Turns out that Dr. Cross is a very persuasive man."

CHAPTER TWENTY-TWO

Everything improves once Monica is there. The job that felt so tedious is now a breeze. She brings levity to every chore, brightening the mood in the house. Mark has never seen her as a caregiver type, but after the first day she slides right into the position as if it were her life's calling. Mark shows her the binder with all the instructions. She scans it but doesn't refer to it after that. "It's not that hard," she says. "The job title is *home health aide*, not *rocket scientist*." She's happy to handle the meal preparation, and Mark is glad to leave her to it. To make it fair, he cleans up after each meal and does the dishes without complaint.

When he asks what made her change her mind, she grins. "Let's just say the signing bonus made it worth my while."

She got a signing bonus? Mark pretends this is good news, but part of him is pissed off that he didn't get the same thing. Irate, he vows to come out ahead in other ways.

"How did Dr. Cross even find you?" he asks.

"Simple," she replies. "He got the address to our apartment off your application." She also tells him Brenda and Brenda's sister agreed to sublet their old apartment, so there's no need to worry about that. Conveniently, she seems to have forgotten that having her friend move in was his idea in the first place. When he asks the amount of the signing bonus, she's cagey, saying there was a nondisclosure agreement. They used to tell each other everything. Now it's like they're on different teams.

Despite all of this, he's glad she's there. The contrast between Nurse Darby and Monica is as wide as Lake Michigan. Monica is not just someone who cuts up meat and helps Alma brush her teeth. She's a ray of light, making everyone in the household happier. Case in point, she comes across a radio in one of the kitchen cabinets, and after getting the okay from Roy, she finds a radio station that plays "golden oldies," putting a smile on Alma's face. When a big band song comes on, Roy asks Mark, "Would you two mind dancing?"

"Like this?" To the delight of the Walgraves, Mark quickly takes Monica in his arms and whirls her around the kitchen.

Roy smiles, then nudges Alma and says, "Now that's what I call chemistry."

The sleeping arrangements are not ideal. Monica sleeps on a rollaway bed in Alma's room, all the better to hear her if she stirs during the night. Mark would have thought this would be a deal breaker for Monica, who cherishes both her privacy and her sleep time, but she says it's not a problem. Their new night-time routine goes like this: the four of them eat dinner together, then all of them kick back some brandy manhattans before heading off to bed. The older folks go to sleep before Mark and Monica do, leaving time for sex and private conversation in Mark's bedroom. It's the only time they have to talk without the Walgraves within earshot.

On the second night, after Roy and Alma have gone to bed, they have a discussion in Mark's bed after some fairly tame sex. He tells her about his trip up to the second floor, trying hard to convey how terrifying the experience was. He can tell she doesn't quite get it.

Monica says, "Any old house is creepy in the dark. That's the premise for nearly every horror movie, right?"

"This is more than that. If you could have heard the chanting, you'd understand. It gets under your skin. It's like they're in the room with you."

"Hmm," she says, running a finger along his arm. "Doesn't sound that scary. I think I could handle it." Before he can respond, she changes the subject. "So whatever happened with them putting you in charge of everything?"

"I keep meaning to bring it up, but I haven't found the right time yet."

"The right time?" She laughs. "I would think a money-grubber like you would find an opening. Sooner is always better than later."

"It's a touchy subject. I'm trying to approach it delicately."

"Okay. Have it your way." The silence between them looms. "Are you going to ask them about the creepy shit in the ballroom?"

"I want to," he admits. "I'd love to know what that's all about. I'm not going to say I went upstairs, of course. I'm going to say I heard about it from Lisa. That she went up there and confided in me."

"Blaming the dead girl?"

Put that way, it sounds pretty cold. Monica always did know how to cut through his crap. "Something like that." He has no choice. He has to lie. It's not like he's going to confess to breaking the rules.

"Why wait? Why not just ask?"

"I will, I will. Like I said, it's a touchy subject." He sighs. "Maybe tomorrow."

"If you're going to be a con man, you better grow some balls, Mark Norman. The money's not going to steal itself, you know."

He chuckles under his breath. The con man reference—the same thing that raised his ire when spoken by his stepfather—is flattering coming from her. It makes him feel like a tough guy in an old movie. "Don't worry, I'm not holding back. I've got a plan."

Mark thinks she understands his thinking on the subject, so he's shocked the next day at breakfast when she blurts out, "Nurse Darby told Mark that you plan to put him in charge of running the household and making decisions on behalf of the two of you. He's hesitant to mention it for fear of looking opportunistic, but he'd be happy to take on the responsibility. He told me he loves you like family."

Mark's face flames red with mortification and anger. The gall. Monica is going to ruin everything. Roy exchanges a look with Alma, whose face doesn't give anything away. Or maybe Alma is checked out once again.

Mark says, "Nurse Darby did tell me that, but I wasn't going to say anything." He shoots a disapproving look at Monica, who has a smug expression on her face, like, *This is how it's done.* As if he didn't know how to ask, as opposed to wanting to work the subject into a conversation naturally. *Good job being subtle, Monica.*

Roy speaks slowly. "I'm glad Monica brought it up, because we feel like Mark is family as well." He turns his attention to Mark. "We were so fond of Lisa that we initially asked her to take on a fiduciary role, but sad to say, the idea weighed heavily on her." He shakes his head and tells them more about the day they asked Lisa to take on responsibilities for both Alma and Roy. They'd planned on compensating her for her trouble, but the stricken look on her face spoke volumes. "She looked like we'd pointed a gun at her head." After that, they noticed a change in her demeanor. "I believe she found the idea to be a burden. I fear we may have contributed to her breakdown."

Mark quickly says, "I would be happy to serve in that capacity. It wouldn't be a burden at all."

Roy's face lights up, and even Alma smiles, her head bobbing up and down. "That is excellent news. We'll take care of it this very day."

That evening, two of the members of the Redevine Society, Neela and Sam, come to visit after dinner. All six of them gather in the blue room, where Sam opens his leather briefcase and pulls out a stack of paperwork for Mark to sign. He explains that he is an attorney, and Neela is a notary. "We'll be happy to walk you through the process," he says with a smile. With each form Sam explains what Mark will be agreeing to and points to the places requiring a signature and a date.

Mark reads each page and afterward hands it to Monica, who looks over it as well. Both of them look for loopholes that would be to his disadvantage, but the agreements seem pretty straightforward. Alma and Roy authorize Mark to make decisions regarding their health care in the event they're unable to, and they also add him to their bank accounts so he can pay the bills on their behalf. The last and most shocking development is a new will that makes him the main beneficiary of the Walgrave estate.

Mark listens as Sam explains this in a straightforward manner, as if designating Mark, a near stranger, as the one to inherit a lifetime of wealth is no big deal. Sam says, "The Walgraves have no outstanding debt, which will make the estate easier to settle." Mark looks around the circle at the others: Neela gazing at him with approval, Alma staring vacantly across the room, and Roy, who regards him with a kindly smile. Only Monica appears a little surprised at this news.

Mark says, "Just to be clear—in the event that Roy and Alma

pass away, they've chosen me to inherit everything?" Mentally he estimates the value of the house, the antique furniture, and the car. Even if their bank accounts are low on funds, the value of what they own is considerable.

"That's correct," Sam says, showing his teeth in a wide grin.

Monica says, "So there are no relatives or friends who will contest the will? No charities they want to list? It's all just Mark?"

Mark is grateful for the clarification, but he's also annoyed that she's bringing up potential conflicts. She's opened the door for them to change their minds. What if they suddenly remember a nephew who might be a better candidate? Or a deserving charity that would, given their money, make the world a better place? God help him then. He's never been this close to getting a life-changing windfall, and it may never happen again. If Monica fucks it up for him, she's going to be sorry.

Roy shakes his head. "We've given this a lot of thought." He reaches over and squeezes Alma's hand. "My sister and I have outlived all our relatives, and the few friends we have remaining"—he tilts his head toward Neela and Sam—"are all financially established. Mark, on the other hand, is a young man just ready to take the world by storm. When I die, it will be with a smile, knowing that someone deserving will use what I built to forge his own path."

Just like a prepared speech that has been performed many times, the words land perfectly. Who can argue with such a kind, wise sentiment? Mark beams and thanks them profusely. "I don't know what to say," he says. "I'm stunned by your generosity."

"No need for all that," Roy says. "I have faith that you'll use the money wisely."

After everyone is through signing and the documents are notarized, Sam stands up to shake Mark's hand and thanks him.

"You're a good man, Mark Norman," he says. "The rewards are great, but as you can guess, the responsibility is great as well." He reaches into his back pocket, retrieves his wallet, and pulls out a business card, which he hands to Mark. "Any questions or concerns, just give me a call."

Mark is twenty-five years old, but this is the first time he remembers a professional treating him like a peer, and he likes it. He nods agreeably and thanks Sam for handling the legalities. Now he sees Alma and Roy through a different lens. No one lives forever, and these two seem like they're inching toward the finish line.

He has no idea how he lucked out this way, but he's not going to turn it down.

CHAPTER TWENTY-THREE

That night, after the Burmans leave, Roy mixes up the manhattans and is generous with the brandy. As he hands them out, he says, "A celebration. Here's to tying up loose ends."

Mark can drink to that. Monica echoes the statement. "To tying up loose ends." They all clink glasses and sip their cocktails. The drinks are stronger than usual, which suits Mark just fine. What the hell—he's young and in terrific health. His body can take it. It's Roy and Alma who should be more watchful, but as far as he can tell they eat and drink whatever they want. It's not a bad way to live out the end of a life, and in this case, it's better for him. Their demise will ultimately be his gain.

"I can't tell you how much it troubled me that we didn't have a designated beneficiary," Roy says. "I feel like I can die in my sleep tonight and not worry about a thing." He raises his glass to Mark. "Thank you, my boy! You've given me a gift. The gift of knowing that I have a legacy that will continue after Roy Walgrave is long gone."

Mark says, "I'm the one who has gotten a gift, thanks to you." He suddenly remembers to add Alma in his gratitude. "Both of you." She can be such a blank slate that he sometimes forgets to include her. "Frankly, I'm overwhelmed, but very grateful. I will never forget either of you, and I promise to make good use of my inheritance."

Later, after Alma and Roy are tucked into bed and he and Monica are in his bedroom, Monica parrots these words back to him, saying dramatically, "I will never forget either of you, and I promise to make good use of my inheritance."

"What?" he says, feigning indignation. "That's honestly how I feel."

She laughs. "As if you'd forget someone who gave you a fortune. When it comes time, you better split the money with me."

"Why would I do that?"

"Because you wouldn't have it without me. I was the one who spoke up and got the ball rolling."

"Bullshit. I'd planned on broaching the subject myself. You just got to it first." Flat on his back, he laces his fingers together behind his head. Both of them are still fully dressed, but he knows that will be changing any minute now.

"Right." She shifts in bed, so she's now up on one elbow, looking down at him. "I doubt you. You were waiting for the right time, and I didn't see it happening anytime soon. You would have waited forever."

Challenging him is her version of foreplay. "You can doubt me all you want," he says, grinning, "but I was going to ask Roy about it after dinner tonight." Combining money talk with cocktails had seemed like the right strategy to him. He'd planned on plying them with liquor and bringing up the subject once they were feeling no pain. "It wasn't your place to bring it up. You could have messed up my opportunity."

"And yet it worked out just fine."

"Lucky for you," he says begrudgingly.

"You're welcome." She tilts her head so her hair falls over

one eye. "And you still haven't asked them what the deal is with the second floor."

"There's always tomorrow."

"Hmm." She gives him a quick kiss on the cheek. "Show me now." For a second he misinterprets her intentions and thinks she wants him to unzip his pants, but that notion is quickly dispelled when she sits up and gestures to the door. "Come on, big guy, let's go upstairs. I want to see the weird photos and hear the chanting."

"Believe me, you really don't."

"Mark Norman," she says, her intonation teasing, "are you afraid?"

He is, a little, not that he'll admit it to her. He tries a different tactic. "You just got the job. Do you want to get in trouble and get fired?"

She stands next to the bed and pulls on his arm. "They drank a boatload of manhattans and were snoring as soon as their heads hit their pillows. Believe me, no one's getting in trouble. Come on. Don't be such a baby."

When Monica gets like this, there's no stopping her. He reaches over to get the flashlight out of the nightstand drawer, then follows her down the hall. Her movements are so light, she's fairly dancing now, suppressing giggles as she goes. If Alma and Roy wake up, he's not sure what he could say to explain this commotion. When they get to the stairs, she steps up and turns around. One hand on the top of the newel post, she leans over to meet his face. "What do you think, Mark? Feeling brave?"

He shines the flashlight upward underneath her chin, and her face becomes beautifully ghoulish. "Don't worry, miss, I'll protect you."

With a laugh, she pulls him up the stairs. Monica plunges forward into the dark, led by the light coming from the flashlight behind her. She is fearless, which eases his own trepidation.

Even when tipsy, Monica is a force of nature. She laughs when she nearly trips on the stairs, regaining her balance as easily as a tightrope artist.

When they get to the second-floor landing, she pauses, and he takes the lead. She has one hand on his shoulder, as if they're doing some odd dance routine. The heavy air is not as bad as he remembers, and the hallway is fragrant with the scent of wood polish. The musty smell is gone as well, reminding him of the day Nurse Darby vacuumed and cleaned the rooms on the second floor. For once he's glad of the nurse's obsession with cleanliness.

As they move down the corridor, he and Monica slow to look at the paintings hanging on either side of the hallway. Most of them are pastoral scenes, but four are portraits from what looks like Victorian times. Four men and four women, each of them no older than Mark and Monica. Each subject poses formally, dressed in clothing that looks terribly uncomfortable—stiffly starched high collars buttoned close to their throats. Their facial expressions are bland. One man wears a bowler-type hat; the women have hair parted in the middle and pinned up. They don't look happy, but Mark supposes that holding a smile while an artist is painting your portrait would be nearly impossible. "What do you think?" Monica asks, looking at one of the women. "Is she prettier than me?"

"No," Mark says, because that's what she wants to hear. "Not even close."

They continue on. When they reach the double doors to the ballroom, he says, "You still want to do this?"

He can't see the expression on her face, but he hears the confidence in her voice as she says, "Of course I do. That's why we're here." He opens the door, and she quickly steps inside, as if she's been here before.

Once their eyes adjust, there's enough light from the windows to at least make out the way the space is laid out. Mark leads her to the photographs and explains that they are arranged sequentially.

"The Redevine Society," she says, reading the caption and pronouncing the words carefully. "They sure do love their champagne." She looks to him. "I could get on board with that."

"Maybe they're accepting new members."

"Sign me up."

When they get to the posters touting Walgrave's Astounding Wonders, Monica says, "Cool!" She reads aloud: "The amazing Roy manipulates time right before your very eyes. Watch as flesh decays right off his bones!" Taking the flashlight out of Mark's hand, she pauses for a minute to take in every detail of the poster. "I'd love to see that in person." Moving on, she stares at another poster, this one depicting Roy with Alma's head under one arm, her tongue and eyes hanging out. Monica chuckles. "How creative is that? I wonder how they did it?"

"Magic."

"All magic acts rely on illusion," she says. "There's some kind of crazy trickery going on there. What I wouldn't give to know how it was done."

Monica is less interested in the rest of the photos, but she pauses politely in front of each one. When finished, she says, "Time for the Victrola!" Her cheeriness is a relief. When they get to the podium and Mark reluctantly opens the cabinet door, she leans down to get a closer look. "Wow! You weren't kidding. A record player from the past." The beam of light glints off the metal horn. "Well, what are you waiting for? Play it for me."

Mark picks it up and sets it down on the stage floor.

Crouching down, he turns the crank. This time, though, he knows to move the latch to one side. Once the turntable starts to revolve, he lifts the arm and sets it down on the outer edge of the record. The familiar sound of static comes from the horn, followed by the muted sounds of conversation and a woman's tormented whimpering. A man's voice cuts through all of it. "Let us begin."

And then the chanting starts. It's not quite as eerie as the first time. After all, he's heard it before and expects it, but it's still unnerving. Even Monica, who now is kneeling next to him, seems taken aback, saying nothing. She just listens with wide eyes. The rhythm of the chanting comes out in beats, almost drumlike. During the Catholic masses of his youth, his grandmother always recited the words *Sursum corda* in a joyful manner, but in this recording the voices spit them out in an angry fashion. The noise fills the empty ballroom, echoing off the ceiling and walls. Again, it feels as if the voices are all around them. A trick of the acoustics, screwing with his brain.

Suddenly, Monica lifts the needle off the record. "I don't like this," she says. "I don't like it at all." She looks to Mark and with a shaking finger points. "Put it back."

Mark nods and turns off the turntable, then lifts the Victrola and takes it where it belongs, setting it down and shutting the cabinet door. She stays right next to him. After returning the record player to its rightful spot, he stands and brushes off the front of his pants leg. He's about to suggest they go, but in the meantime something else has caught her eye. "What's this?" she asks, pulling the book out from the upper shelf.

"I don't know. I saw it when I was here the last time, but I didn't get a chance to take a look."

Monica sets the book on the top of the podium. Leather bound, it's the size of a yearbook, but the uneven edges of the pages remind him of the tomes found in an antiquarian shop.

The front cover has a symbol stamped on it, one Mark recognizes.

"I know this." He points. "The exact same design is laid out in the tile in the center of the room, under the table. I thought it looked like a Spirograph design. Or an elongated number eight spun in a circle."

"A flower?"

"Maybe."

Monica opens the book to find that the inside cover is filled with handwriting, different styles and ink types. She says, "These are all names and dates, like how people write their family information in a Bible. You know, birth and death dates?"

Mark studies the writing. The way the names and dates are listed share a similarity to a family Bible, but in this case all the names are different. There's no indication that these people are related. The only names he recognizes are the most recent—Alma and Roy are listed at the bottom.

She flips through the next few pages and comes across handwritten text in different handwriting, suggesting it was done by more than one individual. She shines the light on one page and glances at Mark. "What language is this?"

"I don't know." It's the English alphabet, but none of it resembles any language he's encountered before.

"Some kind of code?"

He's not certain. The letters are arranged in a strange way—some of the shorter words don't even have any vowels, so it's a good guess. "Maybe."

The first third of the book is more of the same. Pages and pages of undecipherable handwritten print. Words that mean nothing to either of them. When she flips a page and finds sketches done in black ink, bold lines over pencil, she stops to take a closer look, slowing her pace. The following pages are filled from top to bottom with various drawings: half-human, half-animal beings; people with smiles on their faces but skin dripping off their bones; beheaded individuals holding their grinning heads. Some of the images are of animals with human features, and the other way around, men with gills, women with wings. "Wow," Monica says. "Bizarre."

A few of the sketches remind Mark of the Walgrave's Wonders posters. "Could this be a guidebook for their magic act?"

"Dark magic, I'd say." Monica shudders. "Disturbing." The next page causes her to stop and let out a gasp. "Oh my God. What the hell, Mark?" She tilts the book toward him so he can see a sketch of two naked people, one man and one woman. They lie side by side on a table with what looks like leather straps restraining their wrists. "Talk about kinky."

"Not my kind of kinky."

"What do you suppose it is?" Monica asks. "Human sacrifice?"

Mark shakes his head. "In exchange for what? An exceptional crop season?"

"I don't know. It's creepy." Monica continues to turn pages until she reaches the end. The last page is one continuous column of text, like a poem or song lyrics. She shuts the book. "End of story."

"Wait a minute." Mark takes it from her and flips to the end. "I recognize some of this from the chanting." He runs his finger along the text, confirming that the words *Sursum corda* are repeated throughout. Reading it, he can hear the chanting in his head, the voices pounding out the words in unison.

"Do you think this has something to do with their act?" Monica asks.

"Either that or it's some kind of satanic ritual."

"God, I hope not."

Mark gently closes the book, then puts it back on the shelf. "I've seen enough. Let's go."

"Not just yet," she says, taking his hand and stepping down off the stage. "I have an idea."

Her sultry tone tells him that sex is imminent, something he's normally on board with, but when she continues across the room and hops up to sit on the table, her legs dangling over the edge, he gets a sinking feeling. "Not here," he says.

"Oh yes, right here." She takes the flashlight out of his hand and turns it off before setting it an arm's length away, then tugs at his pants.

There are a hundred reasons not to do it here, especially when his bed is just a few minutes away, but she's already started, which means he's started as well. *It's wrong to do it here* is the thought that crosses his mind, but he's no longer in control of his own body and couldn't stop if he wanted to. Instantly aroused, Mark is easily able to disregard the stifling, hot air and the dust all around them, concentrating solely on the heat between them. Her hands and lips find him in all the right places. Clothing gets cast aside; they come together in a white-hot intensity, both of them finishing at the same time, neither of them even trying to be quiet when they cry out at the end.

When all is done, Mark is flat on his back with Monica on top of him, his feet hanging over the edge. Breathless, his heart pounding from the excitement, he wonders what it would be like to be strapped to this very table, with Monica strapped down right next to him. He can imagine the straps around his wrists, his body laid bare. *What would it feel like?* The sketch didn't show anyone else in the room, but there had to be. Otherwise, who had buckled the straps? He imagines a group surrounding the table, men and women, all eyes on him, every inch of him on display. And then what would happen? Was strapping people down an act of forced humiliation? Some kind of cult initiation? Or was it purely sexual, the beginning of something else entirely?

Under the right circumstances, it might be the right kind of kinky after all.

"Well, Mark Norman, you certainly rise to the occasion." Monica's sexy voice right next to his ear interrupts his thoughts.

He grins and tries to think of a witty comeback, but nothing comes to mind. Instead, he presses his lips against her neck. One last kiss. They'll need to get dressed and clean up any evidence that they've been here, but since he feels like he's melted between Monica and the table, it's not going to happen for at least a few more minutes. She doesn't show any signs of wanting to move just yet either. Her body is hot and sticky against him, but he doesn't mind. Nothing that a quick shower can't fix. Once again, he is reminded of the advantages of having Monica at Alden Manor. She does more than her share of work, for one thing, and her sunny mood is a gift, especially when compared to both Lisa and Nurse Darby. And having sex so readily available is a definite bonus.

What the hell. He's not completely heartless. He may just give her a chunk of the inheritance after all.

He's completely relaxed, and then he feels something or someone grab his foot, digging in, squeezing hard. Immediately he knows it would be impossible for Monica to reach that far. Raw terror fills his chest cavity. His breath catches in his throat as he frantically kicks his foot, but whatever it is has tightly pinched his skin. Pushing Monica aside, he yells, "Something's got me! I'm caught!"

CHAPTER TWENTY-FOUR

"What the hell, Mark?" Monica demands, catching herself.

He hauls himself into a sitting position with the thing still clamped to his foot. Blood pounds in his ears. Through the inky blackness he can just make out a wraith at the end of the table, a smokelike vision, wispy white against the darkness. *Dear God.* It appeared out of nowhere and now has gotten hold of him. "Get it off, get it off of me!" With one last yank, he is able to pull free and scramble away.

Monica snaps on the flashlight. The beam settles on Alma, who is at the end of the table, her hand reaching for his ankle, now just out of her grasp. He can see now that her wraithlike appearance in the dark was due to her white hair and cream-colored nightgown. With her sunken eyes and vacant, unfocused gaze, she appears unearthly. Not human. This sudden turn of events strikes Mark mute. *How did Alma get up to the second floor? And how much did she see?*

Monica speaks in a low tone. "Alma, are you okay, honey?" Her voice is that of a mother speaking to a toddler who wandered out of bed half-asleep. "How are you feeling?"

Alma gestures to Mark, who is now climbing off the table and gathering up his clothing. "Mine," she says.

"What's yours?" Monica says patiently, as if this whole scenario—this postcoital interruption while they are naked in a place that's off-limits—is completely normal.

Alma turns to her and says, "I don't want to be here." The words come out as slurred and slow as syrup poured out of a bottle.

"No, of course not."

Mark pulls on his clothes in record time and takes the flashlight from Monica, who dresses while he talks to Alma. "I'm sorry if we woke you up," he says. "We didn't mean to interrupt your sleep."

Alma gives no sign of understanding, just stands and watches as they frantically get dressed.

When Monica is finished, she comes back to Alma and says, "Time to go downstairs and go back to bed. Okay, Alma?"

Alma allows Monica to walk her out of the room. Mark closes the doors behind them, then leads the two women down the hall. Alma takes mincing steps, meandering from side to side. Monica steers her, cajoling as they walk, telling Alma that she's doing a great job and that soon she'll be back in her comfortable bed.

When they get to the stairs, they halt, and Monica and Mark exchange a glance. Considering how much time it took to get from the ballroom to the stairs, Mark can imagine what an ordeal it will be for the three of them to walk down the flight of stairs. There's only one solution. He hands the flashlight to Monica. "I'll carry her."

"Are you sure?"

He nods and then scoops up Alma, who accepts this new development with a small sigh. She clasps her hands around his neck, and he carefully navigates one step at a time, using the beam of light as a guide. Alma nestles against his chest, making it easier to keep his balance. She's as light as a child. Mark can't help but feel a pang of affection for this old lady, as dependent on him as a newborn kitten. He can't imagine what it must be like to need this kind of care. When they reach the ground floor, he lets out a breath of relief and eases her down onto her feet. She pats his face.

"We're almost there, Alma," Monica says. "You're doing great."

When they get to Alma's bedroom door, Mark whispers, "Do you need my help?"

Monica shakes her head. "No, I'll take it from here." With one arm around Alma's shoulders, she steers her into the room and gently closes the door behind them.

In his own bedroom, Mark peels off his clothing and heads into the shower. A quick rinse and he's back out, toweling off, putting on fresh underwear, and ready to go to bed. The whole evening has been an odd series of events. The secret code, the disturbing sketches, Monica's sudden urge to have sex in a hot, dusty room, and the inexplicable appearance of Alma.

What an obscenely weird night.

Lying in the dark, he feels a nagging sensation, one he's had many times in his life. It's a dark cloud telling him that something bad is going to happen and *it's all his fault*. He's fucked up royally and will be found out. It's a guilty, sinking, sick-to-his-stomach feeling, telling him that he's screwed because of something he's done. Mark breathes in and out, wishing the bad feeling away, and then he remembers how he's dealt with it in the past. If he can identify the root of the problem and work out a solution, the feeling almost always dissipates.

Like checking for a wiggly tooth by searching with his tongue, he weighs each event. The book with its secret code and strange artwork was off-putting, but it's not the source of his worry. The sex? He once had sex with a girl on the lawn in her family's backyard while her parents slept inside and didn't think twice about it. Another sexual encounter occurred in a girlfriend's office right on her desk after her coworkers had gone home for the night. And he is well acquainted with the gymnastics required to round home base in the back seat of a car. In the grand scheme of things, doing the deed on a table in a dusty room is nothing out of the ordinary for Mark Norman.

Alma's sudden appearance? Now that, he suddenly realizes, is the tooth that's troubling him. Not just that she grabbed him in the dark, scaring the crap out of him, but the unknown. How in the hell did she get up to the second floor by herself? And would she tell her brother that Monica and Mark were upstairs in the forbidden room going at it like randy teenagers? So often Alma seems out of it, but there are times when she is incredibly lucid. If confronted, would Mark and Monica admit to snooping around in the ballroom and getting caught by Alma with their clothes off?

No, he decides, he can't possibly confess to such a thing. If Roy hears what he's done, he might change his mind about the will, and Mark would probably get fired as well. And if he's fired, then what? With Brenda and her sister ensconced in their former apartment, he has nowhere to live. His pride won't let him approach his friends, and Mark will die before he'll ask to move in with his family. He'd be out on the street homeless first. Just like Lisa, he realizes, he's now out of options. Alden Manor has him by the balls.

But his newly acquired indentured servitude, for lack of a better term, is just for now, and honestly, he has to believe he's unlikely to lose his job. He reminds himself that Mark Norman always finds a way. He'll lie, if need be. Alma is old and confused, and if Monica backs him up, they can pass off Alma's story as a bad dream. It's completely plausible—actually more likely to be the case than the actual truth.

Now that he's thought it through, the guilt that grips him melts away. He hasn't done anything wrong. In fact, he carried a woman down a flight of stairs, which was damn near heroic. All he needs is a full night's sleep. Tomorrow they'll see how much Alma remembers and deal with it from there. He might be worrying for nothing.

He's been asleep for several hours when the sobbing wakes him. He lies still, listening for a moment. Most likely it's Alma, in which case Monica will handle it. The clock radio says it's three a.m., way too early to rise. The crying continues with some urgency. It wears on him, pulling him from his bed after several minutes. He doesn't bother putting on pants over his briefs. He'll just have a quick peek.

Out in the hall, the noise is even louder, and he can tell now that it's coming from upstairs. His body moves as if self-propelled. When he reaches the entryway by the front door, he pulls the curtain back to look outside and takes in a startled breath when he sees the stranger from the other night. Again, the man stands facing the house, a cardboard mask obscuring his face, but this time he's close. Right in front of the porch. He shakes his finger at Mark, as if to say, *I know what you've done.*

Mark flips him the bird, then drops the curtain and turns away. *Well, screw him.* If Mark had time, he'd go outside and rip the mask right off that asshole's face and then beat him to a pulp, but he can't do it right now. The sobbing is getting louder, and *someone* has to check it out. Up the stairs he goes, his hand sliding up the banister, his feet moving as if on autopilot.

By the time he gets to the closed ballroom doors, the sobbing is more subdued but still audible. His hand is on the knob when he hears more: the muted buzz of conversation, of multiple conversations, friendly chatting like people at a cocktail party.

What? He checked after dinner to make sure all the exterior doors in the house were locked. *How did all these people get inside?* He glances down, wishing he'd taken a moment to put on his bathrobe.

He opens the door and blinks at the unexpected glare of light from the three chandeliers. Once his eyes adjust, he's aware there are half a dozen people gathered around the table. Someone is lying there, strapped down. It's a moment before he recognizes Lisa, openly crying, twisting and turning in a futile struggle to free herself. Mark feels almost light-headed in his confusion. Lisa is dead. Her fall was fatal. He saw the medics zip her into the body bag. Is he dreaming? But somehow this doesn't feel like a dream. All of it is so real, right down to the way his heart is racing in his chest.

Mark walks into the room. "What's going on here?" The room is no longer hot and dusty, but as comfortable and clean as a hotel banquet hall.

The six people, three men and three women, turn his way, and suddenly all of them are wearing cardboard masks, the eyes and mouths unevenly cut out as if to cover drooping facial features. A man's voice says, "Mark is here!" and the others call out his name as well.

"Mark Norman!"

"Good to see you, Mark!"

"Come and join us, Mark."

Lisa seems oblivious to his presence, but she cries inconsolably, like a child who misses her mother. A confused thought crosses his mind that maybe her death was temporary and now she's back.

All six of the masked people walk toward him, and suddenly his head is consumed by a throbbing pain while his heart races crazily out of control. "Stop right there," he says, but the words come out in the tiniest of squeaks, and the people keep coming until they're surrounding him.

"No need to be alarmed," one of the women says. "We're friends of yours." His feet refuse to move, even as she moves closer and runs her hand down his chest, then underneath the elastic of his briefs and all the way down, cupping his balls. He reels with shame at the way he responds physically, the way the bulge in his underwear grows as she touches him, as if he's enjoying having a masked woman fondle him in front of other people, which isn't the case at all. It's weird as hell, and it's not his fault that his body is reacting. He wants to tell them that it's just a physical reflex, as automatic as a knee jerk from a doctor's tap with a rubber hammer, but he can't say the words.

"Come and join us," one of the men says, leaning in. Even with the mask covering his face, Mark senses the man leering.

He sucks in a deep breath and manages to spit out, "No." Saying the word gives him the strength to push the woman away. She laughs, and then all of them are laughing at him, and he knows it's because of how weak he is, how pathetic. *Loser. Never going to amount to anything.* He doesn't even care about Lisa anymore or the fact that they shouldn't be there. Everything in him tells him he just needs to get away. His legs move slowly, but at least they're moving, and after he leaves the room, he slams the doors behind him. Mark feels safer now. He thinks they can't leave the room, that there's some sort of rule about it—whatever put them in there keeps them contained—but he's not entirely certain, and it's all very confusing.

And then everything fades away.

At five thirty a.m., he wakes up, reeling with shame. He sits up, trying to make sense of what he remembers from the night before. The state of his underwear tells him at least some of it was true. Were there really masked people up in the ballroom? He can actually see them in his mind's eye, which makes him think there might be some truth to it. Maybe there's a secret way into the house? A passageway that allows people to come and go without detection? He sits in bed, sifting through what he remembers, and then thinks, *No. Lisa was there, and Lisa is dead.*

He knows Lisa is dead because he saw her body carried away in a black body bag.

None of it happened.

It was a nightmare, plain and simple. Not too different from his puberty dreams, the ones where he noticed neighbors staring through his bedroom window witnessing him masturbating. The shame of being seen by Alma has imbued the same kind of guilt he felt as a young teenager. The people with masks, Lisa being strapped to the table—this is just subconscious gibberish laced together from the images in the book and the appearance of the stranger on the sidewalk. All the oddities of the last few days have gotten mixed together in his head, manifested as bizarre dreams. He remembers something Lisa said: *It's like the house is putting ideas in my head.* He shakes his head to dispel the notion and is able to shake the images and shame from his mind.

Only if you let it, Lisa. Only if you let it.

Mark isn't like Lisa, who got rattled by the littlest things. Sadly, this was not the job for her. She was frail-minded to begin with—not like Mark, an adult man, someone in charge of his own destiny.

Enough thinking about the dream. He's awake now and already has made sense of what happened the night before. In a way, he's glad for his disrupted sleep and early awakening. Being up so early gives him time to mentally prepare for the possibility that Alma may narc on them. He will get dressed and get busy in the kitchen, making breakfast before anyone else gets up. Scrambled eggs are within his capabilities. He'll make enough for all of them and keep them in a casserole dish in a warming oven. That, along with some fruit and toast, would be a great start to the day.

Having the meal prepared will win him points with Monica, he knows. Women love this kind of thing.

Hopefully, Alma will have forgotten the previous night's escapade, but if she brings it up, his strategy will be to chalk it up to a dream, after which he'll change the subject. He's running things now.

CHAPTER TWENTY-FIVE

Breakfast is ready by the time everyone else gets up, and just as Mark expects, Monica looks pleased. As she helps Alma into the kitchen, her eyes widen in surprise at the already set table and the freshly cut fruit platter placed in the middle. "You've been busy," she says with a smile. Alma, still in her nightgown, leans heavily on Monica in an alarming way. As if reading Mark's thoughts, Monica says, "Alma's feeling a little under the weather today."

Alma doesn't look like she'll be ratting anyone out anytime soon, so maybe they won't have to worry about her after all. "I'm sorry to hear that," Mark says, getting the eggs from the warming oven and setting the dish on the stovetop. He did a halfway decent job, if he does say so himself. The scrambled eggs are plump, and he also grated some cheese to sprinkle on top. No one could find fault with this breakfast. Now he stands sentinel at the toaster, waiting for the first batch to pop.

Monica makes up plates for both Roy and Alma and is setting them on the table as Roy enters the room. "Morning, all," he says, leaning on his cane. "Did you all sleep well?" The old man has a twinkle in his eye. His question is to all of them, but he seems to be addressing Mark, who tries not to flush red. It's almost like he knows.

"Like a rock, thank you," Monica says as she turns to the stove to get her own plate ready.

Mark says, "Quite well, thanks," but his gaze is on Alma, whose eyes are closed, head wobbling. While he watches, she drops her fork and begins to lean precariously to one side. Mark takes a dive from his place by the toaster just in time to catch her before she hits the floor.

Monica turns and witnesses his Herculean save. "Oh my God." She rushes over to help, as Roy struggles to his feet to do the same.

Roy says, "Carry her into the bedroom!" And to Monica, "Call Dr. Cross!"

Mark's breakfast is quickly forgotten. He lifts Alma and follows Roy into the bedroom. Limp in his arms, Alma is heavier today. Her arms dangle down, and her eyelids flutter. "Maybe we should call for an ambulance?" Mark suggests as he sets her on the bed. Alma is a mess, barely conscious, her limbs splayed out like a rag doll. Mark's no medical expert, but his guess is she's having a stroke.

If ever there was an emergency, it would be now.

"No." Roy shakes his head. "Alma and I have discussed this, and she wants to be at home until the very end. Dr. Cross will know what to do."

In other words, she'd rather die at home than in the sterile environment of a hospital. Mark nods in understanding.

Roy strokes his sister's head and says, "Just hold tight, dear. Monica is calling Calvin, and he'll be here soon."

Alma groans, and her eyes widen. With much effort, she gasps out a few quiet words. "I don't want to be like this."

"I know, dear. Soon it will all be better, and you'll feel like your old self again." Roy turns to Mark and says, "Will you go to the front door and wait for Dr. Cross?"

"Of course." Mark suspects Roy just wants to be alone with his sister, but he doesn't mind being sent out of the room. He's never been adept at dealing with sick people. His stepfather actually accused him once of being completely absent of empathy. Mark doesn't think that's true at all. He's pragmatic. It just doesn't serve a purpose for him to take on other people's misery. Someone needs to be coolheaded in a crisis.

As he watches through the glass for Dr. Cross's car to pull up, it occurs to him that Alma is dying and doing it before she can divulge his misdeeds. In a way, the timing couldn't be better. It's entirely possible that the effort of going upstairs in the middle of the night may have contributed to her decline, which, he thinks, is lucky for her because she's been miserable for some time now, and there is no point in dragging it out.

Or at least she *seems* miserable. Anyone would be, living like that.

And when Alma passes away, will Roy be far behind? *One down and one to go.* And once that happens, Mark will be a rich man. Or a richer man, anyway, depending on what it's all worth.

When death is good, life is better.

When Dr. Cross arrives, he rushes from the car and up the walkway. His long legs take the steps two at a time, and when Mark opens the door, he dashes inside. "Where is she?" he demands.

"In her bedroom, lying down."

As they walk, he peppers Mark with questions, wanting to know what caused her collapse, if she's running a temperature, and if she's spoken at all.

Mark answers to the best of his knowledge. When they reach Alma's bedroom, Dr. Cross tells him to go to the kitchen to make a cup of tea and then closes the door behind him. Mark wanders into the kitchen, where he finds Monica sitting at the table, her head in her hands. "What's wrong?" he asks.

"What's wrong?" She sits up and looks at him incredulously. "What do you mean, what's wrong? Alma is dying, that's what's wrong."

"People die, Monica. Old people are even more prone to death. It's sort of their thing."

She shakes her head. "You are one cold fish, Mark Norman."

"Just stating the facts. People are born, they live, and then they die. That's life." He pulls up a chair and sits next to her. "Besides, you just met her. How broken up can you be?"

Monica's eyes meet his, and her brow furrows. "She's a sweet lady, Mark. It's easy to get attached. Besides, once she's gone, is Roy really going to need both of us here?"

Oh, so that's it. She couldn't keep up her Mother Teresa act for long. "It hasn't happened yet, so don't worry about it. By the way, Dr. Cross asked if you'd make a cup of tea."

"For him or what?"

Mark shakes his head. "He didn't say."

When Dr. Cross comes into the kitchen fifteen minutes later, he sinks into a chair. When Monica offers him a cup of tea, he gratefully accepts. Apparently, the tea *was* intended for him.

"How is she?" Monica asks, her face showing concern. Both she and Mark are leaning back against the kitchen counter, giving the appearance of diligent employees, taking a short break out of respect for the situation, but ready to work at a moment's notice.

Dr. Cross takes a sip. "I gave her a shot, which should help, but I think it's safe to say the end is near."

Mark says, "I'm so sorry," before Monica can.

She shoots him a sideways glance of irritation before echoing his words and asking, "Should I go sit with her? Take in some tea or some breakfast?"

"Maybe later, but right now Roy would like some time alone with her. He's pretty broken up." Dr. Cross's mouth stretches into a brief, sad smile. "Those two are like two peas in a pod. I've never met a brother and sister with such a close connection. He's going to be lost without her."

"How much longer does she have?" Mark asks.

"No way to know with any certainty." Dr. Cross shakes his head sadly. "It could be hours; it could be days. I don't think it will be more than a week, though. She's been such a trouper up until now, but she's so frail. Her body has just had enough."

"If there's anything we can do to help," Monica says, "just let us know."

"I'm glad you asked." As it turns out, Dr. Cross has a whole list of things for them. He wants Monica to call the other members of the Redevine Society, since they'll want to spend time with Alma while they can. For Mark, Dr. Cross has other ideas, so many chores that he pulls a pad of paper out of his pocket and jots down a list. Prescriptions will need to be filled, so a trip to the drugstore is the first priority. Mark will also need to stop at a medical supply store to finalize an order for a hospital bed. "I'll call ahead with the specifics. All you'll have to do is sign for it and arrange for delivery." Lastly, he wants Mark to go grocery shopping. "I'll write down a few ideas, and you can add to it if you think of anything else," Dr. Cross says. "She won't be able to eat much, but I'd like to have soft foods available for her. Canned soup, applesauce, that kind of thing."

"Of course," Mark says. He sounds sympathetic, but mentally he's already behind the wheel of the Excalibur, driving away from Alden Manor. He will not mind avoiding the doom and gloom of a deathbed scene. "Whatever you need."

"Should I go with him?" Monica asks.

"No, you should stay here," Dr. Cross says. "Alma needs you."

CHAPTER TWENTY-SIX

Just like before, driving the Excalibur makes Mark want to shout with glee. He finds himself slowing down when he spots a yellow light ahead, for the sole purpose of actually stopping at the intersection. Waiting at traffic lights while driving this car is one of the best experiences he's had on four wheels. Mark makes a point to keep his gaze straight ahead, hands on the wheel, playing the part of one cool guy. Inwardly, though, he's taking note of the surrounding cars and the pedestrians on adjacent sidewalks, all of them staring in admiration. Hell, some of them actually stop and point in awe like he's John-fuckin'-Travolta.

If driving the car is this exhilarating, owning it is going to be the bomb.

Soon. Very soon.

Picking up the prescriptions takes an hour and a half. While he's waiting for his order to be filled, he flips through *Newsweek* and wishes they didn't keep *Playboy* behind the counter. What he wouldn't give for a skin magazine right now, but if he asks for one, he'll have to buy it, and he's not paying good money to be a looky-loo when he's got the real thing back at the house.

After he gets the white paper bag filled with two different types of pills and one bottle of codeine, he gets back in the Excalibur and drives forty-five minutes, following Dr. Cross's written directions to the medical supply store. The store isn't there, though, so he circles the block and tries again. No dice. He heaves an irritated sigh and pulls up the car in front of a pay phone. Standing in the phone booth, he keeps an eye on the parked car while flipping through the pages. When he finds the listing for Fogleman's Medical Supply Store, he sees that the address is completely different from what he was given by the doctor. Fishing a quarter out of his pocket, he calls the store and winds up talking to an earnest young man who tells him they changed locations more than a year before. After confirming the new address and getting detailed directions, Mark is back behind the wheel, heading that way.

If Dr. Cross had thought to confirm the address, Mark wouldn't be getting the runaround right now. Most people would be irritated at the doctor's blunder, but Mark is only mildly annoyed. Given the choice, he'd rather be out and about driving this fabulous vehicle than back in the gloom of Alden Manor.

Someday, he thinks, this may even make an interesting story to tell acquaintances at a bar. A tale about the time he ran around town looking for a hospital bed while a woman lay dying back in a run-down mansion. If anyone could make it sound amusing it would be him, but right now, this errand is just one more thing to do. At the medical supply store, he's led through the showroom, where Curtis, the earnest young man he talked to from the pay phone, shows him how the bed operates. "This is our top-of-the-line model," he says with a little too much enthusiasm. With his unruly hair and glasses that don't sit right on his nose, Curtis is clearly the type of guy who would have sat alone in the lunchroom in high school, but now, as an adult, he has found his calling in medical supplies. Curtis is happy to show him how the bed works. "You can raise and lower the side rails. And the bed itself adjusts so the patient can be elevated to a sitting position." He demonstrates and then addresses Mark directly. "Is this for a family member, by any chance?"

Mark nods. "My grandmother. A very sweet lady."

"The doctor who called in didn't specify her medical condition."

"It just happened. We believe she had a stroke."

"Oh, I'm so sorry," Curtis says, and he looks mournful on Mark's behalf. "That has to be difficult."

"It is difficult, but we're all doing our best. You understand, I'm sure."

"I'm sure that having a loving grandson brings her comfort." When they set up a time for delivery, Curtis is apologetic but explains that the bed won't arrive until the day after tomorrow. "We have a guy out on vacation, and then the other delivery fella took a sick day, so we're backlogged. If we can deliver it sooner, we definitely will. I'll call if that's the case."

Mark signs the form and assures him it will be fine. If it's not fine, Dr. Cross will have to figure out another option. He's just the errand boy. With the carbon copy in hand, he leaves the store and heads to buy groceries. The doctor gave him a few twenties, a hundred dollars in all, which turns out to be plenty. Mark fulfills the list and buys a six-pack of Schlitz to keep stashed in his room. The store receipt will be conveniently lost on the trip back.

When Mark returns to Alden Manor, he sees several cars parked in front. The Redevine Society, no doubt. After parking, he walks down the sidewalk with the paper grocery sack in his arms. Arriving at the house, he looks around to ascertain he's not being observed, then sets the six-pack of beer behind the row of bushes lining the front porch. He steps back to make sure it's hidden from sight. *Perfect.* He'll retrieve it later.

While he stands there, a male voice rings out. "Hey there, mister. How's it going?"

Mark turns to see Doug leaning against the building next door, one leg bent and flat against the brick façade. One hand comes up to his mouth to inhale from a cigarette, the other hand dangles at his side, holding something between two fingers. It appears to be a piece of cardboard. A mask, no doubt, which would make him the weirdo who appeared in front of the house that night. Mark knows he should ignore this idiot, but there's a smug part of him that wants to put him in his place.

"Were you the one who was standing outside the other night wearing a mask?"

"Like this?" Doug holds up a piece of cardboard so Mark can see the holes cut out of it.

So it was him. *Asshole.* "What's your problem?"

"I got no problem." Doug laughs. "The mask is a metaphor, rich boy. Think of it as a sort of a warning." He scratches his eyebrow with his middle finger. "Things aren't always what they seem, especially in that house. Even the birds get the whiff of death. They get too close, it's the end for them." With one pointed finger, he mimics the shooting of a gun. "I think you'd be able to figure it out."

"You don't scare me," Mark says, anger rising from his chest. "And if I see you on the property again, I will beat you to a bloody pulp." He squeezes his right hand into a fist.

"Duly noted." Doug blows out a puff of smoke and cackles. "You're on your own now."

"Just leave me alone." And with that, Mark bounds up the steps and into the house. Inside, he's surprised to hear what sounds like party chatter coming from down the hall. The Redevine Society, no doubt, and they sound fairly boisterous.

His eyes narrow in confusion. With Alma's collapse and imminent death, he expected somber tones, crying even, but not this. He can't make out the words, but the voices are definitely upbeat.

The front door makes a loud thud as he closes it behind him, and the sound of conversation immediately ceases. When he's halfway down the hall, he's met by Dr. Cross, who is exiting the blue room. "Mark, glad to see you're back." he says, his tone serious. "Let me help you with that." He takes the grocery bag out of Mark's arms.

Mark glances through the doorway and sees Roy sitting with Monica and the other four members of the Redevine Society, all of them seated with drinks in their hands. "What's going on?"

"Come with me."

When they get to the kitchen, Dr. Cross sets the bag on the table. "I'm afraid I have some sad news. While you were out, Alma passed away."

Mark's eyes widen. "She *died*?"

"Yes, I'm sorry to say she did."

"But I was just here and she was fine." Well, not fine, exactly, but not that close to dying.

Dr. Cross gives him a sympathetic look. "Sometimes it happens suddenly. I know you were fond of Alma and this is a shock, but honestly, I think it's for the best. She hasn't been feeling like herself for quite a while now." Dr. Cross peers into the grocery bag. "Why don't you put these things away, and then I'll take you for a showing."

"A showing?" Mark carries the bag over to the pantry closet.

"To pay your respects."

He's not entirely sure what that will entail, but he nods in response anyway. With his back to the room, Mark empties the canned food and applesauce onto one of the shelves. He pulls the change out of his pocket and puts it on the table, pushing it toward the doctor. "I'm sorry, but the receipt flew away in the parking lot," he says apologetically.

Dr. Cross shrugs. "No matter." He tucks the money in his pocket. "Come with me." He turns and leads Mark into Alma's bedroom. They end up standing next to the bed where Alma lies, flat on her back, eyes closed, her hands folded with fingers interlaced. She is still wearing her nightgown, but the sheet is pulled up past her waist. Dr. Cross fusses with the cover, smoothing out the wrinkles. "Doesn't she look peaceful?"

"Yes, she does." Mark is lying. Alma doesn't look peaceful. She just looks dead. Furthermore, looking at her still body is creeping him out. A stray thought runs through his mind: *What if she suddenly opened her eyes and yelled, "Surprise!"* That would be the ultimate, unexpected practical joke. He'd definitely crap his pants if that happened. "Very peaceful." He hopes the act of paying respects is not a lengthy process. "I'm glad she's not in pain anymore." He's not sure that she *was* in pain, but he knows that's something people say when old folks die.

"You can touch her if you like," Dr. Cross says, gesturing toward the body.

Mark recoils in horror and tries to cover it up by running his fingers through his hair. "Oh, that's okay. I'm fine right here."

"I think you should take her hand." Dr. Cross speaks firmly —maybe too firmly. "It's important for a sense of closure."

Mark scans his face, looking for a sign that he's kidding, but he doesn't see it. He shifts uncomfortably. "No, I'd rather not."

"You don't need to be afraid of death, Mark. It's part of life, something every person faces sooner or later." And before Mark can respond, Dr. Cross grabs his wrist and pulls him forward until his hand is pressed against Alma's cold fingers. "See. Nothing to fear."

Mark sucks in a sharp breath. *What the hell?* He yanks his

hand out of Dr. Cross's grasp and takes a step back. "I'm not afraid. I just don't find it necessary." He's shaking in anger, but thinking of the long-term repercussions, he reins it in. Dr. Cross holds sway over Roy, and it wouldn't be smart to get on his bad side. Mark glances down at Alma. "She was a sweet lady." His gaze goes to the doctor, and he firmly says, "I'm sorry for your loss."

Dr. Cross's demeanor lightens, and he claps Mark on the shoulder. "It's a loss for you too, Mark. Every human life that's extinguished takes away from all of us."

"Of course."

"Would you like to say a prayer with me?"

"No, thank you. I like to pray in private."

Dr. Cross gives him a nod of approval. "Suit yourself. Well then, come along and let's join the others. We're having a celebration of Alma's life."

CHAPTER TWENTY-SEVEN

As they approach the blue room, it sounds like there's a party in progress. When Mark and Dr. Cross enter the room, the conversation doesn't pause. Mark sees multiple open bottles on the coffee table. Every seat in the room is full. "Mark, my boy!" Roy calls out, his hand over the top of the handle of his cane. "Have you met everyone?" Mark scans the room and takes note of who is there. Monica is squeezed in between Neela and Sam on the couch. Lara and Baird Whitlock occupy the wing chair opposite Roy's own, with Lara perched on Baird's lap, her arms around his neck. The occupants of the room are configured much like other parties Mark has attended, and all of them have a champagne flute in hand.

"Yes, I've been introduced to everyone." He tries to catch Monica's eye, to get some sign that she finds this gathering unconventional, but she's currently engrossed in something Sam is telling her. A joke, judging by the way she laughs at the end of his statement.

Sam gets up and pours a glass of champagne, handing it to Mark. "It might seem odd that we're not crying," he says pointedly to Mark, as if he's read his mind. "We are sad to lose our friend, but we also believe that a life well lived is worth celebrating."

"Well put." Roy hoists his glass high and says, "I'd like to make a toast to Alma Walgrave. She lived life with passion, and she died a good death."

"Hear! Hear!" Monica says, and all of them follow suit.

"Hear! Hear!"

"To Alma!"

"To a life well lived!"

They all take sips at the same time, and Monica gives him a sly smile, which he returns. He can't wait until they can talk privately later on. Behind him, Dr. Cross comes into the room carrying two kitchen chairs. Mark didn't even realize the man left, but now he's offering him a place to sit, and Mark gratefully accepts. As he sits down, he suddenly remembers something. and so in a hushed voice, he tells the doctor, "They're going to be delivering the hospital bed the day after tomorrow."

"Not to worry," Dr. Cross says. "I've already canceled the order."

Mark drinks his glass of champagne, a silent participant at a gathering honoring a body in a bedroom down the hall. When the doorbell rings half an hour later, he starts to rise from his chair but is ushered back down by Dr. Cross. "That would be the funeral home," he says. "I'll handle it."

The group continues talking. Their voices are loud, nearly rowdy. Sam tells another joke, this time loud enough so the whole room can hear it. Mark wants to commit the joke to memory because it's pretty funny, but ten minutes later all he can remember is that it was told with an Irish accent and had something to do with building a wall and having sex with a goat. Monica, who was made for this kind of social interaction, laughs like a party girl. Mark usually holds his own at social gatherings, but he feels out of place. He's just an employee, not an actual friend. Should he excuse himself and go to his room? No, here comes Sam with a newly opened champagne bottle coming to top off his glass for the umpteenth time. They obviously want him here, or they wouldn't keep plying him with alcohol.

When the funeral home staff wheels a gurney topped by a black body bag past the open doorway, Baird calls out, "Good-bye, Alma. Safe travels."

Lara adds, "It's been swell," and the group laughs.

When Dr. Cross returns to the room, he sits down on the kitchen chair next to Mark. "The worst is over," he says, which strikes Mark as odd. Isn't the worst thing not having the person you love around anymore? But maybe it's different when the one who dies is old and confused. Alma was never going to get better. Still, at the very least, it must be a loss for Roy.

"Is Monica going to have to leave?" Mark asks the doctor in a quiet voice.

Dr. Cross gives him a puzzled look. "Why would she leave?"

"Because Alma is . . . gone? I mean, wasn't that why she was hired? To take care of her?"

"Oh, I see what you're thinking. No, Monica will be staying. There will still be plenty to do around here, and someone will need to keep Roy company here at home while you run errands."

Mark considers this to be good news. Monica would be furious if she was sent away after having given up her apartment and job.

Neela calls out, "Roy! Tell these young people about your early years traveling with your magic act."

"You had a magic act?" Monica asks and glances over to Mark, her eyebrows raised like, *What a surprise!* Her tone of incredulity is convincing; Mark gives her that much. She says, "We'd love to hear about it."

"They were world-famous," Baird says. "Traveled everywhere."

Roy beams with pride. "You young folks should have seen Alma and me back in the day. We performed in theaters all over the world." He takes a sip of his champagne. "We did illusions that had never been done before and haven't been done since. No one could figure it out. Over the years we were offered big money to reveal how our tricks were done, but a magician never reveals his secrets." He smiles.

Mark suddenly remembers something. "Lisa was under the impression that you were a salesman and Alma worked as a seamstress."

Roy tilts his head to one side, thinking. "Lisa did have a tendency to get confused, bless her soul. I will tell you that Alma made our costumes. Her skill with a needle was considerable."

There's barely a pause before Monica asks, "What countries did you tour?"

"Too many to name." Roy chuckles. "If I had to list them, we'd be sitting here all day."

Monica leans forward. "England? France? Czechoslovakia?"

"All of them and more."

Her eyes shine. "I would love to travel like that. I wish I could have been there."

Mark thinks she's laying it on kind of thick. Probably hoping Roy will put her in the will, but that's not going to happen. Not if Mark has anything to say about it.

Roy says, "It seems like so long ago now. The years went by so fast." Bracing his elbows on his knees, he intertwines his fingers. "If we were performing today, we'd be in Las Vegas. I hear that they're opening up to magic acts now. Alma and Roy could give Siegfried and Roy a run for their money." He smiles, as if picturing it in his mind.

Neela says, "You were the magician and Alma was the assistant, isn't that right?"

He nods. "She was so much more than my assistant, though. We developed the tricks together. We practiced until our movements went as smoothly as a finely tuned watch. We traveled thousands of miles and always got along. She was a true partner. My better half. I'm going to miss her so much." His voice cracks as he looks toward the ceiling.

Sam gets up and hands him a white handkerchief. "We're all going to miss her," he says gently. "I find comfort in the fact that someday we'll all be together again."

"Amen to that," Lara says from her perch on Baird's lap.

Roy dabs his eyes. "It's just not fair that she went first. It should have been me." He looks up and gives Mark a grim smile.

"Oh, don't say that," Monica says. "Alma wouldn't have wanted you to be sad."

Mark thinks she's being a little presumptuous for someone who just met Alma and Roy, but the others agree with her, so apparently he's the only one who notices.

Sam tells another joke, and everyone laughs. Baird says, "That's the third time you've told that joke, Sam, but I still love hearing it." He takes a sip of champagne and shares a smile with his wife. The love these people have for each other is palpable.

Maybe it's the champagne, but Mark feels an odd affection for this group of friends. An admiration for how they care for each other. He's never bothered to cultivate friendships, but he can see the value in it. This is something he'll need to aim for in the future. People who will take care of him when he's ill and mourn him when he's gone. There's a pause in the conversation. Mark asks, "What was your most famous trick?"

Roy's face lights up. "There were so many, my boy. But if I had to pick one"—he raises his index finger—"it would be the headless woman. I would pop Alma's head off her neck, and she would walk about the stage with her head tucked under her arm." He chuckles at the memory. "You should have heard the screams. At every performance at least one person fainted, usually a woman. And a few times, an audience member vomited at the sight."

"How did you do it?" Mark asks. "I mean, how did you make it look like Alma was headless? Off the record, can you tell us?" He glances around the room. "You know all of us can keep a secret." Mark is not asking just to make conversation. He remembers the poster showing a headless Alma. The sight of her head tucked under her arm was grotesque and yet compelling at the same time. He's dying to know how it was done. Mirrors? A mannequin? Some kind of projection? There has to be a simple explanation. Everyone in the room looks to Roy, who opens his mouth as if about to speak. For a second, Mark thinks he's going to spill. After all, the old man is so close to the end of his life that not telling means the secret will go with him to his grave, and what would be the point of that?

But Roy seems to think better of it; he closes his mouth and shakes his head. "I prefer to keep it to myself," he says. "So much in life is known. When all is said and done, there needs to be some mystery."

CHAPTER TWENTY-EIGHT

The evening wears on. At some point boxes of pizza are delivered, and Mark eats his fill of pepperoni and cheese. Even Roy manages to eat a slice—a small miracle, given his false teeth. The drinking evolves from champagne to cocktails, and the room fairly rocks with laughter. When Mark privately asks Dr. Cross about a funeral, he gestures to the room and says, "This is it. A group of friends celebrating her life. Just the way Alma wanted it."

Mark sees the group acting silly and drunk. He wonders if this is really what she would have wanted. They haven't mentioned Alma in hours, instead telling jokes and reminiscing about travels and fine-dining restaurants. They try to include Mark in the conversation, but it's fairly pointless. What would he be able to contribute to a conversation about taking a train trip across Europe? These people are like something out of the Agatha Christie novel he had to read in high school.

At the end of the evening, Roy tells them to leave the glasses and bottles for the next day, but Neela and Lara insist on cleaning up. Monica gathers up the pizza boxes and pizza-stained paper napkins and leaves the room to dispose of them while the men stay behind to talk. Mark knows he should be doing *something*, but he can't think of what, exactly. His mind is muddled by the tidal wave of alcohol he's consumed. The room spins before his eyes, and he can't keep his thoughts straight.

Once everyone reconvenes, there is a flurry of goodbyes as the two couples decide to leave for the night. Lara and Neela gather up their purses and give Roy a kiss on the cheek. Sam and Baird shake Roy's hand. Only Neela acknowledges Alma's death as she says goodbye, saying, "My condolences on the loss of your lovely sister."

After they've gone, Dr. Cross says, "Why don't I help you with your bedtime routine, Roy, before I head out? We'll let these young folks turn in for the night."

Mark is relieved at this turn of events. He'll be lucky to get himself into bed, much less anyone else.

And yet, he does. He makes it to his room and shuts the door behind him. After taking a leak and brushing his teeth, he strips down to his underwear and climbs under the sheets. His last thought before he drifts off to sleep is that he's lucky to have avoided the bed spins. Those are the worst.

In the middle of the night, a knock on the door wakes him. His eyes flick open, and for a second he thinks the sound is a figment of his imagination. No. There it is again, three firm raps coming from the other side of his bedroom door. It could only be Monica or Roy, and Monica wouldn't knock—she'd just come in. He suddenly remembers that he didn't leave his door ajar in case Roy needed him during the night. But Monica would certainly hear him, wouldn't she?

He fumbles out from under his covers and pads to the door. Opening it, he's stunned to see Lisa, dressed exactly as she was the day they met: a white peasant top, red-checked flare-legged pants, and a gold cross necklace around her neck. The light in the hallway allows him to see every detail. She is real, so real he can see the freckles on her nose. His mouth is frozen from shock; no words come out. She crooks one finger, beckoning for him to follow her. Numbly, he does.

Down the hall she glides. While he trails her, his mind reels. Lisa, it seems, is not dead after all. She faked her own death and is now back to prove a point. She takes him across the hall and into Roy's bedroom. They stand alongside the old man's bed, looking down on his sleeping body. He's on his back, mouth sunken from lack of teeth, the wispy hair around his ears sticking out in an unattractive way. His snoring is erratic, as if he can't find his rhythm.

Lisa holds a pillow in two hands and mimes holding it over the old man's face. A demonstration of suffocation. She goes through the motions again and looks to see if he understands. Mark nods. She hands him the pillow and points at Roy as if to say, *Now you do it. And make it count.*

Mark sucks in a quick breath. He shakes his head and drops the pillow to the floor.

Yes. He can hear her voice in his head. *This is the only way to stop it.*

He responds out loud, "No." He's crossed lines before, but he's never killed anyone. It's not that he's incapable of ending a life. It's just not necessary. Soon enough the old man will be gone.

Do it. She puts the pillow back in his hands.

"No."

Roy shifts in his sleep and murmurs one word. "Alma." His voice is hoarse, and it's a pitiful sound. Clearly, the old guy misses his sister. This is what happens when you become too reliant on someone else.

The walls of the room become shadowy and begin to close in on them. At the same time, the smell of rotting meat and urine fills the air. Mark feels something slick on his hands.

Taking a closer look, he sees that it's blood. Before he can wipe it off, Lisa grabs his arm and shoves him closer to the bed. Out of the corner of his eye, he watches as she morphs into Dr. Cross. The pillow vanishes at the same time.

"Go ahead," the doctor says. "You can touch her." The body in the bed becomes Alma, her flesh mottled purple-and-blue like a bruise. "Don't be afraid. Death is a part of life. It's going to happen to all of us." His fingers tighten their grip, digging into Mark's skin. "Just do it. Touch her. It will help you to understand how death works."

The smell of rotting meat gets stronger, filling his nostrils and making him gag.

Repulsed, Mark pushes away from Dr. Cross, who throws his head back and laughs. Alma's corpse sits up and giggles, then reaches out both arms to embrace him. "Come to me," she croaks. Wheeling, Mark flees the room. In the hallway he bumps into Doug, who is wearing his cardboard mask and leaning back against the wall, one leg bent flamingo style. "Told ya!" he says. "Remember, it's better to take action than to be a victim." He reaches out and pats Mark on the cheek.

"Get the fuck away from me," Mark tells him and continues on. Behind his back, Doug chortles.

Once he's in his bedroom, Mark closes the door and locks it, then pulls the covers up to his chin for protection. He is fairly certain this is a dream, but knowing that doesn't help if he can't make it stop. Ruefully, he remembers how Lisa warned him about the bad dreams. As it turns out, she was right.

No, wait, she wasn't right. She was a sad, crazy girl, and now she's gone. Or is she gone? Everything is all mixed up, and he doesn't know how to untangle it.

He closes his eyes and wishes for this nightmare to end.

Sleep eventually comes, and he only wakes up when Monica comes into the room and climbs into bed with him. He's too tired to even open his eyes, but her voice croons into his ear. "I've been waiting for this all day." Her hands and tongue do all the things she knows he likes, and when she's on top and the two of them are finally in a rhythm, she says in an insistent, sultry voice, "Mark, look at me."

He struggles to get his eyes open, and when he does, he's struck dumb by the sight of Alma's face right above his, her leathery skin and wide grin showing yellow teeth. Her skeletal hands clamp on either side of his face, and her skinny, naked body is pumping up and down on his. He's repulsed but frozen in place. Her tongue flicks out between cracked lips, and she purrs in Monica's voice, "You really do rise to the occasion, don't you?"

Only minutes before her tongue was in his mouth and had worked its way down his body. Thinking about it grosses him out. He stifles the urge to throw up, knowing the vomit would stick in his throat and suffocate him.

"You love it, don't you?" the specter asks mockingly.

"Get your fucking hands off of me!" His shout rattles in his brain.

Alma slaps his face and laughs. "Mark Norman, you're such a little bitch. Grow some balls, will you?"

Mark closes his eyes. *God.* The word rises, a prayer. *Please make it end.*

CHAPTER TWENTY-NINE

When Mark's alarm clock goes off, his room is bright from the morning light, and he's fairly certain he's not dreaming anymore. He shudders thinking about the nightmare. It was the worst one yet. Between Lisa's outlandish claims and too much drinking right before bedtime, his mind has conjured up some true horrors. He needs to put Lisa's ideas out of his head and dispense with the alcohol before bedtime. Mark's no killjoy. He can put away beer with the best of them. But hard liquor? He's learning that it doesn't sit well with him. That nightmare with Alma is a powerful incentive to lay off the sauce. He can still feel her bony pelvic bones slamming against him, and he can perfectly recall the sight of her breasts swinging like pendulums, while her face leered inches from his own.

He's not letting that happen again.

Mark is still tired and his head pounds, but as hangovers go, he's had worse. After quickly getting ready, he pops a few aspirin and heads to the kitchen, where he finds Monica and Roy at the table eating breakfast. "Good morning," he says.

"Morning," they reply in unison. Both of them are reading

the paper and drinking coffee. Roy has the business section, Monica the local news. Both are properly attired for the day. In fact, Monica is wearing a dress, as if she's going to a social function.

"What's for breakfast?" Mark asks.

Monica lowers the paper. "We had crepes with lingonberry jam. You can have whatever you want." Her tone is even, and yet he gets the feeling she's annoyed with him. She's never made crepes for him, so apparently Operation Win Roy Over has begun.

"You didn't make an extra crepe for me?"

"No, sorry."

Mark shrugs and makes some toast, grabs a cup of coffee, then sits down to eat. While he's chewing, Monica remarks on a funny local story. "An area man was spotted walking on the sidewalk in his neighborhood wearing only his pajama bottoms. When police stopped to question him, they discovered he was sleepwalking." She turns to Mark. "Can you imagine?"

Roy says, "Some say you should never wake up someone who is sleepwalking. That it will be too big of a shock for them. Might give them a heart attack." Roy and Monica begin to talk about the pros and cons of waking up a sleepwalker. What if they might fall down some stairs or walk in traffic? On the other hand, if they could be guided safely back to bed, wouldn't that be better? Roy says, "What do you think, Mark?"

He sets down his coffee mug. "I don't honestly know too much about it."

After that, Mark is excluded from the conversation. Roy and Monica talk on and on. They cover the weather, the migration of birds in the fall, and how much women's fashions have changed over the years. Mark gets the distinct feeling he's a third wheel by design. The idea aggravates him, but it's typical of Monica. She's always been one to look out for herself. Glumly, he thinks that next the two of them will get married and Monica will send Mark packing.

Roy interrupts his thoughts. "I thought we could go to the bank today, Mark, if that works for you?"

"Of course. Whatever you want."

"Bring your driver's license for identification purposes. We'll be taking Alma's name off all the accounts and adding you on instead. I'll also give you permission to access our safe-deposit box."

Excitement rises in Mark's chest. This seems almost more official than the signing of the documents the other night. Having his name on the accounts means, he assumes, that he can access the money anytime he wants. It's a level of trust that he hasn't earned, but he'll sure as hell take it. Mark gives Monica a sideways glance to see if this new development upsets her, but she's looking at the newspaper again and not paying any attention at all. He adopts a light tone. "Are the secrets to your magic act in your safe-deposit box?"

Roy chuckles. "No, my boy, I keep all that up here." He taps his forehead. "The bank box is for documents and photos. Some collectible coins. Nothing too exciting."

"Collectible coins? The usual gold doubloons?" Mark jokes.

"Of course. All my pirate treasure."

And just like that, Mark is back in the fold. Monica is going to have a difficult time gaining traction on him. He got here first, after all, and Roy loves him like a grandson.

When Roy leaves to get his car keys, Mark pulls Monica aside and asks the question that's been on his mind ever since he woke up this morning. "Did you come into my room last night?"

Her brow furrows. "No, why would I?"

"You know." He shoots her a smile. "For the usual."

She straightens up and frowns. "Mark, this is not the time for that. Show some respect, please. A woman has died."

He's puzzled but says, "Sorry. You're right." Another thought comes to mind, and he digs his wallet out of his back pocket, then flips it open and pulls out Lisa's gold cross necklace. "Look at this." He holds up the chain so the cross dangles. "Do you think it's real gold?"

Monica takes a step back and frowns. "Where did you get that?"

"It was Lisa's," he explains, holding it out to her. "The chain is broken, but the cross might be worth something. I thought maybe your jeweler friend could take a look."

She shakes her head. "Mark, I have to say I'm disappointed in you, trying to profit off someone who committed suicide."

He's not used to this particular mode of disapproval coming from Monica. She gives him the business often enough, but it's usually in the form of high-handed sarcasm. He says, "It's not as if she needs it anymore." He is trying for a joke, but from the look on her face the effort falls flat. "So you don't want it?"

"No, I don't want it." She shudders like he's offering her a dead mouse. "Get rid of it."

When Roy returns, he tells Monica, "We won't be back until after lunch, so you might as well eat without us."

Gesturing to the breakfast dishes, she smiles and says, "Take your time. I have plenty to keep me busy here."

The two men head out the door to the Excalibur, still parked out front from the day before. Once Roy is buckled in, Mark clicks his own seat belt in place, and they take off. Already he's starting to think of this as his car. Roy's presence in the passenger seat is temporary. Soon enough Mark won't need anyone's permission to drive this vehicle.

Driving down the block, Mark stops at the next intersection and sees Doug coming from the opposite corner, languidly striding across the street. He's in front of the vehicle when he faces the car, wagging a mocking finger and contorting his face like a kid, then sticking out his tongue. Mark hits the horn, but Doug just laughs and keeps going, hopping up on the curb and striding down the sidewalk. "I hate that guy," Mark says.

"What guy?" asks Roy, who's been looking out the passenger-side window.

"That one." Mark points as they continue on. "The old hippie who hangs around by the building next door. Every time I see that guy, he says crazy things about me being in danger."

"Do you think he's on drugs?"

Old people always think young people are on drugs. "Maybe. Whatever his problem is, he's damn annoying."

Roy shrugs. "I find that if you ignore annoying people, they eventually go away."

"I'll give that a try." Inwardly, though, Mark vows that if Doug continues to harass him, he'll break his jaw. He's had just about enough of him.

Mark is determined not to let Doug ruin his mood, since today is a very good day. At the bank his name is added to four accounts, and he is given an extra key to the safe-deposit box. The bank manager, Mr. Barden, views Mark with suspicion, taking Roy aside to ask if Mark has somehow coerced him into adding him to his accounts. Roy adamantly says no, clapping Mark on the back and saying, "Mark Norman may not be related to me, but he is family all the same. I would expect that when he comes in, you'll give him the same courtesy you've always given me."

Inwardly, Mark beams. It feels wonderful to get the respect he deserves.

From the way the bank teller and manager treat Roy, Mark gets the impression that Roy has quite the impressive bank account. He desperately wants to ask how much money the accounts contain, but admirably, he holds back. Patience is key here. He doesn't want to look greedy. Besides, what does it matter? Someday it will all be his, but today is not that day. Everything will come to him eventually.

When they're done, Roy says, "This calls for a celebration." It's too early for lunch, so they drive around town with the windows down, enjoying the fresh air and sunshine. When it gets closer to lunchtime, Roy announces that they should return to Grenadier's, the fancy restaurant they visited on suit-buying day.

The dining room is the same: framed, spotlighted landscapes on the walls, dark-suited waiters milling about, and linen tablecloths on every table. Most of the other patrons are businessmen, drinking cocktails and talking seriously about landing new accounts and brokering deals. At Mark and Roy's table there are no cocktails, and the conversation is quite different. After their roast duckling with orange glaze is delivered, their waiter ceremoniously drapes linen napkins across their laps. Once he's gone, Roy waxes philosophical on the meaning of life. "I'm going to impart some of my years of wisdom right now, Mark, and I hope you're paying attention."

"Yes, sir."

Roy lifts his fork. "Today is momentous because in entrusting you with my money, I'm also handing over the baton, so to speak. Life has seasons. You are in the spring of life, while I'm experiencing the worst of winter days. For you, life is just beginning, while my days are drawing to a close."

"Not necessarily, Roy. Some people live to be ninety or a hundred. You could live for many years yet." This is, Mark knows, the polite thing to say.

"No." Roy shakes his head. "The end is near. I can feel it."

"I'm sorry." What else is there to say?

"Don't be. Death is inevitable for all of us."

"Time and tide wait for no man."

"Exactly," Roy says, laughing. "I can tell you that faith is what keeps me going. The only reason I'm not devastated to have lost my sister is that I have my faith to comfort me. I don't know how people function without it."

A server comes and tops up their water glasses from a silver pitcher with a napkin tied around it. All the better to absorb condensation, Mark thinks. "Faith is important," he agrees.

Roy continues. "Here's something else for you. Most people think that the end of their life is their darkest hour. Some even call it the dark hour, but I like to look at it a little differently."

"Oh?" Mark raises an eyebrow.

"The way I look at it, life is like a party."

"A party?"

"Yes." He shakes his head vigorously. "When you first arrive at a party, you might enter the room a little hesitantly. You're finding your way into a place you've never been before, scoping out the hors d'oeuvres, deciding what you want to drink, and looking around to see who else is in the room. After some time, you feel more comfortable and start to have fun. Then the music comes on and everyone begins to dance." His eyes gleam. "And it feels wonderful to move to the beat. You might take some beautiful woman in your arms and think that she's perfect, and the potential is there that you might hit it off. You're having an amazing, glorious time, and you wish it would never end."

Marks smiles. "I'd like to go to that party."

"Oh, but you're already there, my boy. You just don't know it."

"This is the first I've heard of it," Mark says, attempting a joke.

Roy says, "That's because most people don't realize how all this works until it's over. And it *will* be over, believe me." He takes a sip from his water glass. "Eventually, if you stay too long, the party gets to be a slog. The other partygoers get on your nerves. The music is too loud, and you become tired of it, weary of the people and the nonstop talking and the smoke-filled air. The jokes cease to be funny, and you've eaten enough delicious food, had more than your share of liquor. And that's when you decide you've had enough. It's time to leave the party. Other people, fresher, younger folks may enjoy it, but it's not for you. You need to go home." He smiles at Mark. "And that's how life is like a party."

"Because at your age you've been at the party too long and want to go home."

"Right you are."

"And home is a metaphor for heaven."

"Presumably. I guess that remains to be seen." Roy spears a piece of duckling and pops it into his mouth.

"Well, thank you for the wisdom."

"You're welcome. It's the least I can do, considering all that you're doing for me."

After lunch, Roy announces he's in no mood to go home. "The house is empty without Alma," he says glumly. Mark cheers him up by taking him for another lengthy drive. Eventually they end up at a local florist, where Roy insists on buying a present for Monica. "She made the most delightful breakfast," he says. "I haven't had crepes in years. I want to show my appreciation." He picks out a potted gardenia covered in blooms. Once it's paid for, Mark carries it like he's holding a baby.

When they arrive back at Alden Manor, Mark pulls the car into the garage and helps Roy out of the vehicle. Monica comes to greet them, and Roy presents her with the flowers. She buries her nose in the flowers and says, "How thoughtful of you. I love them! I'll put them in the blue room so we can all enjoy them."

For dinner that night, Monica makes spaghetti and meatballs, with garlic bread and a tossed salad. Despite having had a good-sized lunch, both Mark and Roy chow down. Roy tells her, "These meatballs are delectable."

"An old family recipe," she says with a smile, dabbing her mouth with a napkin. "It's all in the seasoning."

Mark smiles at this new Suzy Homemaker act of hers. Not bad for the only girl in her fourth-grade class who didn't have an Easy-Bake Oven. "I didn't want one," she once explained to him. "Even then I thought it was the tool of male chauvinists trying to keep women in their place."

After dinner, Monica insists on making the brandy manhattans. "You know I used to bartend," she tells Roy.

He chuckles. "A woman of many talents. I think we'll keep you around."

"You better!" Her back is to the room because she's facing the drink cart, but there's no mistaking her flirtatious tone.

Mark says, "I think I'll take a pass tonight."

"A pass from what, my boy?" Roy asks.

"The manhattans."

"You must be kidding." Monica turns, holding a silver tray. "I've already made one for you." And sure enough, three drinks grace the tray, each one garnished with a cherry and orange wedge. The garnish is a nice touch, but it doesn't make the drink any more tempting for Mark.

"I've been drinking too much lately," he says apologetically.

"Ah," she says and nods. She lowers the tray to Roy, who takes a drink, and then she walks over to Mark, holding the tray toward him. "Just take one to sip on. Since I already made it." Mark hesitates, and she adds, "For me?"

"Don't force him," Roy says. "Not everyone is made for hard liquor."

Mark cringes at the unmanly notion that he can't hold his liquor. He takes the drink. "I guess one won't hurt."

As Mark pretends to sip from his drink, Roy tells Monica his theory about life being a party. She is totally enthralled with this metaphor, listening with rapt attention. Mark regards her attempts at ingratiating herself with a dose of humor. Try though she may, the papers have been signed, and Mark's name is the one on the bank accounts. Monica can flirt and flatter to her heart's content, but she's still a young female, and despite all the efforts of the women's libbers—the protesting, the bra burning, and the chanting for equality—it's a man's world, and he's going to make damn certain he's the one who comes out ahead in this deal.

The taste of the manhattan has lost its appeal now that he associates it with the nightmare from the night before. Mark wonders how he'll dispose of the drink, and then he gets his opportunity when the doorbell rings.

Startled, Monica jumps up out of her chair. "Are we expecting anyone?" she asks Roy. Mark notes the use of the word *we*, as if it's her house.

"Not that I know of," Roy says.

"I'll go see who it is."

As she leaves and Roy's attention follows her, Mark empties his drink into the gardenia plant. He's glad to be rid of it, and he'll be happier still when he can brush his teeth and get the taste of geriatric sex out of his mouth. When Monica comes back a few minutes later, she's holding a cardboard mask and has a puzzled look on her face. Holding it up, she asks, "Any idea what this is all about?"

Roy leans forward to get a closer look. "What is it?"

She shrugs. "I don't really know. When I opened the door no one was there, but this was on the porch." Turning it over, she reads something written on the back. "*Things aren't always what they seem.*"

Mark can picture Doug sneaking onto the porch, ringing the doorbell, and running away like a complete wuss. Presumably

Mark's threat worked and Doug will keep his distance, but Doug can't resist getting in the last word. "Probably just someone's idea of a prank," he says. "I'd throw it out."

Roy nods. "When you're right, you're right, my boy. Most likely just a child playing a joke."

CHAPTER THIRTY

Monica mixes one more round of manhattans before they retire for the night. Mark begs off, but he eventually agrees to take a glass after she says, "You used to be more fun, Mark." There is no opportunity to dump the second one, but he only drinks half, and he's glad when she doesn't push the subject further.

Roy tells both of them he's fine to get to bed on his own this evening, so while Monica takes the glasses to the kitchen, Mark goes straight to his own room. He has just closed the door behind him when the rush of alcohol hits his bloodstream. When the vertigo hits, he grabs the wall to stay upright. This is pathetic and inexplicable. How could half a drink make his joints so loose that walking across a room takes a gargantuan amount of effort?

He is exhausted, but at the same time he feels jittery, his heart fluttering like the flapping of birds' wings. He needs to calm the fuck down if he wants to get any sleep tonight. He painstakingly makes his way to the bathroom, brushes his teeth, rinses and spits, then braces himself by holding both sides of the sink. He looks at his reflection in the mirror. His hair, which had been so carefully styled earlier, is a mess, and his eyes are sunken in their sockets. While he stares at his image, he feels a catch in his chest, taking his breath away. That is weird. Is he totally losing it?

If Lisa felt like this for weeks, no wonder she wanted to put an end to it.

Mark falls back on the bed, too weak to take off his clothes or get under the covers. It's not the job that's getting to him, he thinks, it's the lack of sleep. Maybe he's getting sick as well. His mouth is dry, and he feels a lump at the base of his throat when he swallows. He's nauseous and dizzy.

How long can he keep this up, falling prey to disturbing dreams at night and working while exhausted during the day?

Quitting's not an option, though, not this close to the finish line. As the room spins, he thinks about how Dream Lisa advised him to smother Roy with a pillow, and suddenly it doesn't seem like the worst idea in the world, not if it would make this craziness stop. Roy's a nice old man, but he's nothing to Mark, not really, and didn't he tell Mark just today that he was ready to leave the party?

If Mark were a different sort of person, he would do it. Roy is lucky that Mark is sensible.

Afraid of having more bad dreams, he fights sleep, but it comes anyway. When he feels himself slipping under, he makes a wish that he doesn't have any nightmares tonight.

It begins with the sensation of being moved. The image of Alma being wheeled out on a gurney comes to mind, and for a moment he wonders if he's being carted off to the morgue. But no, he's not on a gurney. The movements are erratic, like he's a wounded soldier being carried on a stretcher. Through a slit in his eyelids, he looks up and sees that the army medics are Baird and Sam, and they're carrying him down the hallway toward the front of the house. At least in this dream, he's clothed.

Sam makes a small grunt. "He's heavier than he looks."

Even though it's hard work, Mark tries to look again. He needs to know what's going on. With great effort he manages to open his eyes, seeing the walls of Alden Manor glide past and getting the sense of other people just out of his view.

"Stop!" This voice he knows. It's Monica. "He's awake! I saw his eyes open."

"Not to worry, my dear. I know it's been a long time, but don't you remember that we've seen this before? It's a reflex, nothing more." Mark is glad to hear Roy's reassuring voice, even if he doesn't quite understand what Roy's talking about.

And now his body is tipped, head lower than his feet, and the movement becomes jerky, leading him to believe they're carrying him up the stairs. Roy's voice saying, "Careful, careful," is accompanied by the sound of clattering footsteps. When they get to the second floor, they head down the hall. Behind his closed eyelids he senses a bright light overhead, signaling to him that he's in the middle of a dream. He knows this because the lights on the second floor don't work. Lisa said there were no fuses in the basement fuse box, so they can't work. It's impossible.

When a woman says, "Easy now. We're almost there," he recognizes Nurse Darby's voice, a curious choice for his subconscious mind.

Someone opens the double doors, and the pace quickens, as if they can't wait to get there. His eyes are still shut, but he senses the high ceilings and open space. The dream version of this room lacks the stale air and pin-drop quiet he's come to expect. Instead, he feels air moving across his face as if a breeze is coming through an open window. As confirmation, a car horn honks repeatedly from the street below.

And then he's unceremoniously dumped onto a hard, flat surface. *Thunk* is the sound his body makes as it hits what must be the table in the ballroom. Inwardly, he groans. The resulting bump to the back of his head hurts like hell.

I'm not awake, he tells himself. *This is just a dream. A horrible, awful dream.* He wills himself to drift out of this nightmare and away from all this confusion.

"I'll get his clothing off," Monica says, fiddling with the button on his jeans. The tug at his waist and the brush of her fingernails on his stomach is familiar.

"Wait with that," Roy says. "Help me up first."

And then there are other voices all blending together. He thinks he can pick them out: Baird, Lara, Nurse Darby, Sam, and Neela. Overlapping excited conversations come from the direction of the stage. He hears a woman (Lara?) say, "I thought this day would never come."

Are they all here? The Redevine Society, Roy, Alma, Neela, Sam, Baird, and Lara—all of them here tonight? But no, Alma is dead, isn't she?

Mark hears the sounds of the Victrola being taken from the podium cabinet, along with the noise of someone riffling through the pages of a book. From the way the table shakes and the sound of Roy's old-man creaks and gasps, he can tell Roy has been boosted onto the table and is lying parallel to him. As he listens, the restraints are buckled around each of Roy's wrists.

"Not too tight," Roy says.

"I know how to do this," Monica says, sounding almost insulted.

Mark remembers the illustrations in the book and is sickened by the thought that he's being used for some kind of human sacrifice. Bile rises up his throat and sits in his mouth.

This can't be real. It isn't real. I must be hallucinating, or else I'm losing my mind.

Neela's sweet voice says, "This is so exciting! We're so close." He feels her hand brush his hair away from his forehead. "You picked a real winner this time."

This time? Mark reels with panic and tries unsuccessfully to move his concrete limbs. He feels like he's about to cry.

"He walked through the door like I ordered him from the Sears and Roebuck catalog." Roy chuckles. "Mark Norman. Not a deep thought in his pretty little head, but he is a fine specimen, I'll agree with you on that point."

"Can't hold his liquor." Monica's voice again. "But we'll fix that."

Such a betrayal. Mark swallows, tasting the acid of his fear. *Why are they doing this to me? Roy said I was like a grandson. And Monica? After all we've been through together. Why is she helping them?*

From past experience, he knows that in the morning he'll realize that this episode is just a gibberish concoction of his own mind. Dreams don't have to make sense.

But what terrifies him is that it doesn't feel like a dream.

Words run through his brain, nagging at him. *It's better to take action than to be a victim.* Who said that? He strains to think but can't remember. Does it even matter? Around him the voices chatter, oblivious to his fear.

He hears Monica say, "Mark's turn."

Roy says, "Get those clothes off before you put the restraints on."

Run! Every instinct he has is shouting the order. *Run as fast as you can!*

His body resisting, it takes everything he has to open his eyes, but he manages, blinking against the bright light coming from the three chandeliers overhead. He has a blurry view of

Monica as she walks toward him. She stops abruptly, shouting out, "He's awake! His eyes are open!" She sounds frantic. "He sees."

As the clatter of footsteps come his way, Mark knows it's now or never.

Adrenaline kicks in and he pushes off the table, willing his legs to hold him. He doesn't know what's actually happening, but one thing is becoming clear: they want to kill him.

And he knows something else too: he doesn't want to die.

"Get him!" Roy calls out in his quivery voice. A glance backward shows Roy stretched out on the table, not a stitch of clothing on him.

"Stop him!" calls another voice.

Mark runs, and now that he's on his feet he's propelled by absolute terror. As he approaches the doorway, he remembers that closed doors will keep them trapped in the room, so he pauses to shut them before he sprints down the hall.

His theory is wrong. The doors don't hold.

They're coming after him now. He doesn't look behind him, but judging from the sound, it's Sam and Baird and they're gaining on him.

Oh God, oh God, oh God. Please help.

He's not praying, exactly. More like begging anyone who might be listening.

But no one's listening.

He's halfway down the stairs when he trips and tumbles all the way to the bottom. Head. Ass. Legs. Over and over again, each body part takes a turn slamming against the steps.

Finally, he lands at the bottom with a sickening thud.

Scrambling to his feet, he goes to the front door, turns the lock, and opens it, leaping off the porch and hitting the ground hard, twisting his ankle. He leaps up, ignoring the shooting pain in his ankle, and dashes forward, aware of Baird and Sam right behind him. He screams into the night, "Help me!" and keeps going, running blindly into the street.

When he's almost across to the other side, he sees a car turn the corner heading right his way. Behind him, Baird and Sam are stepping off the curb, seconds away from grabbing him and dragging him back into the house.

He needs more distance.

Or more time.

Mark makes a quick decision and backtracks into the center of the street, waving his arms. The headlights come closer. Baird and Sam pause, deliberating.

He thinks they wouldn't dare do anything to him in front of a witness.

The car screeches to a stop, just inches away from Mark. He slams his palm on the hood of the car for emphasis and screams, "Help me! You've got to help me."

The car door opens, and out steps Dr. Cross. "Mark, what's going on?"

Mark exhales in relief. He gestures to Sam and Baird. "I have to get out of here. They're trying to kill me."

Dr. Cross looks from Mark to the two men. "They're trying to kill you?"

Sam raises both hands in surrender. "We're trying to help him. Roy called and asked us to come over because Mark was acting crazy."

Baird adds, "He said Mark was tearing up the whole house. We've been trying to calm him down. He's out of his mind."

Both the men sound so reasonable that for the smallest moment, Mark wonders if this is true. Is it possible he has been sleepwalking? Someone was just talking about sleepwalking. When was that? His thoughts are so jumbled he can't remember.

"We were trying to talk some sense into him," Sam says.

"He just bolted out of the house. You saw him." He points. "He just ran into the street like a maniac."

No. This is wrong. They weren't trying to talk sense into him. He's sure of that. Somewhat sure, anyway. He looks straight at Dr. Cross. "You need to help me. Will you take me away from here?"

"Of course." A shadow of confusion crosses the doctor's face. "If that's what you want. I can wait if you want to go inside and pack up your things."

"No." Mark shakes his head. His wallet is still in his back pocket. The only possessions left behind are clothes, and those can be replaced. He's never going inside Alden Manor again. "I just need to leave. Now."

Dr. Cross nods and calls out, "Gentlemen, Mark is leaving with me."

Mark opens the passenger door, gets inside, and locks the door. He sees Baird and Sam's disappointed faces and thinks about how close he just came to danger. Dr. Cross slides into the driver's side. "Where to?" he asks.

"If you could drive me to my parents' house, that would be great," Mark answers, reciting their address. It's the one place he can think of that will take him in on short notice at this time of night. His stepfather will give him shit for quitting another job, but too bad for that. He'll say he's reconsidered his stepdad's offer of working for the insurance company. He'll even give Brian the credit for pulling him back into the fold. All of them will gloat, and he'll let them. He won't be living with them for very long, not if he can help it.

He just needs to put Alden Manor behind him.

As Dr. Cross accelerates and the car glides down the block, Mark breathes a sigh of relief.

CHAPTER THIRTY-ONE

Dr. Cross turns west onto Clarke Street and asks, "What happened?"

Mark shakes his head. "Something strange, I can't even tell you. I just needed to get out of there."

"I see." He gives Mark a quick sympathetic smile. "Are you okay?"

"Yeah, I'm okay."

"You look a bit off. If you want, we can stop at the hospital and get you checked out."

Mark still feels off—in fact, the dizziness is back—but he just shrugs. "All I need is a decent night's sleep." The air-conditioning in the car feels good. Now he can breathe again. The car radio is playing Petula Clark's song "Downtown." Hearing it makes him realize he hasn't listened to contemporary music in what seems like ages.

Interrupting his thoughts, the doctor says, "So I take it you're quitting the job?"

"Yes." Through bleary eyes he watches as they drive past street after street, each intersection another step away from Alden Manor. As much as he was glad to leave his childhood home before, that's how much he wants to return to it now. He's willing to sleep in his old bed again, anything to get this feeling of dread out of his system. When Dr. Cross eases to a stop at the red light on Forty-Eighth and Clarke Street, Mark closes his eyes and rests his forehead against the window.

He's dozing when he feels the jab in his left arm. For a second, in his confusion, he thinks, *Bee sting.* But when he looks, it's Dr. Cross pushing the plunger of a hypodermic needle into his upper arm. Mark pulls away, shouting, "What the hell are you doing?"

Dr. Cross says, "Sorry, Mark. Had to do it." He drops the needle on the floor by Mark's feet, then grabs the steering wheel and makes an illegal U-turn, narrowly missing an oncoming truck.

Oh my God! Mark doesn't know what drug is now moving through his system, but he has his hand on the door release, ready to bolt as soon as the car slows. Dr. Cross turns off the main drag and is now accelerating at top speed down side streets. The residential streets are middle-of-the-night dead, which is fortunate, because he's ignoring stop signs and driving like a lunatic. "Slow down," Mark yells, but Dr. Cross doesn't react at all.

With his hand tightly gripping the door release, Mark weighs whether or not to jump out at this speed. Would he survive the fall? It's possible, he thinks, but it's also possible that he'd land too close to the car and get run over by the rear wheels. Not the outcome he wants.

He thinks he can outlast the drug. He's still wide awake, after all. The car has to slow down or stop at some point—hopefully soon. He glances down the street looking for a police officer. *They're never around when you need them,* is the last thought he has before he realizes he can't move his body at all.

His head lolls to one side, and his hand, the one that was on the door, falls next to the seat.

He's paralyzed.

The car slows to normal speeds, heading back in the direction from which they came. Back to Alden Manor, he realizes with a sickening knot in his stomach.

When the car comes to a stop, Dr. Cross rolls down his window and calls out to someone. "Hurry!" He unlocks the car doors and unbuckles Mark's seat belt. The passenger door opens, and Baird half drags, half lifts Mark's limp body. Everything in him wants to fight, but he's got no bones or muscles anymore. He hears Dr. Cross's voice: "The paralytic won't last long. Maybe another five minutes. You have to get him upstairs right away."

"We're on it," Sam says.

Mark watches the night sky move across his field of vision. As they go up the porch steps, Mark sees Doug peer around the corner of the house, shaking his head sadly. He mouths the words, "Tried to tell ya," then retreats out of sight.

Monica opens the door, saying, "Finally. What took so long?"

They drop him onto the stretcher, which is laid out on the floor in the entryway. Dr. Cross comes in behind them. "Careful!" he says sharply. "We don't want any damage done."

"He's fine," Sam says. "Nothing but a few bumps and bruises."

The two men grunt as they make the trip back up the stairs. This time Mark can see everything, and he knows it's real. What kind of craziness is this? A million ideas run through his head, each one worse than the one before it. Human sacrifice? Sex cult? Organ donation? Cannibalism? Whatever it is, they've somehow gotten Monica involved as well.

This is insanity.

When they plop him on the table this time, he rolls to one side, coming face-to-face with Roy, who is still naked and restrained on the table. "Mark, my boy," he says, his voice jovial. "I'm glad you decided to come back and join the party."

Dr. Cross says, "Get him buckled in right away before the paralytic wears off."

Mark gets rolled onto his back, and Lara and Neela work to pull his clothing off and get the restraints secured around his wrists. His sight line includes the dangling prisms on one of the chandeliers, sparkling in the light. Neela leans over him, and he smells her floral perfume. It's a light, pleasant scent.

He senses the air on his bare flesh and feels like puking.

Lara says, "I don't like his crazy eyes." She's talking about him.

"They're not crazy eyes," Dr. Cross says. "He's afraid."

"Well, can you fix that?" Lara cinches the final buckle and pulls on it to ensure it's secure. "Give him something to knock him out? I can't stand looking at his face. It's creepy."

"He and Roy will be getting the same sedative." A minute later, Dr. Cross's face looms above Mark's own. He smiles and dabs Mark's arm with an alcohol wipe. He feels the jab of the needle, stinging, cold. "Just relax, son. It'll be over soon. You're going to be just fine."

Mark is not convinced. In fact, inwardly he's screaming. But it doesn't seem to matter, because the room is receding and he's now floating away on a cloud, slipping away to somewhere far more pleasant. Dr. Cross reaches over and closes Mark's eyelids. "Sweet dreams, Mark Norman."

CHAPTER THIRTY-TWO

It begins gradually. First, he's aware that he's coming out of a deep sleep. The sensation is that of rising up from the bottom of the ocean toward the light. This is accompanied by the realization that he's alive.

Breathing.

Heart beating.

He's survived. *Thank God.*

Voices float faintly toward him from off in the distance. He recognizes them as Dr. Cross and the other members of the Redevine Society, so he guesses that this new reality is a continuation of what he previously experienced. Mark is still not quite clued in, but he's hopeful he may actually get out of this unscathed.

His fingers press down on the surface he's lying on, and there's some give to it, which tells him he's on a mattress. His wrists are no longer constrained.

With great effort, Mark manages to open his eyes just wide enough to see the ceiling of his bedroom at Alden Manor. His vision is slightly blurry, but he manages to turn his head to one side and sees Dr. Cross, sitting in a chair and reading a book.

The doctor closes the book and sets it down on the nightstand. "Oh good, you're awake." He calls out, "Nurse Darby, I need you."

Nurse Darby strides into the room. She's attired in her nurse garb, and just like before, her white shoes squeak with each step. She and Dr. Cross work together, the doctor checking Mark's eyes with a small flashlight, while Nurse Darby presses her fingers into his wrists while looking at her watch. After a minute, she says, "Pulse rate, seventy and steady."

Dr. Cross puts a stethoscope to his chest, while Nurse Darby wraps a blood pressure cuff around his upper arm. They're concerned about his health and are taking care of him. Mark sees this as a positive sign. He tries to speak, but it comes out in a whisper. "What did you do to me?"

"Just relax. It's almost over," Dr. Cross says.

"How much longer?" Nurse Darby asks the doctor.

"Long enough for the sedative to clear out of his system. I think we're almost there."

Mark's body is currently useless, and his thoughts are fuzzy as well. It takes all his mental effort to make sense of this. In his mind he replays everything that has happened to him since the day he arrived at Alden Manor. How Roy and Alma declared he was like family. The new clothes and haircut. How Roy made him executor of his will.

And the words of wisdom imparted by Roy over drinks.

Life has seasons.

You remind me of myself when I was a young man.

Dress for success, that's my motto. It's how young men come to rule the world.

You can spend your whole life wishing you were someone else, or you can just become that person.

Roy was so kind and encouraging. A cross between a grandfather and a mentor. He chose him to inherit his estate, for God's sake. Had none of it been real?

On the opposite side, there was Doug and his nonsensical warnings.

They're gonna get you.

People go in that house, they don't come out the same.

Bad things happen to people who go in there.

Lisa, too, had her qualms about this house. Her crazy, frantic journal entries captured her frame of mind perfectly. He understands how she felt now. He's never experienced terror like this before. Fear jolts down his spine all the way to the soles of his feet, making it hard to breathe.

He shuffles through the memories over and over again, looking for something that might help explain what's happening here, but he comes up blank. He's alive but can't discount the possibility that they took out one of his organs. A kidney or lung, maybe? Other than that, he can't even imagine.

After Dr. Cross leaves the room, Nurse Darby takes over his spot in the chair, watching over Mark. Maybe she'll help him? They were never friends, but she bossed him around plenty, and he always did what she wanted without complaint. That has to count for something.

His mouth feels heavy, but he manages to say, "I don't understand what's going on." He's speaking as loudly as he can, but it comes out in a rasp. "Help me. Please help me."

"No talking," she says sternly, tapping her watch. "Very soon you will understand."

Mark blinks, trying to get the room to be less fuzzy, without success. It's as if he's wearing glasses with lenses coated with Vaseline. Everything is hazy, which gives him a headache. He closes his eyes and finds himself drifting off.

He's roused when Dr. Cross shakes him awake. "It's time," he says. The rest of the Redevine Society is gathered around the bed, all of them with expectant expressions. The doctor shines a penlight into his eyes and says approvingly, "I think we're nearly there."

"What are you doing to me?" Mark rasps. "What's happening?"

Dr. Cross ignores the questions and instructs him to squeeze his hands and wiggle his feet. Obediently, Mark complies. He can't do much more than this, but once he gets his strength back, there's nothing he won't do to get out of this real-life nightmare.

The doctor says, "All set. He's aware of what's happening. We're good to go." Mark watches as he beckons to someone off to the side. He hears the person step forward, but he doesn't see who it is until he's just inches away.

Mark blinks, unable to fathom what he's seeing—his own face staring back at him. Even with his blurry vision, there's no mistaking the dark hair combed into a pompadour and the strong jaw and intense, heavily lidded eyes accentuated by dark lashes. He's struck speechless, trying to make sense of the vision above him.

"Hello, my boy. You're not looking so good." The words come out of the imposter's mouth, so close he can smell the brandy manhattan on his breath. "I'm glad you're awake now because I think it's important that you know this was your choice. You traded your future for the promise of easy money." He chuckles. "A shame you were so greedy. But on the bright side, I think you'll be pleased with what I do with your life. Now that I have this beautiful body, there's no stopping me."

Mark reaches up to push the hallucination away, and when he does, he catches sight of his own hand and is shocked. In disbelief, he turns it from side to side, bringing it closer so he can get a better look. It's a gnarled claw of a hand, with raised veins and liver spots. The hand of a man in his eighties. One ready to leave the party. Bile creeps up and burns his throat. His mouth feels oddly full because of the dentures fitted over his gums. *Looks can be deceiving.* "No." A tear rolls down his cheek.

"I think Mark is beginning to understand," Nurse Darby says.

The group chuckles as Monica says, "Too little, too late."

As he catches sight of their jeering faces, he gets a flash of insight regarding a notation in Lisa's journal, a sentence she'd underlined three times, the last time so emphatically that the pen tore through the paper. *The Redevine Society is a cipher.* He understands now that she wasn't referring to the people in the group. What she meant was that the name is a cipher—or more accurately, it is an anagram.

R E D E V I N E

Mentally, he reshuffles the letters like moving tiles on a Scrabble board:

NEVER DIE

"The Redevine Society" transposed is "The Never Die Society." No wonder their photographs show the eight of them raising their glasses in a toast, saying, *To never growing old.*

It's the last thought he has before the pillow comes down over his face. There is no point in struggling. He no longer has the strength.

EPILOGUE

Everything about Las Vegas astounded Brian, from the Hare Krishnas chanting at the airport, to the free champagne handed out at the casinos, to the dazzling, pulsating neon signs that lined the Strip. He gaped at the showgirls with their enormous feathered headdresses and took in all the excitement of the game tables. He even gambled a little too. Nickel slots, for the most part, and one time at the roulette wheel. Although he walked around the casino floor for hours on end, he didn't get sucked into the big-money bets. Leave that for the wheeler-dealers, the guys who had something to prove. He was there for one reason and one reason only, and he didn't want to get sidetracked.

He'd flown to Las Vegas to talk to his brother, but once he arrived he'd found that this proved more difficult than he'd anticipated. Brian had so many questions for Mark. Why the radio silence for more than fourteen months? Their mother had been frantically worried. Even their stepdad had expressed concern about Mark's well-being, and that was big of him after all the grief that kid had given them over the years.

Mark had been AWOL for more than a year when the

family had seen a newspaper article in the Sunday paper talking about the hottest new magic act in Las Vegas. The large photo had caught their eye, and the article confirmed that the magician in question was Mark. His stepdad pushed the newspaper across the table to Brian and asked, "What do you know about this?"

Brian read the article and shook his head. "Nothing, really. I mean, I met his girlfriend, Monica, once, when I went over to their apartment. She seemed nice. I didn't know they'd left the state or that they were still together." That they were still a couple was astounding, given Mark's track record with women.

"How did he learn to do magic?" his stepdad asked, scratching behind his ear.

Brian shrugged. "Beats me."

According to the article, it wasn't just the usual rabbit-out-of-a-hat magic. The illusions Monica and Mark performed were unusual, even by the standards of professional magicians. The act consisted of one confounding thing after another: Monica tap-danced upside down on the ceiling; Mark's body decayed in a matter of minutes until he ended up as a clothed skeleton walking up and down the aisles; and shockingly, the two of them exchanged heads so that Mark's head was on Monica's body and the other way around. "The most disturbing, incredible show I've ever seen," said Margie Hightower of Omaha, Nebraska. "I'd love to see it again!"

The article also quoted an official of the International Brotherhood of Magicians as saying, "Some of these tricks haven't been performed since the heyday of Walgrave's Astounding Wonders fifty years ago. No one figured out how it was done back then, and today it's still a mystery."

The newspaper went on to say that Norman & Grau's Magnificent Marvels had outgrown the Sahara Lounge and was now headlining sold-out shows at the Las Vegas Hilton. In an attempt to contact Mark, his parents tried both writing and calling the hotel. The switchboard operator said that without prior approval she couldn't connect the call. It was doubtful, too, that their letters were forwarded to him. At least that's what they'd assumed, since they'd never heard back.

When Brian had seen an ad in the paper for a three-night, four-day package deal to Las Vegas, he'd booked it for himself without telling his parents.

It wasn't until his third day in Las Vegas that Brian managed to score a ticket to Mark's show. He had to pay a scalper three times the listed price, and that was for a matinee. The seat wasn't even all that great either. It killed him to shell out that much money, but by this point he was desperate. Earlier he'd stopped at the front desk and asked to speak to Mark, explaining that he was his brother, but since Brian wasn't on the approved list, they refused to put him through. His next idea was to spend time hanging out at the lounge, waiting to see if Mark would come by, but that didn't happen either.

Brian couldn't believe how hard it was to connect with his brother. You'd think he was Liberace, the way they protected his privacy. If they knew Mark the way Brian did—as the family screwup—then they'd know he was nothing special.

But then he saw the show, which put his brother in a different light. Once the lights went down and the curtain came up, Brian was transfixed. Mark proved to be the ultimate entertainer, commanding the attention of every person in the room. The lights, the music, and the costumes were all superb, but they were just window dressing compared to the magic, which, Brian decided, absolutely, positively had to be real magic. There was no other explanation. How did Monica grow wings right in front of them and fly overhead? It could only be from some supernatural power.

Brian had trouble reconciling the man in front of him with

the whiner he'd known his entire life. On stage, Mark was confident and relaxed. He seemed, Brian realized, to be completely in his element. It was clear that Mark was having the time of his life.

After the show, the audience leaped to their feet. The applause was thunderous, the cries of "Encore!" deafening. Mark and Monica came out holding hands and bowed, while their adoring fans wolf-whistled, stamped their feet, and screamed for more. The pair accommodated the request with one more trick, sending floating, glowing bubbles out into the audience. Those lucky enough to touch one giggled with delight at the chiming sound the bubbles made when popped.

When the show was over, the lights went on. While everyone else trooped up the aisles toward the exits, Brian walked against the flow of the crowd in the direction of the stage. He approached an usher and introduced himself, saying, "I'm Brian Norman, Mark's brother. I'd like to talk to him."

"Sorry, no one goes back unless they're on the list."

The list again. Good grief, if family members weren't on the list, who was? Brian sighed. "Can you just tell him I'm here?" He removed his wallet from his back pocket and handed over his driver's license. "Show him this, if you need proof."

The usher reluctantly took Brian's driver's license and looked it over for what seemed like a long time. Finally, he jogged up the stage steps and disappeared behind the curtain. While waiting, Brian flipped through the program. A few minutes later, the usher returned, beckoning for him to follow him.

When they reached the dressing room, Brian found Mark sitting in front of a vanity mirror, combing his hair into a pompadour, while Monica sat nearby, eating apple slices. When Mark saw Brian standing in the doorway, he got up and extended a hand. "Brian! It's nice to see you. What brings you to Las Vegas?"

Brian shook his hand, confused. "What brings me to Las Vegas? I can't believe you're asking me that. Mom and Dad have been worried sick. No word from you in over a year. We thought you were dead. What gives, Spud?"

Mark's smile wasn't one he'd ever seen his brother use before. It was the smile of a man with the winning hand in poker. "I don't answer to *Spud* anymore. It's *Mr. Norman* now. As for not being in touch, I believe that's my prerogative." He gestured to Monica. "You've met my better half, Monica Grau?"

"Of course," Brian said, nodding in her direction. "It's nice to see you again, Monica." She gave a little finger wave, then resumed eating.

Noticing the program in Brian's hand, Mark said, "Did you enjoy the show?"

For a second, Brian forgot his mission. "Did I enjoy it? Hell yeah! It was unbelievable. Absolutely incredible. I had no idea you were so talented. You have to tell me how you did it. I promise I can keep a secret."

Mark laughed. "A magician never tells his secrets. I can tell you, though, that I learned all of these illusions from Roy Walgrave, a brilliant and generous magician."

"How did you meet him?"

"Remember the job I had working as a home health aide? You came to see me at the house?"

"Yes, I remember."

"Roy Walgrave and his sister were my employers," Mark said. "Turns out that Roy was so impressed with my potential that he made me the sole beneficiary of his estate, and he also passed on all his magic secrets to me. I guess it wasn't such a loser job after all."

Brian felt his face flush red upon hearing his own words

quoted back to him. "Oh."

"Now, if you'll excuse us, we have a tight schedule. It was nice seeing you, Brian. Say hello to the folks for me."

Mark had him by the elbow now and was escorting him to the door. His grip was surprisingly firm. Brian said, "Wait! I leave tomorrow morning, but I was hoping we could do dinner tonight."

"No, sorry, that won't work out. We have a show tonight."

"I know. I meant after the show?"

Mark shook his head. "We're otherwise engaged, but thank you for the offer." He continued to maneuver Brian by the arm until they were out in the hallway.

Otherwise engaged? What the hell? Pretty high-and-mighty talk, given his background. "I came a long way," Brian said. "And I think—"

"I realize that, but no one told you to come." Mark grinned. "And you did get to see an incredible show, so the trip wasn't a total waste."

The hallway's walls were lined with posters of all the acts that had appeared there to date, signed by the celebrities themselves. Barbara Streisand, Robert Klein, Elvis Presley. Someday, Brian realized, Mark's picture would be among them. His little brother up there with all the greats. So unreal. "Can I at least give Mom and Dad your phone number? They'd love to talk to you."

Mark shook his head. "I don't think that's advisable. If I need to reach anyone, I'll be in touch. Thanks so much for stopping by."

Brian hesitated, racking his brain for something that might change the trajectory of this conversation. He'd won every argument he'd ever had with Mark, so it was inconceivable that he was now getting the bum's rush. This new version of his brother had him rattled.

From down the hall, a large man called out, "Mr. Norman, I have a message for you from Mr. Sinatra. He called confirming drinks after the show."

"Am I supposed to call him back?" Mark asked.

"No, he just said to meet at his usual table."

"Will do, Bob." Mark gave Brian a gentle, friendly push. "Thanks again for stopping by. Have a safe flight home." He turned to go back into the dressing room.

Flustered, Brian said, "Was he talking about *Frank* Sinatra?"

But Mark had already closed the door. Brian trudged down the hall, back the way he'd come. The last few hours had been unreal. He thought about the show, the way the announcer's voice had come over the loudspeaker: "Ladies and gentlemen, you are about to witness Norman & Grau's Magnificent Marvels. Please welcome to the stage Mr. Mark Norman and Miss Monica Grau!" Before they'd even performed one trick, the audience had loved them, cheering and applauding as if just spotting Mark and Monica on the stage was enough. And when the act began, the fervor had built into a tidal wave of adoration.

He thought back to something he'd overheard as he was taking his seat. A woman in the row behind him said this was the hottest act in Vegas and possibly the best magic act in the history of the world. He shook his head. Somehow, in the last year, Mark had been completely transformed. He looked happier than Brian had ever seen too.

Apparently, the whole family had underestimated Mark. Who knew he'd be capable of such showmanship? Brian shook his head in silent wonderment. Somehow his younger brother had managed to acquire the kind of confidence that filled an auditorium. And hobnobbing with celebrities? Totally unexpected. Who could have seen that coming?

If he'd known Mark was going to become such a big deal, he'd have been a hell of a lot nicer to him growing up.

ACKNOWLEDGMENTS

Thanks to Jessica Fogleman, Grace Greene, Michelle San Juan, MaryAnn Schaefer, Barbara Taylor Sissel, and Caitlin O'Dwyer for their invaluable contributions to this book.

ABOUT THE AUTHOR

K.J. Young is the pseudonym of an author known for heartwarming novels of love, puppies, and the kindness of strangers.

Welcome to her dark side.

If you enjoyed this story, she'd be overjoyed to see your thoughts in a review. If you didn't think it was that great, well then, never mind.